Also available from Chencia C. Higgins

To Buy a Vow
To Build a Vow
To Break a Vow
Things Hoped For

Janine: His True Alpha
Lenora: His Omega Mate
Alicia: His Troublesome Fate

No Strings Allowed
No Love Allowed
The Week Before Forever
No Games Allowed
Holiday Honey
K.S.L.

Benefriends
Beyond Benefriends

Glasses
Fast Breaker
The Reset

An Illicit Seduction

Her & Them

The Color Spectrum: Ebony
Love On The Luminous
Costume Cutty

Remember Our Love
Loud & Lew'd
Consolation Gifts

D'VAUGHN AND KRIS PLAN A WEDDING

CHENCIA C. HIGGINS

carina
press

carina
press®

Recycling programs
for this product may
not exist in your area.

ISBN-13: 978-1-335-53494-1

D'Vaughn and Kris Plan a Wedding

Copyright © 2022 by Chencia C. Higgins

This edition published by arrangement with Harlequin Books S.A.

For questions and comments about the quality of this book, please contact us at
CustomerService@Harlequin.com.

Carina Press
22 Adelaide St. West, 41st Floor
Toronto, Ontario M5H 4E3, Canada
www.CarinaPress.com

Printed in U.S.A.

For my babies who aren't "out."
Your experience is valid.
You are valid.

D'VAUGHN AND KRIS PLAN A WEDDING

Do you have what it takes to say I Do?

All Genders Welcome!
Ages 25-40

Are you single?
Are you queer?
Are you good at lying?
Do you have six weeks to spare?

If you said yes to all of these things, then you should audition to be a contestant on Instant I Do, the reality show where strangers are paired together in a race to win 100K each! Send us a headshot and a video no longer than thirty minutes telling us why we should pick you!

See you at the altar!

Week One

Chapter One

D'Vaughn

The Real Deal

"Are you just going to stare at it?"

Blinking out of my reverie, I looked up from the hefty, legal-sized, manila envelope that had been delivered directly into my hands not even an hour earlier, and stared at my best friend, my lips turned down pitifully. Pushing an obviously annoyed breath out through her nose, Cinta stomped across the living room and snatched up the envelope from where I'd placed it on the coffee table. Spinning on her heels, she stomped back across the room and leaned against the round bistro table that made up the dining area of the tiny apartment that we shared. Shooting a quick glare at me, she ran her fingernail underneath the seam, opening the envelope and pulling out its contents.

My heart lurched in my chest at the thick stack of papers now in her hands. *That had to be a good sign, right?* They wouldn't send me a ton of paperwork just to tell me that I hadn't been selected...right? Instead of voicing my thoughts, I stared anxiously at the woman who knew me better than anyone, watching her eyes rove the first page.

"What does it say?"

Ignoring me, Cinta pulled the first page off of the stack and tucked it on bottom, continuing to read in silence.

"Cinta," I called, getting annoyed that she was reading on while I was still in the dark.

She continued reading, moving the second page to the bottom. That was the last straw for me, because there was no way in hell she'd read the second page that damn fast.

"Cinta!" I screeched, shooting onto my feet.

Brows lifted, she swung her gaze over to me. "Girl, why are you yelling?"

I just stared at her, my face scrunched into a pout. Taking pity on me, she giggled and waved the papers at me.

"If you wanted to know, you could just read them yourself."

I took a single step toward her, lifting my hand to reach for the papers before pausing and shaking my head.

"I can't, Cinta," I whined, fear causing my voice to tremble. "I'm scared. Just tell me if it says yes or no."

Pursing her lips, she shuffled the first page back on top of the stack. "Well…" she drawled, her lips drooping with remorse, "I'm sorry to say…but both of those words appear on the page."

Releasing an indignant shriek, I flew across the room and snatched the stack of papers out of her hand. As my eyes flew across the first paragraph, my heart skipped at least three beats and my brain felt a little fuzzy.

Congratulations, D'Vaughn! We received your audition and believe you would be a wonderful addition to season three of Instant I Do.

The papers shook as my hands began trembling and the words blurred as my eyes watered. I looked up to find Cinta beaming at me.

"You're in, boo!"

I was in?

I couldn't believe it and wasn't sure if I should jump for joy or crumble onto the couch and cry.

Auditioning to be a part of *Instant I Do* had been a long shot. I wasn't a particularly outgoing woman and, although I was attractive, it was no secret that reality shows tended to put a certain style and shape of woman in front of the camera. Petite, with flawless skin. Dazzling smiles and relaxed hair. Skin so fair it was almost translucent. So aggressively heterosexual they were willing to fight another woman over a man offering community dick that was mediocre at best. In the more than twenty years that I'd been watching reality TV, it was clear what was the norm, and I was none of those things.

Well, I did have a dazzling smile thanks to three awkward years of orthodontia in junior high, and I was known to rock a bone-straight wig every now and then. That's where the similarities between me and the "norm" ended. Beyond that, I didn't tick any of the other boxes.

Yet, I held papers in my hands that said they'd chosen me. Far too often, even the calls for queer representation tended to leave out people who looked like me, but not this time. They'd accepted me in all of my cocoa-brown-skinned, plus-sized, and lesbian glory, so I suppose they were doing something different for season three. Brushing away the warm trails of tears from my cheeks, I read on. The first page informed me that I was to be a contestant on the show and then listed the contract, nondisclosure agreement, filming schedule, and terms and conditions that made up the rest of the stack. There was also a party I was required to attend where I would meet the other contestants. Moving back over to the couch, I sat down and spent the next hour silently reading through every page.

When I finished, I turned to Cinta with a wide smile on my face.

"Is this really happening?" I asked in a dazed voice.

Nodding, Cinta grabbed my forearm. She'd read everything just as I had, and knew the minute details of what I'd been tasked with for the next six weeks.

"Not only is it really happening, Vaughn, it's happening right now!"

"I can't believe this."

"You'd *better* believe it. I told you that you'd be great for that show."

"Yeah, but I don't—"

"It's not about how you look, D'Vaughn, even though you're gorgeous. I have no doubt that you could go all the way with this thing because you *never* bring anyone home. *Instant I Do* is all about convincing your family that you're marrying a stranger, right? Well, you're perfect for that because your family has no idea what your type is, so they'll believe whatever you tell them."

I gave her a skeptical look. In theory, what Cinta was saying might be true, but she was forgetting one crucial detail.

"Except…"

Cinta waved me off. "That's a small detail."

Furrowing my brows, I gave her a disbelieving look, only to have her raise her eyebrows. After a moment we both burst out laughing. I shook my head.

"A small detail, huh?"

She held her index and thumb an inch apart. "I might've went a tad overboard, trying to downplay it."

Snorting, I shot her another glance before straightening the papers in my lap. I had to sign them all and then have them notarized. "You think?"

Cinta sighed and leaned back against the couch. "It's likely to be a shit show."

Pushing a heavy breath out of my nose, I nodded. My hands shook with nerves at the knowledge that my deepest struggle was coming to an abrupt end. Placing them on my bouncing thighs, I dug my fingers into the flesh, grounding myself as I swallowed that anxiety down. This was necessary. It was past time for my family to know everything about me so that I could lose the stress on my shoulders and breathe easier. I hadn't possessed the ability to do it on my own, and now I was getting the backing of an entire network.

"Yep. It's probably the main reason they selected me. I mentioned it in my audition and their eyes probably lit up when they heard that. It's guaranteed drama."

"And that's what makes up these shows."

"It's what gets them millions of viewers every week," I corrected. I wasn't naive enough to think that my particular situation didn't have a hand in securing my spot on the show. In fact, I'd used it as bait, knowing that my personality was otherwise too plain to be given a shot and that I needed a hook. It wasn't in any of my paperwork, but I was sure that it had worked like a charm.

It got me in; now I just needed to make sure that it didn't get me kicked off the show.

♥♥♥♥

Party Time, Excellent

The party was at a mid-rise condo on the outskirts of downtown, within walking distance of both Minute Maid Park and BBVA Stadium. I parked on the street and used the code from my paperwork to get inside of the gated building. There were two men already on the elevator when I stepped on, probably coming up from the parking garage one level down, and after nodding their way, I moved into the back corner and fiddled with my phone as a distraction. Inside of the canvas bag hanging from my shoulder was the signed sheaf of papers. Per instructions, I'd had them notarized before sealing them in the tamper-evident envelope that was also included in the box. It was all incredibly official and very, *very* real.

My stomach rumbled with nerves and I hoped that the men couldn't hear it. I stepped off the elevator and onto the eighth floor, taking my time as I walked down the eerily quiet hallway until I reached the right door. I knocked twice and stood back, willing my knees to stop knocking and my heart to stop racing. When the door opened, the sound of music and laughter reached me, and my nerves escalated. While I preferred to avoid large gatherings of people I didn't know, I wasn't the most awkward person in social situations. I knew how to hold my own.

Dropping my head back, I stared up at the giant of a man who stood on the other side of the door. He smiled and moved back, gesturing for me to enter. Clad in boot-cut jeans and a clingy, scoop-necked shirt, he looked significantly more casual than I assumed everyone would be.

"Hi there. D'Vaughn, right?"

Nodding, I stepped inside of the posh apartment and promptly froze when I caught sight of the camera pointed right at me. A second man, this one dressed in soft khakis and a white shirt that blended in with the wall behind him, stood in the corner of the foyer holding the large piece of equipment on his shoulder and motioned for me to keep going. I'd been expecting this, of course—today's event had been at the top of the list on the film schedule—but it still caught me a little off guard. Releasing a breath, I dipped my chin once, shooting the man who'd opened the door a quick glance before I continued into the apartment and observed the bright, inviting decor in the foyer. There was a chandelier overhead that highlighted the art on the walls and the two large plants in attractive, glazed ceramic pots on stands.

"That's me," I confirmed with a close-lipped smile.

The man behind me closed the door. "Welcome, D'Vaughn. We're glad you could make it. I'm Kevin Henderson, one of the executive producers of *Instant I Do*."

Relief gripped me. No wonder he was dressed down; he was staff. Turning around, I held out my hand which he shook with a firm grip. "Pleasure to meet you, Kevin."

Smiling, he nodded. "Did you bring your paperwork?"

I reached into my bag and pulled out the sealed envelope, handing it over. His smile widened.

"Ah, excellent!" After tucking the envelope under his arm, he showed me the closet where I could hang my coat and bag, and then pointed me straight ahead, down the short hall of the foyer. "You'll find everyone else in there. Go on in, grab a drink, and mingle."

Facing the direction from which the noise level came, I hesitated, causing Kevin to chuckle.

"I promise you that no one in there will bite you."

Lifting a brow, I turned to him with pursed lips. "How can you be so sure?"

"We ran extensive background checks on each of you," he informed me, a somber look on his face. "No one was a biter back in elementary school."

Throwing my head back, I busted out laughing and he shot me a wink. In five short minutes, Kevin had managed to eradicate more than half of the nerves plaguing me, and I suddenly felt more at ease than I had all day. It was almost enough for me to forget about the man standing seven feet away, capturing our entire exchange.

"Okay," I conceded with a nod of my head. "I'll take your word for it."

He nodded toward the hall and, without saying another word, I took a deep breath, smoothed my hands down the front of my dress, and headed toward the noise. The sound of laughter erupted just before I entered the living room of the condo and I was grateful that just about everyone's attention was focused on the teller of the joke instead of the doorway that I had walked through.

The great room of the condo was divided in half, with a sleek, chrome-filled kitchen to the left, and a sunken living room decorated with a stylish leather sectional on the right. Cameras on tripods sat beneath boxed lights in each corner of the room, and two people dressed in all black circled the space while carrying cameras with furry microphones mounted on top on their shoulders. In the living room were six people standing in a semicircle, deep in conversation. They stood against one side of the room, next to one of the three large windows that overlooked the busy streets below, with the lit baseball stadium towering over residential and commercial buildings just a few blocks away. Nearly everyone in the group held a glass in their hands, and I decided that was a smart move. Holding a drink would not only occupy my hands, but it would give me a reason to speak as little as possible.

There was an island in the kitchen with an under-mount sink and an eye-catching graphite countertop that currently doubled as a wet bar. It was covered with a cluster of glassware, an assortment of alcohol, a bucket full of ice, and several mixers and accompaniments. Shooting a cursory glance at the group of people on my right, I noticed one of the cameras swing toward me and hooked a mean left, heading straight for the island, and filled a ten-ounce tumbler with Jameson, chilled ginger ale, and a couple cubes of ice. I forced myself not to look up.

"*Remember to act natural,*" Cinta had reminded me as she helped me get ready for tonight. It was so much easier said than done.

Clutching the edge of the counter, I took a fortifying sip

from my lowball glass, allowing the crisp bubbles from the soda to coat my throat before I deigned to face the other people in the room. According to the paperwork I'd received, there would be a total of five couples this season, so it was likely that one of the six people already present would be my fiancée for the next six weeks. It probably wouldn't do me any good for my first impression to be that of a wallflower. Taking a breath, I girded my loins and moved across the room, being careful when descending the short flight of stairs into the living room. The absolute last thing I needed was to faceplant onto the gorgeous cherrywood floors.

I approached the group at a snail's pace, feigning as if I didn't want to spill my drink, but stalling until the last possible second. With my eyes over the rim of my glass, I observed the group. All eyes seemed to be on one woman who looked to be thriving under the attention. She was tall, with long pink hair that looked like it grew out of her scalp as it framed her mahogany-toned face and hung down to her waist. Cinta would have drooled over a wig so beautiful. A white bodycon dress molded to her substantial curves, curves that put mine to shame and made my heart flutter with joy at the same time. I'd fully expected to be the biggest person on the show this year, but whoever this woman was blew that theory into the stratosphere. Seeing another undeniably fat woman warmed my soul and made me tip an invisible hat to this season's producers.

The woman tossed her hair over her shoulder and lifted the wine goblet she held into the air. "We need to toast to *Instant I Do finally* gaying up the show!"

The group burst out laughing, and everyone raised their drinks into the air, knocking their glasses against one another in a ripple of clinks. Lifting my glass to my mouth, I giggled softly. I agreed wholeheartedly with her sentiment, and had said as much in my audition video. To my surprise, her eyes flitted over to me and she pursed her artfully painted lips, a playful look in her brown eyes, which were framed by thick lashes.

"Oh, no, ma'am! There is no way you're going to hide your gorgeous self over there, honey." Breaking the circle, she crossed the living room, her six-inch heels clacking elegantly against the hardwood floors as she made a beeline for me. Wrapping a hand around my wrist, she tugged me over into the circle.

All eyes were on me, and I knew without looking that at least one camera was likely zooming in on my face which was quickly growing hot with embarrassment. The last thing I'd expected was to have the attention of everyone present. In fact, it was something I had planned to actively avoid.

"Everyone," the woman announced to the small crowd, "we have a new arrival."

Lifting my drink in lieu of waving, I smiled and offered a lame "Hi."

The pink-haired woman turned to me. "What's your name, honey?"

"D'Vaughn."

"Nice to meet you, D'Vaughn. I'm Diamond."

"Hi, Diamond," I responded, a smile creeping onto my face. Diamond's energy was so infectious that it seemed impossible to not smile when around her.

Glancing around the circle, I found nothing but friendly faces smiling back at me. I received waves and greetings in return, continuing the job of putting me at ease that Kevin's friendliness had started. By the time we were all introduced, I felt immensely more relaxed.

"Miss D'Vaughn," Diamond began, stepping back to eye

me from head to toe. "I gotta say, you are wearing this mint-green dress, honey!"

Smiling, I dipped my head and murmured, "Thank you."

A couple of people chimed in to agree, and my face warmed all over again. The short-sleeved, A-line dress with sweetheart neckline cinched at my waist before flaring out down to my knees. Cinta had made it for me as a celebration gift after I submitted my audition video, and when I'd tried it on there hadn't been a doubt in either of our minds that it accentuated my best assets. I took a sip of my drink, trying to think of a way to shift the conversation away from me, but before I finished my thought, loud speaking interrupted me.

"Aye! Party over here!"

Following the shout, we all turned toward the entryway as two people appeared. As I laid eyes on them, I involuntarily sucked in a breath, swallowing liquid down the wrong hole. Of course, I began coughing, bringing everyone's attention right back to me. I could have melted into the floorboards.

"I'm fine," I wheezed, waving everyone off as I tottered back into the kitchen to grab a handful of napkins.

Turning my back on the rest of the room, I tried—and failed—to clear my throat as quietly as possible. I was wondering how much worse things could get when a hand came to my back just as a cold bottle of water was pressed against my left palm. Gratefully, I closed my eyes and sipped from the bottle, sighing with relief when my cough slowly ebbed away. When I felt like I could breathe without choking, I sighed and turned to the kind soul who'd helped me, thanks already forming on my lips. The words died, however, when I found the very person who'd caused me to start choking in the first place.

The finest person I'd seen in a stone's age stood directly at my elbow, with her hand on my back and her face mere inches from mine as she bent to get a good look at me. We were the same height, which meant she was just a few inches taller than my five-five when I wasn't wearing heels, with smooth tawny skin that was dusted with light brown freckles across her face. Her hair was a mass of dark brown locs that hung around her face in crinkly waves. Her arms and neck, exposed by the short-sleeved button-down that she wore, were covered in colorful tattoos, and I counted at least six piercings just on her face and ears.

"You alright, beautiful?"

Her voice was as rich and smooth as the Jameson I'd been sipping on, and my tongue felt heavy in my mouth. I tried to say something so that I wouldn't just be standing there, staring at her stupidly, but nothing came out. Defeated and even more embarrassed, I nodded.

Offering me a small smile that made my heart flutter a bit, she tilted her head to the side. "Are you sure?"

I nodded again, wondering why the previously loud room suddenly seemed so quiet.

"I won't believe you unless you say something," she teased, her eyes crinkling at the corners.

"I'm fine," I croaked before taking another sip from the bottle in my hand. It wasn't clear if the water was now for my throat or my thirst, but it got my eyes off of whoever she was, and I considered that a victory. In my peripheral I watched her subtly lean away from me and drag her warm, brown eyes down and up my frame. I couldn't tell if she liked what she saw, and I quickly averted my gaze when she brought her attention back up my face.

"Alright, beautiful. I'mma get out of your face, then."

Allowing myself to look her way, my eyes immediately fell to her mouth and I saw her smile widen in real time before she stepped back, putting a few extra inches of space in between us. She shot a glance over her shoulder before turning back to me and nodding slowly.

"I'll see you around, yeah?"

Again unable to formulate a response, I nodded and watched her walk away. Once she was out of the kitchen, it was as if the volume in the room had been raised back to normal levels, and I turned around to see that conversations had continued on in my absence. After getting myself together, I rejoined the group just in time to witness another round of introductions go up for the benefit of the two new arrivals. Unsurprisingly, Diamond took the honors, pointing out everyone and giving a quirky little tidbit about the person based off of what she had observed over the night.

There was Margo, the pansexual princess who was a little uptight, but had a great ass; Kirk, the bisexual boy-next-door with thick black curls streaked with blond highlights and a megawatt smile; and Tanisha, the lesbian femme who only dated other femmes and was obsessed with matte lipstick. Beside Tanisha was Nicolas, an unassuming guy who had declared with a shrug that he had no preferences "as long as the hole is wet." Finally was Bryce, who looked like a graduate of the Diamond School of Fashion. He wore a shiny bandeau top and miniskirt combination that matched both the sky-high stiletto heels on his feet and his robin's-egg-blue razor-cut bob. His beat was a level of perfection that made me want to burst into tears, and the bag he carried was from a line that was famous for its limited pieces. It was clear from first glance that Bryce didn't follow the culture, he *was* the culture.

Diamond went person-to-person in the small circle until she made her way to me.

"This is D'Vaughn. She's adorable and likes to hide from the spotlight."

"OMG!" I gushed. "How did you know?"

"I have a sixth sense about these things, honey," she declared, winking at me before turning her attention to the newcomers, the cause of my coughing fit and the person whose words had caught my attention in the first place.

"Now," Diamond continued, "since I haven't had a chance to suss you out, why don't you two introduce yourself to the class." She pointed at the gorgeous butch. "How about you go first, handsome."

The tattooed woman chuckled. "Thanks for the compliment, beautiful." She winked at Diamond before continuing. "I'm Kris. I was born and raised in Spring, but I live in the Montrose area now." She tapped a finger against her chin as she looked up at the ceiling. "Hmm, what's something interesting about me?"

Diamond propped a hand on her hip. "This humility has got to be an act."

Kris chuckled and my heart did that fluttering thing again when her cheeks lifted. I shot a quick glance around the circle, certain that I couldn't be the only one affected by her.

"It's no act. I'm incredibly boring on most days. Oh! Here's something interesting about me. I auditioned for *Instant I Do* because I want to find the love of my life."

My eyes widened to saucers, as did almost everyone else's. The group fell silent with varying looks of disbelief on our faces. After taking a look around, Kris laughed and nodded.

"I guess I don't have to ask if anyone thinks that's crazy. Come on, y'all, it's a love show."

"It's a marriage show," Margo corrected.

"Right," agreed Nicolas. "Love and marriage are not mutually inclusive."

Kris shrugged. "In my opinion, they should be."

Nodding, I observed her for a moment before adding, "It's a popular sentiment."

Kris met my eyes. "Indeed it is, beautiful. And it's probably what got me selected this season."

"Aside from the pure perfection that is your face, I'm almost certain that's the case, honey," Diamond mused, before moving on to the other person who'd arrived at the same time as Kris.

They were a burly individual who towered over everyone else, wearing boot-cut jeans and a plaid button-down that was rolled up at the sleeves. Their face was beat with a crisp cat-eye liner, and an eyeshadow and blush that matched their shirt. They introduced themselves as "Jerri with an *i*" and instructed us to use they and them pronouns when referring to them.

After introductions, the conversation shifted to expectations for the upcoming season. A few people wanted to hear more about Kris's quest for love, but I needed to avoid her for my sanity's sake. It was bad enough that I almost choked to death at the sight of her, I didn't need to add "perpetually struck mute whenever she's around" to my contestant profile on the season opener. Somehow, I was dragged into a conversation with Kirk and Jerri, but quickly begged off to refill my drink. To my dismay, they followed me, grabbing drinks of their own as they talked over my head about gender roles and what was expected of us during the season. Since I hadn't been familiar with the show prior to auditioning, I was genuinely curious, but had nothing to add to the conversation so I kept quiet. The tenth contestant arrived, and with them came a final round of introductions. This one was quick and dirty, with Diamond calling out names and folks waving from wherever they were in the room.

About an hour into the night, my feet started to protest my upright position. Although the dark green platform heels were usually comfortable, that was mostly when I was moving around. Standing in one place and allowing my weight to settle made the shoes near torturous. Fully capable of appearing to be engaged in the conversation while sitting, I made my way over to the couch and eased down on the end, leaning my knees to the right and crossing my feet at the ankles. Almost immediately after I sat down, three other people joined me on the sectional, with Tanisha sitting next to me.

"Hey, Dee!" she chirped, pleasantly.

Dee wasn't a nickname that I went by, but I figured I'd let it slide for the night. If Tanisha ended up being my fiancée for the next six weeks, I'd correct her when we discussed strategy.

As if she had heard my thoughts, Tanisha sighed and leaned into me.

"You know, you are exactly my type."

My brows rose and an uncontrollable smile lit my face.

"Really?"

She nodded, brushing her microbraids over her shoulder and twisting in her seat until she was facing me. Her ombré lips pursed as she eyed me from head to toe, the undeniable interest in her eyes warming me from the inside and making me blush.

"Yep. To a T." She gestured at me. "All this pretty brown skin and those dimples? I love it. Then, to top it off, you're thick *and* know how to dress? Perfection."

Bringing a hand to my face, I covered my eyes, my cheeks hurting from how hard I was grinning. "Please stop."

Tanisha grabbed my hand and lowered it from my face. "Don't do that. Don't cover up that gorgeous face."

Dropping my eyes to my lap, I stared at the glass in my hand. I was on my second and final drink of the night, but I might be tempted to have another if Tanisha didn't let up.

Scooting closer to me so that our thighs pressed together, Tanisha bent her head to look at my face. "You're either not used to being complimented, or you're shy as hell and my attention is embarrassing you. Which is it?"

Lifting my eyes to her face, I tried to suppress my smile. "You are embarrassing the hell out of me right now."

With a nod, she scooted away from me just enough so that we were no longer flush against each other. "Alright. I'll ease up; but you should know that if you were my fiancée, I wouldn't."

"Well," I began, lifting one of my shoulders, "it's a possibility."

She shook her head. "Making you my fiancée would be too easy. When I said you're my type, I meant that you're the kind of girl I could fall in love with. This show is about convincing our family and friends that we are doing something unbelievable. Nothing about me and you together would be unbelievable."

I stared at her, lips parted, as I took in what she'd said. Tanisha's words made my heart beat a little faster. I could see her point, though. Although I didn't have a "type" in the traditional sense, my dating history tended to trend toward women who looked like Tanisha. With her caramel skin, pouty lips, and curvy shape, it wouldn't be hard to convince those who truly knew me that we were a thing, and from the attraction I felt toward her, and her flirtatious nature, I wouldn't even have to pretend that I was into her. But truthfully, my aim wasn't to convince my loved ones I was into a stranger—not exactly. I was here to do something that I'd been unable to do, but was wholly necessary. It mattered not if my match didn't make sense.

After I agreed with her, we moved on to a different topic, and she did as she said she would, easing up off of me. Able to breathe, I was in the middle of listening to Tanisha describe her perfect date, when I felt someone tap on my shoulder. Looking up, I saw a dark-skinned woman with a pixie cut smiling down at me.

"Hi, D'Vaughn. I'm Bethany, one of the executive producers for the show. Can you come with me?"

Nodding, I stood from the couch and sat my empty glass on the coffee table atop a coaster, before smoothing my hands down my dress and following Bethany across the living room. When we reached the foyer, she made a right down a hall of closed doors before stopping at the last one on the right. She turned to me, a bright smile on her impish face, and spread her arms on either side of her.

"Are you ready?"

Cringing, I hesitated. "Uh…ready for what?"

Sensing my unease, Bethany shook her head and touched my arm. "No worries, D'Vaughn. It's just a little chat."

"Um, okay then. Let's go."

Bethany pushed open the door, entering the room first. I followed behind her, stepping inside of the bedroom and casting an assessing glance around. There was a full-sized bed bracketed by two nightstands against one wall, and a round, plush rug in the center of the floor. In the space between the bed and the door was a chair with one of those professional light umbrellas trained on it and a microphone dangling above it. A few feet in front of the chair was a huge camera mounted on a tripod. The lens of the camera was aimed at the chair.

Bethany gestured for me to have a seat and I did so gingerly, pressing my knees together and crossing my ankles demurely as I eased down into the chair, my palms sweating more than a little bit. It was a bit nerve-wracking sitting directly in front of a camera, but it was something I was going to have to get used to, at least for the next six weeks. Standing off to the side of the camera, Bethany smiled at me.

"Thanks for giving me a moment, D'Vaughn. This won't take long."

I nodded, curious about what I'd be doing. "No problem," I offered as if I'd really had a choice.

"This little setup here—" she waved at the camera and microphone "—is for what we at *Instant I Do* like to call the Jitter Cam."

That didn't sound promising. "Jitter? Like…wedding jitters?"

Nodding, her smile widened as she winked at me. "Exactly like that! And just like wedding jitters are a natural and normal part of the wedding process, we want your interactions with the Jitter Cam to be as natural as possible. You'll see different variations of this setup over the next six weeks. At random intervals each week, you'll take fifteen to thirty minutes to talk about what's going on, how the wedding planning is progressing, how you feel about your fiancée, et cetera, et cetera. Sometimes it will just be you and the camera, and you'll have the opportunity to speak your mind. Other times, it'll be interview style, with your executive producer asking you questions off camera."

"I'll be doing this several times a week?" That didn't sound too bad. I'd grown up watching *The Real World*, so the concept of a "confessional" was something I was familiar with.

"Generally, you'll only do one Jitter Cam per week, but it isn't unheard of to be pulled into a second or even third session after completing certain tasks during the week."

I nodded. "That sounds pretty painless. What's the catch?"

Tossing her head back, Bethany let off a short bark of laughter. "There isn't a catch. I promise."

Narrowing my eyes, I tilted my head to the side. "Well, we just met, so I have no idea if that promise is worth anything."

Still laughing, she shook her head. "You have a point. The good news is that you can talk about that as soon as I'm out of the room."

My eyes widened. "Wait, like…right now?"

Grinning, Bethany nodded. "Yep. There's no time like the present."

I pursed my lips. "That's the catch."

Her shoulders shook as she laughed again. "Nope. Still not a catch. We need to capture your reaction to the party."

"But the party isn't over."

"Which means everything is fresh. Don't think about it too hard; just give your initial reaction to what you've experienced thus far, and your first impressions of everyone. When the timer goes off, you can come on out."

I nodded and watched as she left the room, then I turned my attention to the camera in front of me. Taking a deep breath, I squared my shoulders and folded my hands in my lap.

Here goes nothing.

Jitter Cam 01-D'Vaughn

Um. This isn't awkward at all. Let's see. Well, so far things seem cool. The party is a nice way for everyone to get to know each other, but I guess I don't really see the point of it, since I won't see eight of those people after today. Speaking of those people, Diamond is a trip. She's hilarious and the complete life of the party. Whoever ends up as her fiancé had better be someone who won't fold under her dynamic personality. I know it won't be me, since she's a straight, trans woman. She's gorgeous though, and I hope she makes it all the way.

Um...Kirk is pretty funny. I think him and Jerri have hit it off. Actually, you know what? Kirk is a huge flirt and was up in Margo's face as well. Margo is...a lot. I mean that in the nicest way possible. She's very...severe...for lack of a better word. She reminds me of the stereotypical schoolmarm from a boarding school. Just unyielding and hard to please. Yikes. That sounds terrible. If you see this, Margo, I apologize. Anyway, um...I wonder what made her audition for the show, but I guess I don't have to wonder why she was selected. It would be a miracle if she can convince people that she is in love with someone, let alone getting married.

Oh, and Jerri is freaking hilarious. Whenever I'm around them, I laugh until my ribs hurt. Kris is...fine as hell. That's it. Just sexy as all get-out for no damn reason. Like...good luck to whoever is paired up with her, because you're going to need the strength of the gods to keep from drooling whenever you look at her. Matter of fact; let me say a prayer right now.

Lord, keep your hand on Kris's fiancée. They need you now more than ever because they won't be able to convince people they're marrying her if they're staring at her dumbly at every turn. Gird their loins and strengthen their poker face. Cross my heart and hope to die, stick a needle in my eye. Amen.

My mama would kill me if she heard me joke like that while praying. Lord, forgive me. Mama, if you see this, forgive me too.

Hosea seems cool, but something about him feels…disingenuous. Like…he's cisgender and *Very Manly*. He presents as heterosexual, but I wonder if he isn't hiding behind that facade. Now that I think about it, he strikes me as the type of person who isn't out to their family. As a fellow mothball, I recognize that in him and I'll be saying a prayer for him tonight. If he *is* closeted and is using this show as the vehicle to come out to his family—like *I'm* doing—I hope that he doesn't lose anyone close to him. I hope that the people he loves, love him enough to accept that being gay is a part of who he is and always has been.

Let's see. Who am I missing? I haven't really had a chance to talk to Bryce or Nicolas but I can't lie. Bryce is flamboyant and seems to have his eyes set on Hosea, which would be great television if they actually got paired together. Nicolas seems cool, if a little gross. He doesn't seem to be leaning toward any one person though. I'm still squicked out by that 'wet hole' comment. Why are men like this? Honest question.

Last but not least, there's Tanisha. Um…I…like her? I don't know why I said that like a question. I'm not unsure about it. I *like* her. It's weird to say that about someone I literally just met, but it's true. I like her energy. She's gorgeous and she smells *so good*, and she isn't stingy with compliments. I don't really have a type but if I did, it'd be her. Of course, I didn't say that to her, but I didn't have to, since she told me straight up that I was *her* type. That, um…that was nice to hear. She was pretty adamant that we wouldn't get paired, but maybe she'll be wrong. Who knows?

Welp, those are my initial thoughts about everyone. Here's to the next six weeks. Hopefully I'm not knocked out before we even make it to the weekend. I was gonna come out to my mama eventually…one day, maybe, but it would be so much easier to do with a camera around, since she'd rather die than present anything other than a solid family unit in front of others.

Ah, well. Wish me luck.

Chapter Two

Story of a Girl

I had no expectations.

Not when it came to the person I'd be paired with to plan a wedding while also convincing our families that we were madly in love for the next six weeks. The party had been fun, like hanging out with a group of friends from high school after not seeing them for ten years, but I wasn't sure if I really connected with anyone. There were a few women that I found attractive, but I didn't go there expecting to make a love connection. I saw the event for what it was: a chance for the producers to scrutinize our interactions and pair us off. Because of that, I spent an equal amount of time speaking to everyone, even the guys, and kept my flirting to an almost nonexistent level.

It was strategic. I wanted the people behind the scenes to have to put in some real work when they chose for me. The first two seasons of the show had some odd pairings; couples who likely never would have crossed paths ordinarily. Despite that, each season had at least one couple that made it all the way, yet they all chose the money instead of marriage when it came down to it. I wanted to do something different.

Before the party came to a close, each of us was issued a handheld sports camera with instructions on how to record ourselves the following morning. To keep the integrity of the "reality" portion of the show, *Instant I Do* used a combination of external and internal footage, with larger events where family needed to be involved being captured by camera people, and a set amount of filmed hours submitted by the contestants weekly. I was no stranger to a camera and already knew the best areas in my home to get the best footage, so I wasn't put out by those instructions at all.

When there was a knock on my front door at nine the morning after the party, I had a pretty good idea of who it was. The same courier who'd delivered my initial paperwork handed me a slim envelope before smiling and disappearing down the walkway that led to my front door. I watched as he hopped into the passenger side of a Smart car just before it took off soundlessly down the street. Closing and locking the door, I carried the envelope with me back into the kitchen, where I'd been having breakfast with my older sister, Rhea.

"Who was that?" Rhea asked, cutting into her omelet and taking a bite as she zeroed in on the item in my hands, one eyebrow lifted in curiosity.

I slid into my seat and placed the envelope on top of the empty place setting to my left. I was both eager to see its contents and skeptical about the name I would find inside, so I decided to finish eating first.

"The delivery guy for the show," I responded nonchalantly. If he wasn't a courier, he was definitely on staff for the network.

Rhea stopped chewing and swung her now wide eyes from me to the envelope and then back to me. Facing my plate, I kept my eyes on her as I resumed eating, lips twitching, but laughing internally as the excitement on her face grew.

"You're not gonna open it?" she finally asked, after more than a minute of me not saying a word had gone by.

"Of course," I responded breezily, scooping the last of my scrambled eggs into my mouth. I took my time wiping my mouth with my napkin and taking a sip from my glass of orange juice before finally picking up the envelope. It was all a show because I wanted to rip into the letter to see what it held, but I wouldn't be a younger sibling if I didn't needle her when the opportunity presented itself.

"Me vas a volver loca, lo juro," she muttered as she rolled her eyes.

"If I haven't driven you crazy after all of these years, a few minutes of waiting won't do the trick," I chuckled, using the handle of my fork to slice the top of the envelope open.

I made a show of shaking the envelope and widening the hole to peer inside before eventually reaching in and retrieving two sheets of paper. My eyes flew across the first page. It held the address to a restaurant that wasn't far from the home I shared with Rhea, and told me what time to be there. It was the location where my *fiancée* and I were supposed to meet for the first time. The meeting would be filmed, and after an hour and a half of me and my fiancée getting to know each other over lunch while a camera captured the moment from a distance, a member of *Instant I Do* would join us and give us an overview of their expectations. The second page was of more interest to me. At the top left was a headshot paper-clipped to the sheet. I removed the picture and stared at it, a slow smile creeping onto my face.

I'd been paired with D'Vaughn Miller.

I remembered her clearly from the night before. It might have been my strategy to appear uninterested in anyone, but I'd definitely noticed her, and not just because she'd had a coughing fit as soon as I'd arrived. D'Vaughn was freaking gorgeous, and from the way she dressed, she absolutely knew it. It'd been obvious at the party last night, with the light green dress she'd worn, which accented her bust and flared around her hips, to the forest-green platform heels that made her legs seem longer than what they were. Her skin was the color of canela or cajeta, and that made me think that she probably tasted sweet as well. Unbidden, my thoughts took a nosedive into the gutter, and I dragged a hand down my face as if I could wipe them from my mind.

Rhea snatched the picture out of my hand as I read the second page. It told me what the picture already had. D'Vaughn had been chosen as my fiancée and we had to spend the next six weeks convincing our closest family and friends that we would be getting married, while simultaneously planning a wedding. All initial expenses for the wedding were to be covered by the network, but of course, no one would know that. The wedding was to take place exactly six weeks from tomorrow, and we would be given tasks to complete each week until we reached the wedding—*if* we reached the wedding.

Each couple had been assigned an executive producer who would stick by our side throughout the six weeks, guiding us through our assigned tasks, offering support, and monitoring how good a job we did at convincing our families that we were getting married. The e.p. was also our first cheerleader, taking weekly reports back to a panel of judges who made the ultimate decision on who stayed or continued on. I'd frowned a little when I got to that part in the contract. Although I'd watched other seasons of the show, that was new information to me. How could my future be determined by a handful of strangers—people who didn't know my family the way I did? My papi was a stoic man, and even though I'd known him all of my life, I still had a hard time deciphering how he felt about a great many things. If he didn't say it with his mouth, there was always a possibility that our assumptions about his feelings were false.

According to the detailed report, mine and D'Vaughn's e.p. was Kevin Henderson. I'd met him briefly at the party, but we hadn't spoken to each other beyond him greeting me at the door and telling me and Jerri to have a good time. Supposing that I'd get a better read on him once we had a chance to speak later, I shrugged it off and looked up at Rhea, watching her volley between reading the report and looking at D'Vaughn's picture.

"She's cute."

Giving her a side-eye, I shook my head. "You know damn well she's more than cute. Shorty's bad."

Rhea shrugged noncommittally. "I didn't want to say too much, in case you weren't feeling her."

Laughing, I rolled my eyes. Of my four siblings, Rhea and I were the closest. Not only were we just ten months apart, but thanks to the finagling of our Tia Claudia, we'd been in the same grade throughout our years in school. Coupled with the features and body type that we'd shared up until recently, we'd had to deal with people thinking that we were twins for almost twelve years. It didn't help that Mami had loved to dress us alike.

Rhea had always been my best friend, and it became clear that we were more alike than either of us had realized when she announced to our family that she was a lesbian when we were in middle school. The announcement had surprised even me, because despite how we would discuss everything under the sun, she'd never mentioned that. Never even hinted at it.

But neither had I.

She became my example of living as your full and true self, and seeing her dress in clothes that looked like they came from Raul and Raymond's closet only solidified that for me.

After Kiana had fallen asleep the night before my birthday, I'd dragged Rhea into the makeshift fort that we'd erected in the corner of the bedroom the three of us shared, and spilled my guts about the things I'd been feeling for a while. I came out the following day, just before my party, and was immediately carted to the store by Mami to fill my closet with the same sweatpants and sneakers she'd just purchased for Rhea. Mami wasn't going to let a little butch lesbianism keep her from dressing her niñitas alike.

Without a doubt, I'd been blessed. At no point in my life had I ever felt alone, but beyond that, our parents never made us feel like something was wrong with us. They never turned their backs on us. Even Papi made a point to speak to us separately, and express to us that even though he didn't fully understand, he still loved us. He went on to joke that he went from having two sons, to four, since both Rhea and I preferred baggy Wranglers and jerseys to the floral dresses and stockings that Mami dressed Kiana in. It could have been offensive, but at thirteen, I took it as it was—his acceptance. To have something so important from a staunchly traditional and religious man, it meant the world to me.

"So, what's your game plan?"

Furrowing my brows, I gave Rhea a questioning look. "What do you mean? I'm in it to win it." I'd been talking her ear off about this since I'd first seen the casting call, so she—more than anyone—knew what I was on.

Rhea shook her head, wiping her mouth with a napkin before sitting back in her seat. "I know that much. I'm asking you what your goal is. Are you gunning for the money, or are you still hoping to find the love of your life through the show? I mean…" She shrugged. "A hundred thou ain't nothing to sneeze at."

Knowing my sister, she wasn't done speaking, so I quirked a brow and stared at her, waiting.

"I'm just saying," she began, "are you still using this as a way to get a girlfriend?"

I rolled my eyes at her oversimplification. "Why are you trying to play me, Rhea? You know this isn't about getting a girlfriend."

"Remind me of what your goal was, because I distinctly remember it sounding basic as hell. You have hundreds of women in your DMs right now, but you think you need to go on a reality show to find 'the one'?"

Groaning, I dismissed her words with a wave of my hand. "Man, come on with all of that. You know as well as I do that the women in my DMs aren't there to find forever with me. It's about the moment—the opportunity—and that's it." The tiny bit of social capital I'd stumbled upon via social media made me just another rung along the bottom of the status ladder. More women than I wanted to admit had tried to use me as a stepping stone to launch their careers as influencers, only to find out the hard way that no one of importance gave a damn about a random weight-lifting stud whose favorite pastime was eating tacos after the gym.

Shaking her head, Rhea stood from the table, her plate in her hand as she headed toward the kitchen. From my spot at the table, I had a clear view of the sink, and I watched as she washed the dish and set it on the wire rack on her right before turning back to face me.

"When you saw the casting call and decided to audition, I didn't say anything because I thought it would be a dope idea. Now that you're actually in, I can't let you go on without at least voicing my concerns." She shook her head. "I know you'll do what you want, but I can't be silent."

I frowned and folded my arms across my chest. "Why do

you sound so down about this? You're talking as if this terrible thing is going to happen and you're trying to keep me from danger. It's a reality show, Rhea, not a train wreck waiting to happen."

Her dark brown eyes bored into me, and I could see that she was thinking deeply. I was baffled by this. *What did she think was going to happen?*

"Man, listen. You know I get my feelings about things every now and then. When my intuition speaks up, I make sure to listen. Ever since you found out that you were selected, I've had this feeling that I can't describe."

"What am I supposed to do with that? You can't even tell me what, exactly, it means." I didn't want to downplay her feelings, but this was exasperating.

"I want you to really think about what you plan to gain at the end of all of this. What if you fall for this girl and she doesn't feel the same? What if she falls for you, but you realize that you can't stand her? If you make it to the altar, are you going to try and force something that isn't working just so that you can be the first to say I Do? Or are you going to take the money and call it a lucrative six weeks?"

I stared at her, torn between anger and frustration. Or maybe they were one and the same. Outside of the party, and the little footage of me opening the envelope minutes ago, I'd barely begun filming the show and Rhea was already turning on the sprinklers to delay the parade. It didn't make sense to me, but I didn't want to get into it with her. Rhea could go on for a while if I let her, and I had no intentions of letting her. So, I sighed, shook my head, and smiled at her.

"I hear you, Rhea. I'll think about everything you've said."

She narrowed her eyes at me, clearly skeptical at how quickly I'd acquiesced, but finally, she nodded.

"I know you're not trying to hear me right now, but I'm

just looking out for you." Walking back to the table, she offered me her fist.

She was both right and wrong. Rhea was the more practical one of the two of us. She considered the bottom line and mapped out the most logical way for us to get from point A to point Z, while I was content to let the chips fall where they may. Because of that, she couldn't wrap her head around the seemingly strategic move that participating on *Instant I Do* was for me. Beyond what it could do for our brand, my gut told me that I could find a love that had—until now—seemed elusive. Rhea was buggin' because she didn't understand the plan, but I didn't have the words to explain that I was trying the least obvious route to love because the regular shit hadn't been panning out. Or maybe I did have the words, but what I lacked was the desire to see her give me a disbelieving look since, in her eyes, I'd never lacked for admirers. The thing was, I wasn't looking for an admirer. I didn't need a reality show to help me find someone to fuck. What I wanted was someone who could make me feel even a fraction of the way my parents felt for one another, and if I could give some random chick in my DMs an opportunity to be that, there was no reason to turn my nose up at a reality show contestant who was closer to wanting the same things as me simply by being present on the show. I couldn't expect Rhea to understand that though, so instead of trying I left it alone and dapped her up, laughing when she threw her arm around my shoulder and dropped a kiss on my temple.

"I appreciate you looking out," I assured her, "but I can't go into this thinking it won't work because then it's guaranteed to fail."

She nodded again. "I get that."

"Good." Pulling out her grasp, I stood and carried my plate

to the sink. "Now, if you don't mind, I have a date with my fiancée that I need to prepare for."

♥♥♥♥

Day Date

The restaurant was an unassuming place, with a narrow store-front that was tucked between a quirky consignment shop with vintage mannequins in the windows and a pet groomer. I'd walked right past it at first, not realizing my mistake until I reached the end of the block and had to turn around. The marquee was no bigger than a stop sign, hanging above the glass-paned door that opened to a steep set of stairs which led me to a half-filled dining room. Two people stood behind a counter near the door, smiling as they welcomed me.

I responded in kind before sweeping my gaze around the room. Just under a dozen tables were scattered around the room in a pattern I couldn't decipher, more than half of which were occupied by patrons who carried on conversations over their meals. Two of the four walls were exposed red brick, and the remaining two were made of floor-to-ceiling retractable windows, letting in an abundance of sunlight which allowed me to scan each table. D'Vaughn was nowhere in sight.

Turning to the counter, I opened my mouth to give them my name when an impressive figure approached me from further inside of the restaurant and entered my peripheral. His eyes were trained on me and he wore a friendly smile on his familiar face which immediately put me at ease and caused me to smile in return.

"Kris," he greeted, holding a hand toward me. "You made it."

Nodding, I shook his hand. "You're my e.p., huh? The one stuck with me for the next six weeks."

Kevin's grin widened and he took an awkward sort of bow

while our hands were still clasped. "At your service, but don't make me regret it."

Chuckling, I pulled my hand from his. He straightened and gestured for me to follow him. There was a tiny coatroom off the entrance to the restaurant. It was March, so the room was mostly empty, save for a television setup which was clearly out of place. Perched on a stool in the center of the room was an older man with a salt-and-pepper afro that was mashed slight by a pair of heavy-duty, over-the-ear headphones as he stared at two monitors that sat atop a built-in counter. He looked up when we entered the room and immediately reached for the black rectangle sitting on his left. The device—which was the size of a box of playing cards—was attached to a long, thin cord which held a small flesh-colored ball at the end.

"This is Joe," Kevin offered as he closed the door behind me and guided me over to the man. "He's our sound engineer and makes sure that we can hear you even when we aren't standing over you with a boom mic."

Stepping off of the stool, Joe lifted the device into the air. "Do you mind if I put this on you?" His voice was a calming rasp that, when paired with his deep umber skin and warm, brown eyes, reminded me of Papi.

My brows met. "Oh, I didn't know it was optional."

He held my gaze, his expression serious but not unkind. "Wearing a microphone isn't optional, but having it put on by me is."

As I realized what he was saying, the corner of my mouth lifted and I felt a surge of respect for him and the network.

"If you tell me what all 'putting it on' entails, I can decide."

With a nod, Joe explained how the device clipped onto the back of my pants, while the cord was snaked under my shirt so that the ball could fit into my ear. Lifting the back of my shirt, I allowed him to secure the device just inside the waistband of my shorts before following his directions to carefully thread the cord between my undershirt and the lightweight polo I wore. After pushing the soft ball—that Joe assured me was newly unpackaged—into my ear, we bumped fists and I gave him my thanks.

Kevin motioned for me to follow him out of the coatroom.

"We're—*you're*—going to go out onto the patio. There is a small crew out there and D'Vaughn's already here. I'm going to give you two some time to get to know each other and then I'll join you in about an hour. Don't worry about the cameras, just act as if they aren't there. You're both mic'd, so relax and use your regular speaking voice. Feel free to order whatever you'd like. It's on me today."

Smirking, I gave him a sidelong glance as we moved toward the entrance to the patio. "On you, huh?"

He laughed lightly, lifting his broad shoulders up near his ears and dropping them swiftly. "I'm swiping the card. The network pays the bill."

My stomach rumbled as I passed a table and spotted a plate piled high with a club sandwich cut into perfect triangles and a basket of house-fried kettle chips. Patting the protesting organ, I nodded.

"It just so happens that I brought a mean appetite, so I'll definitely be taking advantage of that."

I made it to the door two steps before Kevin, but we reached for the handle at the same time, his long arms and massive hands taking up a large portion of the push-bar. Eyes wide, I looked up at him.

"Damn, dude," I breathed in awe. "What's your wingspan?" He didn't have an exact foot on me but it had to be close.

Laughing, he pulled his hands from the door.

"I don't have a clue. That's not something they check for at the doctor these days."

Shaking my head, I cracked up at the genuine confusion in his voice.

"Don't worry about it, man. I'll see you in a bit."

I tipped my chin up before pushing the door open. I stepped onto the patio, my eyes sweeping the space. It was mostly empty, save for a couple people sitting off in the corner near the street under a large umbrella. They were laughing and talking and didn't even look up at my entrance. On opposite sides of the patio were the two people that Kevin had mentioned. One stood behind a tripod mount and the other held a smaller camera on their shoulder.

The other end of the enclosed patio was where I was supposed to be. I started toward D'Vaughn, my lips curving into a smile as I observed her from a distance before she took notice of me. A thick wax-print headband pushed her curly hair out of her face, exposing the sun-kissed skin on her face as she perused the one-page menu in her hands. The tablecloth on the wrought-iron table was short, and I could see that her legs were crossed in front of her, one foot bouncing in the air. On her feet were wedge sandals that tied in a bow at the front of her ankle. The whole scene was cute, and I had a passing thought of how perfect it would be to snap a picture and post it on a rainy day with a caption along the lines of "take me back" or "summertime vibes."

"D'Vaughn," I murmured as I approached from her side. "Hey."

D'Vaughn's head snapped up and wide eyes lined with black liner and framed with thick lashes found me. With her painted lips parted, it was almost as if she was surprised to see me, but that didn't make sense. Without a doubt, she'd received a dossier on me just as I had on her so she had to be expecting me. Blinking rapidly, she quickly pushed back from the table, the legs of the chair scraping against the wooden planks that covered the floor as she stood.

"Hey, Kris."

My smile deepened, putting all of my teeth on display as pleasure surged through me at the sound of my name on her lips. Her voice was mellow; smooth like my favorite brown liquor, and I loved the surety with which she spoke my name. Too often, I met women who, for some reason, thought that pretending to be confused about my name would keep me from realizing that they already knew who I was before we met. This moment was in stark contrast to that, not only because the greeting was personalized, but D'Vaughn used the name I'd given at the party and *not* the name that was likely listed in my dossier. It was a little thing, yet at the same time, tremendous, and I delighted in it.

Now that we were up close, I got a better look at her. D'Vaughn looked comfortable and was dressed for the weather. It was a warm day, already in the eighties even though it was just eleven, and she wore a short-sleeved V-neck top that was tucked into a pair of high-waisted shorts that fell to the middle of her thighs. Unfortunately, this wasn't even unseasonable weather. Born and raised in Southeast Texas, I was used to eight out of twelve months being different shades of summer with the other four being pre-summer in varying stages of dampness. I wondered if D'Vaughn was from the area as well. Her dossier hadn't delved into her background.

Spreading my arms, I asked, "Can I?"

Once again, she blinked, this time confusion lowering her eyebrows just a little. "Huh?"

I chuckled. "I meant, can I hug you?"

Her chocolate-brown irises widened. "Oh!" She shook her head as if she couldn't believe that she didn't catch that. "Yes, of course."

She took two steps in my direction, her arms widening to receive me, and I dipped low, wrapping my arms around her waist and pressing my palms against her back as I gave her a soft squeeze. I kept it brief, not wanting to make the situation awkward since it was so clear that she was already a little flustered, either by my presence or that of the cameras. Separating, we settled into our seats and I took a long gulp of ice water from the glass that was already placed at my setting.

I managed one gulp of the cool liquid before a waiter appeared next to the table, delivering a basket of pita and a dish of hummus before asking if we were ready to order. There were already two menus on the table, so I grabbed one and instructed D'Vaughn to order first while I perused the restaurant's offerings and settled on something to eat. After we ordered, the waiter took our menus and disappeared.

"So," I began, dragging a triangle of pita through the hummus and popping it in my mouth after the silence stretched on long enough for things to become awkward, "this place seems nice."

A measure of relief flashed in D'Vaughn's eyes, and she glanced around the patio. The rooftop extension of the restaurant had no ceiling or walls—save for a seven-foot-wide trellis on the side that faced the street. The open-air concept allowed for a cool breeze to whisk over us, providing instant relief as the sun steadily moved overhead, its beams dodging the clouds to dance along our skin.

"I know, right! As much as I'm in this area, I can't believe I've never been here before. A rooftop patio has a vibe I can always get with." Her smile widened into a grin. "Especially when the weather is as amazing as it is today."

Closing her eyes, she leaned her head back, a move that put her face in position for a persistent ray of light to cast upon her in an almost angelic way. Mere seconds passed as I stared at her, my eyes roving over the rounded jut of her chin, the smooth column of her neck, and the surprising peek of dark ink that danced along the edge of her collarbone that wasn't covered by her top.

She looks amazing, I thought, smiling softly at the serenity on her face. The thought was so strong that I found myself uttering the words aloud.

Seemingly startled, she quickly dropped her chin, facing me as her eyes popped open. Her cheeks flushed as she bit her lip and lowered her gaze to the table for a brief moment before lifting her eyes to once again meet mine.

"Thank you," she murmured, a small smile lifting her lips. "So do you."

Quirking a brow, I rubbed my chin as I eyed her.

"You tryna flirt with me, beautiful?" I teased, tilting my head to the side. Eyes wide, her cheeks instantly bloomed, and she brought her hands to her face, pressing her palms against them. It hadn't been my intent to fluster her—or…maybe it had—but I couldn't suppress my grin even if I'd wanted to.

"Oh my gosh," she mumbled, fanning her face. "I don't know why I wasn't prepared for this."

"Prepared for what?" I asked. "I wouldn't have pegged you for being this shy. That's not the vibe you gave off the other night at all." Diamond might have said that D'Vaughn avoided the spotlight, but throughout the night she was always engaged in conversation with someone.

Her brows knitted. "We barely spoke to each other…" Releasing a slow breath through her nose, D'Vaughn shook her head and took a sip of her water. "I'm not usually…"

She trailed off a second time after flicking her gaze to my left where I knew the cameraperson was slowly circling our table. I waited fruitlessly for her to continue, wondering if she was hesitant to speak because we were being filmed. Leaning forward, I prompted her. "It sounds like a 'but' was coming."

Pursing her lips, D'Vaughn regarded me for a moment before shaking her head again. "That's because there was. I was going to say that I'm not usually a shy person unless I'm around a group of people that I don't know, so I don't know what vibe you picked up on." Wrinkling her nose, she shrugged. "But it's obvious that doesn't matter since God decided to be funny today."

Curiosity lifted my brows, and I brought my left ankle up to my right knee, getting comfortable for what seemed like it was going to be an interesting story. "Care to explain that?"

Lifting a finger into the air, D'Vaughn indicated for me to wait. "Hold that thought."

Bowing her head, she pressed her palms together and closed her eyes. Before I could say another word, her lips started moving and I could hear her faintly speaking.

"Lord, I see You got jokey jokes. Obviously, this is You getting me back for that fake prayer I did for the Jitter Cam, and to that I say, well played."

When she opened her eyes and looked at me, she busted out laughing. That was the oddest prayer I'd ever heard in my life, and the tightening of my features surely displayed that. I knew my face looked crazy.

"Are you religious?" I asked when she composed herself.

D'Vaughn scrunched her nose before wobbling her head left and right. "Um, yes and no. I was born and raised in the church, and still go every Sunday. However, I consider myself to be more spiritual than religious. I mean—" she shrugged "—I regularly participate in certain religious practices, but I don't subscribe much to the teachings of religious folks."

My brows furrowed. "What exactly does that mean?"

"In a nutshell: men are flawed and because of that, I tend

to leave them out of the relationship I have with my heavenly Father."

Well, that was interesting. Despite both of my parents being raised Catholic, I came from a decidedly secular household where we were encouraged to defer to our morals over pleasing a higher power. Since my journey through life was unique to me, I didn't judge anyone who lived theirs differently. However, I didn't have to be deep in D'Vaughn's faith to know how it treated people of our ilk. Part of me wanted to leave the subject alone. There were certain topics that were sensitive and had the potential to turn decent conversations into shouting matches, and religion was without a doubt top two on that list, and it wasn't number two. However, despite the knowledge that traveling down this road could lead to a difficult few weeks ahead, I couldn't move on to something else without asking the question bouncing around in my head.

"How do you reconcile your faith with your sexuality?" I found myself more than a little curious how she handled something I'd seen many struggle with, and whether it had anything to do with her coming on the show. *Was this essentially her giving a big middle finger to the establishment?*

D'Vaughn tilted her head, offering me a smile that brightened her entire face and immediately made me smile in response.

"The beauty in my faith is that I don't *have* to reconcile anything. I know who I am and what I believe, and that is enough for me."

Impressed, I sat back. That definitely answered my unasked question. "Wow. That's awesome," I commented genuinely, "and not something I've heard very often when having conversations like these over the years."

Still smiling, D'Vaughn shrugged and reached for the pita. "Believe me, I get it."

Our waiter appeared and placed our meals in front of us. The aromas wafting up from my plate of chicken kebab, basmati rice, potatoes, and spinach pie made my stomach rumble loudly. Digging in, I glanced up at D'Vaughn, who was hefting a massive gyro into her hands while doing a cute little shimmy in her seat. We ate in relative silence for a while before I picked the conversation back up.

"So, is that philosophy shared amongst your family as well?"

Inhaling sharply just as she was chewing on a few fries, D'Vaughn began to choke. Jumping out of my seat, I rounded the table and patted her on the back. She dropped the remains of her sandwich onto her plate and reached for the glass of tamarind juice in front of her. After taking a fortifying sip, she waved me off as she continued to clear her throat a few times.

"Goodness gracious," she finally murmured lowly. "I'm always choking around you. That was incredibly embarrassing."

Patting my chest, I shook my head. "Try terrifying. You just reminded me that I need to renew my first aid certification."

Cutting her eyes at me, she pursed her lips. "You're welcome," she remarked, her tone dry.

"I take it your family is a touchy subject…"

She shook her head. "The opposite, actually. I love them with all of my heart. My mama raised us by herself on a high school education and yet, *somehow*, my siblings and I never wanted for anything." D'Vaughn paused to sip her drink before continuing. "You know what? That's a lie. I definitely wanted a few things that she told me I couldn't have, but we had the necessities."

Her tone had taken on a dark, affronted register that had my curiosity piqued. "What's one thing you wanted but didn't get."

"Barbie Dream House from page one-eighty-six of the Big Book of Toys," she gritted instantly through clenched teeth.

"It was three feet tall with a working elevator and doorbell." Her eyes were narrowed and one hand was curled into a fist on the table near her plate.

Laughing, I shook my head. She was cute as hell. "Why do you still sound angry about that?"

Her unfocused eyes found my face, and she blinked a few times, clearing the dark clouds from her eyes. The fingers on her hand relaxed and she dropped her hand into her lap. Ducking her head, she gave a sheepish smile that brought another bout of laughter out of me.

"There may be some residual…disappointment lingering around."

That was obvious. "How long ago was this?"

"Christmas of '97," she sniffed, turning her head toward the trellis, which had vines woven through the slats and was the perfect backdrop for selfies and boomerangs.

Trying to keep from saying anything, I bit my lip and nodded. It was a cute story and I wasn't even going to call her out on how smoothly she'd managed to navigate the conversation away from answering my question. Picking up my fork, I prepared to finish off my food.

"I'm not out to my family."

D'Vaughn's blurted confession made a record scratch loud and obnoxious in my head and brought my startled gaze back to hers. Her eyes roved my face, taking in my widened eyes and gaped mouth, and she covered her face with her hands.

"Don't judge me!"

Immediately, I snapped my mouth shut and dropped my fork back onto my plate. Of the many thoughts that came rushing to the forefront of my mind, that hadn't been one of them at all. There were several variations of "well, there went the show" but not one instance of judgment.

"I would never judge you for something like that," I assured her, my tone firm. "I don't know your family. That might be the safest thing for you."

Eyes closed, D'Vaughn lowered her hands from her face and took a deep inhale before cracking her lids. The shame in those chocolate-brown depths broke my heart.

"It's not about safety, I've just been terrified."

Reaching across the table, I grabbed one of her hands, lacing our fingers together. Her skin was soft, palm warm against my mine. "And that's okay. Whatever your reasons, your feelings are valid. You said that you were born and raised in the church, right? That's more than enough of an explanation for why you aren't out."

She tilted her head back, but when I saw a single tear slip from the corner of her eye, my throat tightened. I pulled a few napkins from the dispenser in the center of the table and pressed them into her free hand. As she dabbed at the trail the tear had left, she took a shuddering breath. Although I hadn't had to grow up with the fear of keeping my sexuality from my family, I understood how difficult and draining it could be to have to hide a part of yourself from the ones you loved.

After a few moments, D'Vaughn squeezed my hand, pulled hers free, and lowered her chin until we were once again facing each other.

"Um…I'm sure you've figured it out by now, but I'm using the show to come out."

I nodded. Yeah, I'd gathered that as soon as she'd made her admission. Despite how that not-so-little tidbit was sure to tank our place in this pseudo-competition, I actually thought it was rather genius. If you felt like you were being pulled to come out, why not do it on a reality show? I could already hear Rhea in my head gushing about how the ratings would go through the roof and the sponsorships would come flooding in. That was the content-creator in her that thought in terms of profit.

"I think it's incredibly admirable of you to do it that way." She was freeing herself, but in doing so, was also putting herself in a position to possibly lose the people that meant the most to her. On top of that, she was choosing to be filmed, which guaranteed that it would be broadcasted into millions of homes. Rhea's imaginary voice in my head had been correct about the ratings. Doing it this way meant that D'Vaughn was going to help so many queer people make a decision that may have been difficult for them. So often we needed to witness someone conquer a beast before we realized that we too held the power to best it.

D'Vaughn bit her lip and cast a glance toward the table. She brought a hand to her neck and shook her head lightly.

"That's kind of you to say."

"It's the truth," I insisted, wishing she'd look at me again so she'd see the sincerity in my eyes. I gained nothing by lying about this.

Maybe she heard something in my tone because her eyes shot to mine. There was surprise there at first, but then it softened into gratitude.

"Thank you, Kris. That means more to me than you know." Her voice was thick with emotion, and I had to clear my own throat to keep from tearing up.

"So…" I trailed off, my attempt at changing the subject falling flat. Making a joke didn't feel right following the heaviness of moments earlier. We needed to get back on track, but I didn't know how.

Recognizing my attempt, D'Vaughn offered me a soft smile. "Now, we have to tell our families that we're getting married."

"Yeah," I agreed, "that might be the easiest part of all of this."

Her brows rose. "How do you figure?"

"Telling them is literally as simple as 'Hey, I'm getting married and this is my fiancée.' It's convincing them that this is real where I foresee the biggest issue." I paused, not wanting to be insensitive but needing to know. "How do you plan on convincing your family that you're marrying a woman if they don't even know you're gay?" It seemed an impossible task from where I was sitting.

Releasing a breath, D'Vaughn twisted her lips to the side. "Well, they have no reason not to believe me. I'm a pretty honest person."

My brows shot up and she laughed lightly, rolling her eyes. "Not including this one thing, of course." She waved a hand in the air. "Anyways. What about you? Is it really going to be as easy as making an announcement? Seriously?"

"I mean, yeah. My family knows that I'm gay, but they've never seen me get serious with anyone before. That's why it's the convincing part that I have to work on."

D'Vaughn quirked a surprised eyebrow. "You've never had a girlfriend?"

She sounded almost incredulous, as if she didn't believe that for a second, and I had to laugh.

"Man, come on. I've had girlfriends before. Why does it sound like you're trying to play me?"

Lifting her hands in the air, she shook her head. "Guilty conscience perhaps?"

Tossing my head back, I laughed loudly. "Oh, so you're funny today, huh?"

She pursed her lips, but it did nothing to suppress her grin. "If you say so."

"Anyway, I've dated and have even had long-term relationships, but nothing has ever come close to me even thinking about settling down." Not for my lack of trying. My body was ready to be boo'd up with somebody's daughter and breaking out into random choreography at bottomless brunch while dressed in matching 'fits, but every time I thought I'd found something worthwhile, I ended up sorely disappointed. Heavy on the sore. Out of sheer self-preservation I'd put my heart on ice months ago.

Cocking her head to the side, D'Vaughn propped an elbow on the table, rested her chin in her hand, and stared at me. "So what made you audition for the show?"

Pushing my relatively empty plate forward, I folded my arms on top of the table and leaned forward, giving D'Vaughn direct eye contact. Her question was one that I'd gotten several times over the course of the other night, but something about the way she was looking at me made it feel weightier than a random probing question.

"I figured it was time to change that."

I waited for her follow-up—could almost see the question forming in her eyes—but she blinked a couple of times and looked away. When she turned back to me, her eyes were carefully shuttered, revealing nothing. We'd essentially just met, so there was no way to tell what that meant, but a surge of disappointment hit me that I couldn't explain.

"The clock starts tomorrow," she chirped brightly. "Do you want to break the news to your family first?"

I stared at her for a moment, wondering if I'd just been projecting or if she'd really closed up on me. I'd expected to dig into the relationship conversation a bit more. I wanted to get an idea of where her head was at on the subject, because contrary to what Rhea assumed, I had no intention of going all in for someone who wanted nothing to do with me beyond collecting a check. Been there, done that, got the heartbreak and tag on a sponsored Instagram post. Finally, I shrugged.

"My little sister's baby shower is tomorrow. It's at my parents' house and my entire family will be there. My papi is cooking and he's a master on the grill. Good food and cold beer will soften the shock of me springing a fiancée on them. It'll be perfect."

"Cool. Then we can tell my family on Sunday."

"You sure about that?" The wobble in her voice didn't sound convincing at all, and neither did the scrunched look on her face, as if she'd just swallowed a goldfish and wanted to give it time to make its way down her throat. She shook her head and swallowed that puppy down, meeting my eyes determinedly.

"I signed a contract."

Nodding, I sat back in my seat, flicking my gaze to my left as Kevin pushed through the doors and ducked to step out onto the patio carrying a large tablet in his hand. Instead of heading straight for us, he sat at one of the empty tables, pulled out a stylus, and started writing on the screen. When it became clear that he wasn't going to interrupt our conversation, I turned back to D'Vaughn.

"Well, alright. Let's do this."

Sighing, she folded her arms on the table and leaned forward. "Tell me something I need to know about you. Something your girlfriend would absolutely know."

"Uh…" I looked up at the clear sky, taking a moment to think. "I can bench press ten reps of 265 lbs."

Her brows shot up in surprise. "Oh, wow. Why would your girlfriend need to know that though? Do you only date gym rats?" She wrinkled her nose, clearly put off by the possibility.

I chuckled lightly, unable to stop the sly grin from crossing my face as I stared at her slightly amused, very attractive face. Just the fact that she seemed to genuinely be confused by my declaration brought a bit of giddiness to my disposition.

"I mean…any girlfriend of mine might be very interested in the fact that I can pick her up without straining."

"*Oh,*" she mouthed silently, and I laughed. "I—um. Well, I can't really see a scenario where that sort of information might come up, but I guess I'll—uh…keep that in mind." She cringed and dropped her gaze to the table. It was like those cartoons of children's dreams appearing in a bubble above their heads, the way I could almost see her visualizing how that might play out in her mind. I decide to give her an out.

"Do you have a day job? Tell me about it?"

A soft smile graced her face. It was just a small lifting of the corners of her mouth, but her cheeks bloomed and her eyes lit up and *holy shit* my breath caught in my throat. She was really, *really* fucking beautiful. Picture perfect. She reached up to brush her hair from her face and I shifted in my seat, realizing that I was staring. It had only taken a few minutes of laughing and conversation for me to lose myself and forget the overall reason why we were sitting on this rooftop patio in the first place.

This is a business lunch, Kris. This isn't a date.

Yet. Maybe.

Thankfully, D'Vaughn answered my question, pulling me out of my wayward thoughts.

"I'm a ninth-grade guidance counselor."

"That's dope!"

That already eye-catching smile widened, and she dipped her chin in acknowledgment. "Thanks. It's so important to make sure our babies are on the right path from the word 'go,' you know? On top of that, the school I work for is phenomenal. They even granted me off for today without hesitation. I'm all-around blessed in my career. I truly love it."

Watching her speak, it was incredibly obvious that she did. Suddenly, she was so animated; waving her hands around as she spoke, leaning forward, her lips parted in a toothy smile, her eyes bright and interested. When she finished, her smile remained as she nodded for me to go.

"And you? What do you do for a living?"

Rubbing my chin, I canted my head to the side. "Ah, that's kind of complicated."

"How so?"

"Because it's a two-parter. I have a nine-to-five, *and* I have a side gig where I make my living."

"Okay, wait. That sounds interesting. Start with the nine-to-five."

"I'm a middle school gym teacher. This meeting just happened to fall during my free period."

"Wow! *Really?*" Her lips formed an O. She looked completely surprised, which I get, but still I pursed my lips.

"Dang, beautiful. Why you say it like that?" I asked teasingly. "I don't look like I can shape young minds?"

"Well," she begins measuredly, "you have your last name tattooed in Old English font across your neck like a three-inch-wide choker, and naked, female-presenting deities on each of your forearms." Lifting her hands into the air, palms out, she sat back. "I'm not judging you for it at all. In fact, I'm finding all of the ink incredibly pleasing to the eye. *However*, I just remember schools being more conservative about the teachers' appearance."

She'd low-key called my tattoos attractive but instead of pointing that out, I nodded my head.

"No, you're right. They still are, to an extent. I think I just got a pass because they were more concerned about the fact that I was wearing traditionally masculine clothing and didn't have time on the agenda to get to my tattoos."

Her face immediately sobered as she sat forward.

"They gave you crap about your clothes?"

"The principal did—or rather, he tried to. It didn't last long and now everything's all good." It had taken a while for things to get here though. My hometown was extremely conservative, and I'd spent my youth counting down the days until I could move to Houston proper, just sure that the liberal city was what dreams were made of. As soon as I graduated college, my sisters and I relocated an hour and a half south, only for me to get a job at an ESL magnet and be hit with the same ignorance I'd dealt with when I was a teenager navigating the education system. The realization that no place was perfect had been more than disheartening, and I'd taken my lumps for being visibly queer, but I gave those shits right back because I had no intention of changing who I was.

Nodding, she pursed her lips but didn't say anything else. I could feel her irritation as if it were misty fog hovering around us. Needing to bring the vibe back up, I changed the subject.

"Do you use social media?"

Her frown said *duh, bitch* as she nodded emphatically.

"Way too much. I'm on Instagram so much that I have to set a time limit on my phone that locks the app after so many hours."

"Damn," I drawled. "It's that bad?"

"Worse," she admitted, hanging her head in shame. "I'm constantly telling the timer to give me fifteen more minutes."

"I'm not judging you," I announced, holding my hands in the air. People like her were the reason I was able to build a platform on that app. "What kind of accounts do you follow?" I was indirectly inquiring if she knew about my presence on those apps. So far, it didn't seem like she did.

"Foodie stuff. The self-taught home chefs, professionals, restaurants, bartenders."

"Ah, okay. I follow that kind of stuff too. I also post cooking videos and recipe posts every now and then."

Her brows rose. "Cooking videos? Oh, you're kind of fancy, huh?"

Folding my arms on top of the table, I leaned forward, my eyes on hers. "A little bit."

Narrowing her eyes, she studied me for a moment before reaching into her bag and pulling out her phone. "What's your handle?"

I rattled it off.

"On which platform?"

"All of them."

She dipped her head. I watched as her thumbs flew across the screen of her device before her brows shot up again. When she lifted her head, her eyes were wide with surprise.

"Why do you have two hundred and fifty thousand follows?! Are these real people?"

I laughed. "Hell yeah they're real people! I don't pay for followers, beautiful."

Returning her attention to her phone, she dragged her thumb in a straight line up the screen, scrolling through my posts.

"You post a lot."

I nodded.

"Oh! Is this your sister? Y'all have the exact same face." Turning her phone, she showed me a selfie that Rhea had taken a few weeks ago after we'd finished a workout. Sweat was pouring down both of our faces but we were grinning like kids in a candy store.

"Yup, that's Rhea. Everyone thought we were twins when we were kids. Still do, actually."

"Are you close?"

"Closer than close. We're ten months apart, born in the same year and nobody knows me like she does. She's my best friend."

"Aww. That's sweet," she murmured, eyes back on the screen. Chuckling, I sat back and patted my full belly.

"If you say so, beautiful."

Putting her phone on the table, she pinned me with a look that made me quirk an eyebrow.

"Okay, let's just get this out of the way. I realize that 'beautiful' is your general pet name for like…everyone, but that's not going to work for me. If I'm supposed to be your fiancée, I need a name that's unique *to me*."

Oh. This…confidence—assertiveness—was completely unexpected and attractive as hell. Grinning, I canted my head to the side, eying her. "What do you want me to call you?"

Her eyes narrowed as she pursed her lips. "The real question is what would you call the woman you love so much that you'll marry her before the people who mean the most to you have a chance to get to know her?"

I nodded. "You have a point." Movement across the patio caught my eye and I turned to see Kevin heading our way. Turning back to D'Vaughn, I winked.

"Don't worry about it. I'll get right on that and you'll have a *unique to you* name by tomorrow."

Jitter Cam 02-Kris

Lunch was nice. I think we have a pretty good idea of how this thing is going to go. Was I shocked that I was matched with D'Vaughn? Absolutely. How do I feel about it? Well…

Hmm. I don't know how to say this without it sounding harsh. Before we dug deep into each other's backgrounds, I would've said I was ecstatic. D'Vaughn is cute and curvy, and both of those are very relevant to my interests, which is important when it comes to convincing my family that we're the real deal. On the flip side, she seems pretty reserved, which is completely opposite of every woman I've ever dated. She's different, but I wouldn't necessarily call that a bad thing. You know how they say that opposites attract? We could sell this as something like that. I'd be lying if I said I wasn't down to give it a try.

That excitement though? That was before. Now that we've kind of laid our cards on the table? Uhh, let's just say that I'm not so confident anymore.

I hate to say that, because D'Vaughn seems like a great girl, but it's impossible to ignore the big pink elephant in the closet. I don't judge anyone for how they decide to live their lives, and I meant what I said when I told D'Vaughn that I admired her approach to this, but I can't help but think about how that will affect this competition.

Ugh, I hope this isn't making me sound like an asshole, but

hell. It's the reason we're here, after all. How in the world are we supposed to convince her family that we're in love and getting married when they don't even know that she's gay? Seriously. I need someone to explain that to me because right now, I can't see it. For D'Vaughn's sake, I'm praying they don't disown her on the spot. We've *all* seen or heard the horror stories of how religious families react to learning their children are queer. It's usually not pretty.

Man. I hate this for her. I hate it so fucking much! Why can't we just live and be accepted as we are? Why do we have to be afraid to be ourselves in front of the ones who are supposed to love us the most?

Ay dios mio. My grandmother's gonna kick my ass when she sees that I cussed like this on television. Lo siento, Abuelita! Pero es por una buena causa, lo juro!

Speaking of my abuela, she'll be at my parents' house tomorrow. I have no idea how things are going to go with D'Vaughn's family on Sunday, but at least tomorrow she'll get the opportunity to be around people who accept her for who she is without a second thought. They might question our engagement, but they won't have one negative thing to say about her sexuality.

Shit.

Rhea is going to have a field day with this.

Chapter Three

Kris

Showtime!

D-Day had arrived.

The six-week clock had begun its countdown and now the race to the altar was officially on. I wasn't nervous, but I wasn't *not* nervous. D'Vaughn was due to show up within an hour, and while I'd brought girls around my family before, this was markedly different. For one, I had to lie right out of the gate. The lying itself wasn't an issue—my parents had raised me to lie with a straight face every time I had to look Mami in the eye growing up and deny that Papi's chili con carne was better than hers—but it was the inevitable web of elaborate lies I'd have to weave to make this thing stick which gave me pause. At brunch, D'Vaughn suggested that we keep things as close to the truth as possible to negate tripping ourselves up later on.

It was a solid plan.

It sounded easy enough, but keeping it as simple as possible had never hurt anyone. I was going to have to convince my family that I'd finally found someone that I wanted to spend the rest of my life with. I'd have to keep them involved in every aspect of planning the wedding, and at the same time continue to create content for social media without breathing a word of this. Under no circumstances was I to even hint at the show, and that meant I couldn't post D'Vaughn on my accounts. It was a voluntary, stress-induced sort of challenge that—if executed—could be life-changing.

Rhea and I, along with our baby brother, Raymond, had arrived at our parents' home around nine in the morning to help set up for Kiana's shower. The festivities were set to begin around one, with the rest of the family showing up before noon. After documenting my strength training—and subsequent weight-loss—journey a couple of years ago, my family was used to me carrying a camera around. That worked in my favor when neither of my parents batted an eye when I asked if I could record the shower. I had the handheld camera with me, but there was also a cameraman named Felix sitting in a van on the street, waiting to receive the okay to come inside. With the help of Rhea, we convinced them that we were trying something different with our brand that required a higher-quality camera. Per D'Vaughn's suggestion, it wasn't too far from the truth, evident when Papi fussed at us for making Felix wait outside instead of bringing him in with us.

Raul had arrived before sunrise to assist Papi with cooking, and soon the scent of grilled meat and vegetables filled the air, making my stomach grumble and my mouth water. My parents' home was a three-bedroom, two-bathroom bungalow on the southeast side of my hometown that they'd managed to raise five nearly stair-step children in. Growing up, the larger-than-average corner lot with tons of back and front yard real estate had provided us with a natural playground that doubled as an event hall when special occasions rolled around. Raymond and Rhea assembled six round tables for sitting and three rectangular tables for food and gifts, while Mami and I worked in tandem to cover the tables with yellow tablecloths made of plastic and decorated with cartoon storks carrying brown-skinned babies wrapped in green blankets.

The task was repetitive, and I found myself zoning out as I worked, my mind drifting to the task ahead. Mami picked up on my fidgeting after I'd accidentally tugged a tablecloth too hard while covering one of the tables and ripped the corner. With a frown, she slapped my hand away and used the roll of double-sided tape to hide the imperfection underneath the table. When she finished, she turned to me with her hands on her hips.

"Que paso, mija?"

"It's nothing, Mami."

Her eyes narrowed as she continued to observe me. "Porque estas nervioso?"

Running a hand down my face, I shook my head. Her keen eye never ceased to amaze me, but at that moment, it was more inconvenient than anything. I wasn't yet prepared to start lying, so I decided to deflect.

Keep it simple.

"Why would you ask me that?"

"Look at you," she quipped gesturing at me. "Estas pálido."

At that, I busted out laughing. "Wow, Mami. *You* decided to marry a light-skinned Tejano and now you want to complain 'cause I came out his color. I'm offended."

Shocked, she let her mouth fall open. Her grip tightened on the bag of decorations and for a second I thought she was going to swing it at me, but instead, she spun around, facing the back corner of the yard where my father and brother stood.

"Oye, Reynaldo!"

Instantly, the grin melted off of my face and I took off in the opposite direction as she headed toward my father, complaining about me in rapid-fire Spanish. It was all fun and games until Mami went snitching to Papi. As easygoing as he was, he didn't play about his wife. I had vivid memories of hearing his favorite phrase *"Ella fue mía primero y será mía cuando te vayas"* as a child whenever one of us complained about our parents' constant displays of affection.

Just as I stepped into the living room via the side door that led to the backyard, the doorbell rang. I jogged over and opened it to reveal a crowd of my family. Mami's sisters, Tía Michelle and Tía Christine, entered first, giving me hugs, fingering my locs, and telling me how good I looked as they passed me and headed for the door I'd just entered through. Several of my cousins followed, laughing and making jokes as they carried gifts and balloons out to the backyard. Mis tíos brought up the rear, lugging large pans of deliciously aromatic, marinated meat as they dropped kisses on my cheek in greeting.

The baby shower was set to start in an hour, with Kiana and her boyfriend scheduled to arrive shortly after. I'd asked D'Vaughn to come at twelve thirty so that her presence wouldn't distract from my sister's attention. Checking my watch, I made a quick trip to the bathroom down the hall, returning minutes later to find Rhea letting more people in. A wicked grin came across her face when she spotted me. After directing everyone toward the backyard, she folded her arms and leveled me with a knowing look.

"You know Papi's gonna get on that ass, right?"

Groaning, I plopped down onto the sofa and covered my eyes with my hand. "I already know. Mami knows I was joking. She just wanted to tell on some-damn-body."

"Should've just told her what was up. Instead you wanna pump-fake, knowing Mami don't play that colorism mess. You set yourself up with that one."

Rolling my eyes, I gave Rhea a sidelong glance. "You know damn well I can't say a word about you-know-what."

"Well, yeah. I know that much. I'm talking about a simple mention that you want to introduce her to someone. It would set the stage nicely."

"That's the point, bro. I can't 'set the stage.' It's in the contract that I can't even hint at something going on. Not one peep is allowed until the big reveal. All of this has to be a complete surprise."

"Damn," she breathed, tilting her head to the side and staring off into space. I nodded because *my sentiments exactly.* Yeah, I'd signed up for this, but that didn't make the shit any less nerve-wracking. One of the few weights lifted off of my shoulder was the fact that none of my family had to be on television if they didn't want to. Although everyone would be filmed during the six weeks, once filming wrapped, each person who had camera time would be presented with a waiver, and if they declined to sign it, they'd be edited out.

There was a firm knock on the door and my pulse skyrocketed. It was D'Vaughn. I didn't know for sure, but I *knew.* Glancing at Rhea, I curled my lip at the amused gleam in her eyes.

"Good luck," she sang before jumping up and heading out to the backyard.

Standing, I brushed my hands down the front of my shorts and tugged on the hem of my shirt to smooth out the wrinkles. It was another hot day and I, thankfully, owned enough short-sets to last me until the summer solstice. Crossing the room, I quickly brushed my fingers over my eyebrows and checked my teeth in the long mirror on the wall before pulling open the door with a smile on my face.

D'Vaughn stood before me holding a vase of fresh flowers in one hand and two gift bags in the other. Felix stood behind her and to her left on the other side of the porch railing.

The camera on his shoulder was angled so that he had a clear shot of both of our faces.

"What's up?" I greeted, immediately reaching to relieve D'Vaughn of the bags before pulling her into a quick hug. "Did you find it okay?"

"Yeah," she admitted with a nod. "You gave great directions, so thanks for that."

A car door slammed out near the street. D'Vaughn glanced over her shoulder, and I followed her gaze to where my father's youngest brother was crossing the street and heading our way. Returning my attention back to D'Vaughn, I grinned.

"That's what's up. Hey, I wanted to talk to you before we go in. Is that cool?"

She turned back to me, brows lifted, and dipped her chin. "Yeah, of course."

I guided her away from the door and into a corner of the porch which was sectioned off by a brick enclosure that my father had built by hand with the help of his brothers. I set the bags on the wooden bench just as my uncle stepped onto the porch.

"Hola, Tío," I called with a tip of my chin.

"Buenas tardes." Mateo Zavala swung his light-brown eyes from me to D'Vaughn, taking in our body language, before shooting me a wink. "¿Tuya?"

Bruh. I busted out laughing. As the youngest of my aunts and uncles, Mateo was only ten years older than me, and had a similar taste in women. We learned from Raul's mistakes that if we didn't want Mateo to walk off with our dates, we had to stake our claim early and publicly.

"Sí."

Chuckling, he pursed his lips, an impressed gleam in his eye. Turning to D'Vaughn, he spoke in English. "Good afternoon, gorgeous."

"Buenas tardes, señor," she responded in perfectly accented but slightly stilted Spanish.

Mateo's eyes brightened and he bowed his head slightly. After shooting me a second wink, he continued on inside. I faced D'Vaughn, a grin still present on my face.

"You didn't tell me you were bilingual."

Shaking her head, she held up a finger. "You didn't ask." She lifted a second finger. "I'm not. Estoy aprendiendo. *Slowly.*"

Taking a step back, I gave her an exaggerated once-over. "Check you out!"

Covering her face with her free hand, she laughed lightly before sighing. "So, what did you want to talk to me about?"

"Oh yeah." Gently, I took the vase from her and set it on the ground beside the bench before gesturing for her to have a seat and doing the same. "We didn't really get a chance to go over everything yesterday—"

"That was definitely by design," she murmured in a low voice.

I nodded. "Oh, absolutely. The more we fumble, the better the show. We already know what it is. But before I take you inside and introduce you to my family, I wanted to run some things by you and get your consent."

The c-word caught her attention and she straightened, giving me an expectant look. "Okay," she said cautiously, "go ahead."

"This is going to sound like a cheesy-ass line and clichéd as fuck but it's the truth. My family is incredibly affectionate. We're touching all the time and it's only magnified when we're in romantic relationships. For them to believe that you and I are truly engaged and *in love*, I'm going to have to be all over you. That's where the consent comes in. If that makes you uncomfortable, I don't have to, but it makes our job that much harder." It was something I'd been thinking about since we'd parted ways the day before. I was looking forward to playing the part with her and couldn't wait until I could wrap my arms around her. The hugs had been nice, but I was more interested in finding out if her skin was as soft as it looked. Something told me it was.

D'Vaughn's eyes were wary, even as her face remained expressionless. "Okay…what exactly does 'being all over me' mean?"

"Basic relationship lovey-dovey stuff. Hugging, kissing, caressing, holding hands, etc. All of that."

I shrugged as if it were no big deal, as if I wasn't ready and willing to slip into go-mode with her, and watched her face carefully, making sure her words lined up with her reactions. If she said it was fine but her face protested, I'd nip it. Like I'd told her, it would make this thing ten times more difficult if we didn't "look the part," but it would be counterproductive if she cringed every time I touched her. Surprisingly, she dipped her chin twice.

"Okay."

"Are you sure?" She hadn't hesitated but I didn't want her to feel pressured, plus, I couldn't deny that the fact of her being closeted had weighed heavily on my mind, factoring in my concerns. *Were public displays of affection even something she'd done before?*

She quirked an eyebrow at me, as if she could hear my thoughts, and somehow managed to challenge me with just a look. Tossing my head back, I laughed. *Fine.* All I could do was trust her words since I didn't know her to be able to predict her actions.

"Aight, man. Cool."

Her lips quirked and when she pursed them, I knew she was fighting a smile. I surprised myself with how much I wanted to see it. She wore a brown lip stain that was a couple shades darker than her warm-brown hue but matched the short-sleeve top and biker shorts she wore perfectly. The yellow flower studs in her ears were the same shade as the canvas tennis shoes on her feet, and her twistout was especially wavy. It was almost effortless, how she managed to look sexy in the simplest way.

Yeah…it wouldn't be hard to appear into her at all.

"Let's head inside."

I started to stand, but a short tug on my shirt brought my movements to a halt. D'Vaughn's eyes held a measure of uncertainty that made my eyebrows furrow.

"What's up? Second thoughts?"

She jerked her neck back as if I'd asked an outrageous question. "What? No! I just—" She took a breath and blew it out through her nose slowly. When she spoke, her tone was more measured. "Can we…practice?"

A slow grin took over my face and I settled back onto the bench, draping my arm across the back as I leaned toward her.

Who was being cliché now?

"You want to 'practice kissing' me, huh?"

Lifting a hand, she shielded her eyes from me as she groaned. "Oh my gosh," she muttered. "Why are you saying it like that?"

"How am I saying it?" Pushing the tip of my tongue through my teeth, I lowered my lids and peered at her. She still had a hold on my shirt, and I could feel the faint heat from her hand on my abdomen. I pulled her other hand away from her face, trying to meet her gaze with my own.

Eyes quickly flicking over to Felix before flitting around the porch, D'Vaughn shook her head again as her cheeks flushed. "I just don't want our first kiss to be in front of a crowd of people. I saw how many cars are parked on the street; y'all are having a *party* party. What if you can't kiss? Then I'll have to pretend in front of a gang of peo—"

I was cheesing hard as hell at that point. "C'mon, preciosa," I teased. "You already know what it is. Pretending is the name of the game."

Releasing an exasperated sound, D'Vaughn stopped avoiding me and gave me her undivided attention.

"May I kiss you?"

The soft, even tone she used made me swallow down any more teasing. Eyes on hers, I nodded. She surprised me by clenching my shirt even tighter as she leaned toward me, canting her head to the right as she aimed her lips for mine. I lifted my chin to receive her and let my eyes droop closed as our mouths met. Based on her demeanor the couple of times that we'd met, I'd expected her to be hesitant—almost scared—but D'Vaughn was anything but. Her pink tongue darted out and flicked the small hoop in my bottom lip before her lips pressed against mine in a firm, sure kiss that made my breath hitch. They were soft and insistent, demanding that I open for her and rewarding me when I relented. A soft moan sounded and I wasn't sure if it had come from me or her, but the moment that our tongues touched, the low grunt that permeated the silence absolutely burst from my throat. With one hand clenched at my thigh, I cupped the back of her neck, burying my fingers in the soft curls at her nape as I pulled her face closer to mine and sat up straighter to make the movement easier.

I was *fallingfallingfalling* into her, ready to risk it all on that porch, family be damned, when someone cleared their throat loudly, quickly yanking me out of my reverie. Twisting on the bench, I turned to see my father's eldest sister and a couple of my younger cousins standing near the door. My giggling cousins hurried inside, but Tía Claudia stood with her arms folded, giving me an amused look.

"Tía," I began huskily, stopping to clear my throat before I came to my feet. She lifted a hand in the air, stopping me from going to her.

"Tienes lápiz labial en la boca."

My face heated as I swiped a thumb over my lips. I could hear my cousins break into laughter on the other side of the door. My thumb was empty. Looking up, I smiled in response to the smirk on my tía's face.

"Gracias, Tía."

She entered the house and I turned around to find D'Vaughn on her feet, once again holding the flowers and gift bags. If not for the brightness in her eyes and slight heaving of her chest, I wouldn't have been able to tell that she'd been doing anything but standing in that spot.

"Was that good enough for you, preciosa?" I asked, still feeling a little breathless.

Her cheeks lifted as she smiled and ducked her head. "It was satisfactory," she deadpanned.

Laughing, I shook my head and took the bags from her before grabbing her hand and linking our fingers. I needed to reevaluate my expectations for the next six weeks because D'Vaughn had just surprised the shit out of me, that was for damn sure. I led her into the house and through the side door to reach the backyard. It was already loud as hell and packed with people. I could feel Mami's eyes on us as soon we came around the corner. It hadn't been my intention when I'd sat with D'Vaughn on the porch, but it was clear that someone—either my cousins, my tía, or Mateo—had whispered about us amongst the family.

After leading D'Vaughn to the gift table where I deposited the larger of the two bags, we crossed the yard to the cabana where my parents were lounging amongst their siblings. The talking quieted as we approached, and I squeezed D'Vaughn's hand to signal that it was showtime.

"Mami, Papi," I called over the music, trying to get their attention even though they were both already looking at us curiously. Mateo picked up a remote and lowered the volume of the music. It wasn't much, but it allowed me to speak without having to continue yelling.

"Yes, mija?" Mami questioned, a knowing grin on her lips, her shrewd gaze honing in on my and D'Vaughn's joined hands before lifting to my face. "¿Quién es?"

I answered in English so that the woman on my left would understand everything.

"This is D'Vaughn."

Mami smiled indulgently. "Hello, D'Vaughn. How are you?"

"Buenas tardes, Sra. Zavala." Her voice trembled a little, but she held her head high and extended the vase toward my mother. "These are for you."

Surprise lit Mami's eyes as she took the flowers from D'Vaughn. "These are beautiful, mija," she breathed. "Thank you." The vase was filled with colorful wildflowers that were undoubtedly artfully arranged by the hands of a skilled florist. Mami spent plenty of time in her garden and loved receiving a fresh bouquet.

D'Vaughn beamed before handing the smaller gift bag toward Papi. "And these are for you, señor."

His eyes lit up like a kid on Christmas as he took the bag and set it in his lap. He pulled his reading glasses from the front pocket of his shirt and slid them onto his face. D'Vaughn hadn't mentioned bringing gifts for my parents, so I was just as curious as everyone else to what she'd brought. My father reached into the bag and pulled out two canisters, each the size of a tallboy. He squinted as he read the labels, and after a moment a pleased smile brightened his face. Handing the canisters to Mami, Papi stood up and pulled D'Vaughn into a hug, pressing a kiss on each of her cheeks.

"Muchas gracias, D'Vaughn."

"You're more than welcome." D'Vaughn beamed at him, and I felt a surge of affection for her. She didn't have to bring anything at all today, but her kindness had put undeniable smiles on both of my parents' faces.

Mami passed the canisters to Mateo, who oohed and ahhed before passing them to Tía Claudia, who finally passed them to me. They were hefty and wrapped with leather labels that were branded with the company name and the canisters' contents. Afghani black cumin and bourbon-barrel smoked chili powder. Two ingredients that were prominent in Tejano cooking. The sheer thoughtfulness was touching and her keen choice of gifts stood out to me. I'd only mentioned that Papi was grilling in passing, and yet she'd brought him something that was bound to bring him joy for several months. I was blown away and suddenly had to wrack my brain to remember if anyone I'd dated previously had ever done something so kind. Unsurprisingly, my memory bank came up empty. I handed the spices back to my father, and leaned over to drop a soft kiss to D'Vaughn's cheek, just west of the corner of her mouth. From my proximity, I saw, rather than heard, her quickly suck in a breath. To mask it, she began to nibble on her bottom lip.

"Stop that," I chastened without thinking, using my thumb to free the abused lip. Silently, she stared at me, and as I stared back into those wide brown eyes, I felt like Alice peering into that hole in the ground just before she took a tumble.

Mateo's wolf whistle jostled me out of the pull of D'Vaughn's dark irises, and I grinned at the near embarrassed look on her face. Leaning into her ear, I spoke in a low voice.

"Their teasing is a good thing. Don't worry about it, aight?" Canting my head, I met her eyes, waiting for her to nod before turning back to my family. I was used to them, but this was all new for her. I wanted to sell this thing, but I also didn't want her to feel uncomfortable, which was a possibility even though I knew it was all good-natured.

When I was once again facing my family, I laughed at the expressions on my parents' faces. Papi looked impressed, maybe even proud, and Mami had stars in her eyes. It had been a while since I'd brought someone home, and even longer before it was someone who'd made a good impression from the jump. I could almost see the gears in Mami's head turning, and couldn't wait for her reaction once we made our announcement.

A sharp whistle sounded, and we all turned toward the house to see one of my little cousins running from the side of the house. He made a beeline to the cabana, catching his breath before informing us that Kiana was outside. The music was turned down a few decibels and Mami hushed everyone. Six minutes later, first a belly and then my baby sister appeared, followed by her doting boyfriend, Josue. Cheers went up and the crowd parted like the Red Sea as Mami and Papi headed for Kiana and swept her into a group hug.

Slinging an arm over D'Vaughn's shoulder, I put my mouth near her ear. "That's my baby sister, Kiana," I stated unnecessarily.

It was obvious from everyone's reaction who she was, but I was having fun watching D'Vaughn's reactions to every touch and endearment. She was so damn expressive that it was becoming addicting.

"She's gorgeous," D'Vaughn whispered.

A proud smile stretched across my face as if I'd had a hand in Kiana's appearance. At almost eight months along, Kiana looked stunning, with her belly poked out as if she had a basketball under her maxi dress. Her deep brown skin—the only feature she inherited from Mami—glowed under the midday sun. Both Kiana and Josue had the biggest grins on their faces as everyone embraced them while Mami and Papi led them over to their designated table.

They reached us and I wrapped my baby sister in a delicate hug before stepping back and rubbing my palms over her distended belly. My cheeks hurt from how hard I was grinning. On the other side of that bump was my half-cooked nibling, and I couldn't wait for the timer to start dinging when they were ready to come out of the oven.

"Hold up," Kiana sassed, her hand in the air as if she was pressing pause. "Who is this?"

Peeling my eyes from her belly, I lifted them to Kiana's face to see her curious eyes on D'Vaughn. Licking my lips, I slid an arm around D'Vaughn's waist and pulled her closer to me.

"KiKi, this is D'Vaughn. D'Vaughn, this is my KiKi, also known as Nosy NaNa. You can just call her Kiana though."

Giggling, D'Vaughn dipped her chin. "Nice to meet you."

"Thanks for coming to my shower," Kiana chirped as she surged forward and hugged D'Vaughn quickly, before standing back and propping her hands on her hips. She pinned me with a glare. "I can't believe you'd bring a date to my baby shower, knowing that I'll be too busy to talk to her! You did this on purpose, you jerk!"

Laughing, I held up my hands. "I swear that wasn't my intention." Kiana glared at me for a moment before relaxing and lowering her arms. I waited until she started to turn away and then added, "It's a happy coincidence though."

She whipped back around, but Josue chuckled and ushered her forward as he tipped his head in D'Vaughn's direction. "Nice to meet you," he offered just as they were engulfed in Tía Claudia's arms.

The crowd thinned out the further into the backyard Kiana and Josue traveled. Once they made it to their specially decorated table, Mami and Sra. Munoz bustled over the tables that were piled high with gifts and instructed everyone to gather around.

"Oh!" D'Vaughn exclaimed as I pulled her over to a round table. "You guys do the gifts early? I've never seen that before."

We turned our seats to face my sister and Josue and sat down. "Yeah. It's been that way as long as I can remember. We do it because every time my family gets together, the party lasts well into the night. When the gifts are opened first thing, it allows the mama-to-be the freedom to leave whenever she's ready."

Nodding, D'Vaughn murmured, "Ah. That makes a lot of sense. I imagine cooking a kiddo can tire you out sooner than the average partygoer."

"And you'd be correct. KiKi's only twenty-four, but I doubt she'll make it past nine."

Mami started speaking so we stopped talking and paid attention as the gifts were presented. Everyone cooed over D'Vaughn's gift, which was a spa pedicure set for Kiana and matching robes for her, Josue, and the baby.

"That was really thoughtful," I whispered into her ear.

"Thank you, but I can't take all of the credit. There is a lovely older woman at a department store in the Galleria who steered me in the right direction."

"Well, she ain't here so you get the points tonight."

With her eyes never straying from my sister across the yard, D'Vaughn smiled. I wanted to nuzzle those dimples something serious but held back, not wanting to overdo it so soon. Sure, she'd given me the go-ahead to do the lovey-dovey thing, but something about her made me feel like it wasn't enough. I wasn't touching her enough, kissing her enough, holding her enough. Maybe it was that kiss, or maybe it was residual gratitude behind my parents' gifts. As I reminded myself that

I was once again staring at her, I turned back to my baby sister and resigned myself to figuring it out another time.

After all of the gifts were opened, Josue, Raul, and Raymond carted them around the side of the house to put in the car. Mis tíos pulled the parrillada they'd brought off of the grill and began to process it at the counter of Papi's outdoor kitchen, slicing the beef and chicken into tender strips of perfectly spiced morsels. The aromas had the entire yard heaving a collective sigh, and with that as the green light, everyone began to line up to eat. Mami and Sra. Munoz went first, fixing plates for Kiana and Josue. When they finished, Mami's sisters made sure all of the children were seated with plates of grilled chicken, corn on the cob, rice, and beans in front of them. I turned to D'Vaughn.

"You're hungry, right?"

She was nodding before I even finished my sentence.

"Hell yes. You told me there would be a mountain of food, but even if you hadn't warned me, I smelled the smoke from the grill as soon as I stepped out of my car." Rubbing her belly, she shimmied as she bounced up and down, reminding me of her happy dance from the day before. "My body is ready to receive this blessing."

I brought my fist to my mouth as I cracked up. "Let's get you fed then."

Lacing my fingers through hers, we joined the growing line and were soon back at our table with the chairs turned inward. Paper plates overflowing with seasoned rice and borracho beans, sizzling fajitas, onions, and peppers were in front of us, and a shallow, clay bowl filled with warm tortillas sat between us. As we dug in, Rhea came by and clipped two wooden clothespins on each of us.

"Say the word 'baby' and your pins can get snatched. Hear someone say it and you can take their pins. Whoever has the most pins at the end of the night wins a prize."

"I love this game!"

A smile on my lips, I glanced at D'Vaughn. "Oh yeah?"

She nodded, half laughing as she said, "Yes! It's the only shower game I can actually win."

I sucked in a breath through my teeth and cringed playfully. "Lo siento, preciosa. It looks like whatever winning streak you have ends today. I'll try not to rub my trophy in your face though."

Instantly, her eyes narrowed. "Is that a challenge?"

"Not at all, ba—beau—preciosa. I wouldn't set you up for failure like that." I chuckled, shaking my head at my slip. She almost had me with that one, but I was quicker than that. She'd learn though.

She started to grin, but quickly pulled her bottom lip into her mouth. I sucked my teeth and pursed my lips. There was just something about the way she nibbled on that thing that made me want to suck it into my mouth, and as much as I protested every single time she did it, I was starting to think that she was purposely doing it in anticipation of my reaction.

"Now, what have I told you about that?" Reaching forward, I slid my thumb from the corner of her mouth to the other, gently rolling her lip outward. "You're going to have to pick a new nervous habit, baby. This one is making me want to attack that mouth." Although I couldn't see him, I knew that Felix was somewhere nearby, yet that declaration hadn't been for the sake of the cameras. In fact, it was a truth that had decided to slip out of its own volition.

This time she didn't try to stifle her grin. Sitting forward, she leaned toward me until our lips were only a breath apart. Her eyes were full of mirth as they bored into mine, and I held my breath to see if she was going to initiate the kiss. Except for our practice session earlier, every visible moment of affection between the two of us over the past couple of hours had been at my hand. I started to let my eyes drift closed.

"Gimme my pins," she whispered, brushing her lips against mine in a notkiss that pulled a sigh from me right before I processed her command.

But then I caught it and my eyes flew open.

"Wait. What?!"

"Aww shit!" hooted Rhea, her fist at her mouth as she cracked up. "She got your ass!"

Sitting back in my seat, I sputtered a half-groan, half-laugh as I shook my head and removed the pins from my shirtsleeve. "You set me up."

D'Vaughn giggled as she added my two pins to the ones already dangling from her shirtsleeve. "How in the world could I have done that?"

Sucking my teeth, I lifted the lid of the clay dish and retrieved a couple of tortillas. "By being all fine and shit. You distracted me and I couldn't think straight." That was an understatement. I hadn't even thought of the word all afternoon, yet the moment she's leaning into me and aiming those big brown eyes at me I didn't hesitate to attach it to her. *What was that about?*

Rolling her eyes, she smirked and flicked her fingers at me in a shooing motion. "Girl, bye!"

Still laughing, Rhea walked off to distribute the rest of the pins. As soon as she was gone, Raymond breezed past me, rounding the table and dropping down on the other side. His thick, shoulder-length hair was pushed back from his face with a jersey-knit headband and a pair of wide-rimmed sunglasses.

"I'm finally off the clock!" he declared, stabbing a fork at the mixed-up pile of food on his plate. He shoved a heaping forkful into his mouth, shaking his head. "Moses knows he could've freed me hours ago."

"Bruh," I cracked up. "All Mami asked you to do was take

pictures while KiKi opened her gifts. You're the one who decided you needed different angles and shit."

"I'm a professional, dammit," he snipped, cutting his eyes at me.

Chewing my food, I shrugged. "And it's your professional fault that what was supposed to be a half hour of pictures turned into almost an hour and a half."

He glared at me for a moment before swinging his gaze to D'Vaughn. The glare quickly morphed into an interested gleam that made me suspicious.

"Well, hello there, beautiful."

D'Vaughn turned to me. "I love this family. You are all fantastic for my self-esteem."

Ray and I laughed. I gave myself permission to lean into her then, brushing my lips over her cheek.

"Zavalas have naturally good eyesight. You gotta stick around 'cause I swear it gets better."

There went that lip into her mouth. Tilting her head to the side, she eyed me, an unreadable expression on her face. Finally, she reached her left hand up and brushed her fingers over the steel bar in my eyebrow before trailing them down over my temple, cheek, and cupping my chin.

"I think I might just."

What the hell had just happened? The *falling falling falling* feeling from earlier slammed into my gut as I stared into her eyes. It had only been the lightest of touches and five simple words that she'd bestowed on me, but it felt big. It felt *meaningful*, hitting me in the chest in the form of an inexplicable pang.

It wasn't until Ray gasped that I realized what happened. When D'Vaughn had touched me, she'd used her left hand.

The hand that currently held a decently sized engagement ring.

"Damn!" exclaimed Ray as he leaned forward, both of his

palms flat on the table. "What the hell have I missed?! How do you have a whole ass fiancée when I didn't even know you were dating anyone?"

"Yo, chill!" Glancing around, I checked to see if anyone had heard his loud ass over the music.

His mouth fell open. "No one knows? Not even Mami?!"

"Not yet. I'm waiting to tell them after KiKi has her moment."

"Okay, okay. I get that." Propping his elbows up on the table, he scooped more food into his mouth and eyed us.

"How long has this been going on? When did y'all meet? When did this—" he gestured at D'Vaughn's hand that was now hidden under the table "—happen?"

I turned to D'Vaughn. We'd discussed how to answer this question.

"The time doesn't matter," I said smoothly, "only that we both realized that we were meant to be together around the same time." It was simultaneously a sidestep of the question and a play on words. It was so clever that I deserved a pat on the back.

"Oh." Ray sat back. "So it's true what they say about lesbians, then? By the second date you're moving in, and by the third, you're picking out matching engagement rings?"

D'Vaughn cringed. "Well, I've never moved this fast with anyone before so I can't attest to that." I shot her a quick glance, unsure if I had imagined the dip in her tone. Did she say that for the benefit of the show, or had she felt that same… whatever it was that I'd felt when she touched my face? It was just a look, but it had also felt like so much more than that.

Ray nodded, as if he understood completely. "Well, she does have the Zavala face. This thing can make many a discerning individual lay their well-placed hesitations to the side."

"Ray," I groaned, "shut the fuck up." The last thing I

needed was him intimating that I used my looks to drive women wild.

His grin widened. "Why? Clearly I'm right, or your *future wifey* wouldn't be here sporting that jewelry that she's trying to hide. Unless it was the stud energy." Narrowing his eyes, he peered at us both. "Hmm, you've given me a lot to think about. Maybe I need me a li'l butch to put a ring on my finger." He tapped his chin thoughtfully before taking another bite.

"Uh…" D'Vaughn aimed an unsure glance from Ray to me, lifting her bottle of soda to her mouth. I could read the question in her eyes like the paper on Sunday morning. Before I could clear things up, Ray reached across the table and patted her arm.

"Oh, I was just joking, love. I'm a bottom-bitch through and through, and while those plasdicks might work for *your* holes, *I* need the real thing. I like my meat throbbing or it don't feel good."

D'Vaughn immediately began choking on her drink and I patted her back as I laughed at my brother. Ray could be a lot for even the most outrageous of us all. No doubt D'Vaughn was overwhelmed; her brows were already lifted toward the clouds.

"It feels good enough. Ain't that right, baby?" Turning to D'Vaughn, I ran my nose along her cheek.

"Oh my gosh," she murmured, dropping the glass bottle onto the table before letting her head fall forward into her hands as she groaned.

Ray gasped in faux shock, eyes widening at D'Vaughn's obvious embarrassment. "Oh, you're *shy*? How in the world did you end up with this attention whore?" Ray jutted his chin in my direction.

Snapping her head up, her brows furrowed in confusion as she swung her gaze from Ray to me, and back to Ray.

"*Who's* an attention whore?"

When my baby brother's mouth fell open and he straightened in his seat, I could tell that this time his shock was genuine.

"You don't know?" He turned to me. *"She doesn't know?!"*

"Uh," D'Vaughn hesitated, "know what?"

Suddenly, Ray threw his head back and cackled like the fucking Wicked Witch of the West. Rolling my eyes toward the cloudless sky, I prayed for rain.

"No wonder you're trying to one, two, skip-a-few your way to the altar," he quipped once his laughter eased up enough for him to talk.

"Shut the fuck up, Raymond!" I sputtered. "She already knows about the social media shit."

D'Vaughn frowned and gave Ray a weird look. "Oh. Is that what you're talking about?" She snorted and picked up a taco from her abandoned plate. "Everybody on social media is begging for attention; that's nothing special." Shooting me a glance, she winked. "No offense."

Chuckling, I shook my head. "None taken." Outwardly, I bit my lip and arched an eyebrow at my baby brother. Inwardly, my mind was racing. D'Vaughn knew exactly how many followers I had on social media, had seen just how often I posted, and had just said it was nothing special. She'd snorted! How was it that her nonchalance about my online presence made me like her more?

Ray snapped his fingers as if he were at a spoken word event. "It's the maturity for me, honey."

D'Vaughn covered her mouth as she chewed. "You're something else," she laughed, eyes on Ray.

He smiled widely and posed, lifting his shoulder as he

pursed his lips. "Indeed I am." Scooting back from the table, he gathered his plate and stood to his feet. "Well, I'm going to leave you two lovebirds alone so you can be sickening and make heart eyes at each other in peace. See ya!" After wiggling his fingers, we watched as he weaved through the tables until he reached the one our parents were at.

"He was nice," commented D'Vaughn, drawing a disbelieving look from me.

"Nice? He called me an attention whore! How is that nice?"

Grinning, she shrugged. "He's also the youngest of the family. My younger brother annoys the hell out of me sometimes by picking at me just like that. I think it's actually a part of their DNA."

Taking a bite, I shook my head. "You're giving him quite a big ass benefit of a doubt."

Leaning toward me, she lowered her voice. "In his defense, you *are* weaving a pretty tangled web of lies for a television show. I think you can give him a pass."

"Man," I drawled, pursing my lips, "ain't nobody asked you for all of that."

Tossing her head back, she let out a shout of laughter. "My bad for giving you unprovoked—and apparently unwanted— logic. I promise to hold on to it next time."

Draping an arm over the back of her chair, I dropped a kiss on her cheek. "Thank you, *baby.*"

Her lips curved up but she suppressed the grin as she cut a sidelong glance at me. She didn't say anything else and neither did I as we continued eating. Halfway through my second plate of fajitas, I reached for my beer, only to find that it was empty.

"Aww shit." Pushing back from the table, I tapped D'Vaughn's thigh with my knuckle. I waited for her to tear her eyes away from her plate before I held up my empty bottle. "I'm going to grab another drink. Do you want something?"

She nodded. "Just bring me whatever you're having."

"Cool. I'll be right back."

I started toward the ice barrels, and then had a thought that stopped me in my tracks. I spun around, slipped a finger from my free hand under D'Vaughn's chin, and swiveled her head until she was facing me. Instead of the widened eyes that I expected, her lids were low while her bottom lip was once again trapped between her teeth. I clucked my tongue, freed the trapped piece of flesh with my thumb, and dipped my head to kiss it once, twice, a third time before covering her mouth with mine completely. I'd intended to only give her a couple of quick pecks, but had played myself. It was so easy—too damn easy—to lose myself in D'Vaughn's kisses, and I only pulled away when a long wolf whistle pierced my misty brain.

Opening my eyes, I saw that D'Vaughn had already turned back to her plate, but hadn't yet picked up her fork. Unable to help myself, I brushed the back of my hand against her cheek, grinning at the heated flesh. I understood that part of her apparent bashfulness was due to her past relationships, but I couldn't help how adorable I found it. The fact that she never pulled away from me showed that her declaration to make a change hadn't just been lip service for the camera's sake.

Or maybe she only kept the PDAs under lockdown when around her family, and her reaction was because of me?

I wasn't sure, but something told me that the journey to figuring it out would be a fun one. After shooting a middle finger at the cousin who'd interrupted us, I made my way through the crowd of family members who were dancing in the center of the yard. Once the sun went down and the drinks started flowing, the party was liable to go on all night, regardless of the initial occasion. Baby showers, weddings, summer barbe-cues, graduations. It didn't matter.

Greeting Raul as I reached the coolers, I lifted the lid to observe the contents and make my decision. Settling on a couple of Modelos, I handed them to Raul since he was just standing there observing everyone. He'd kept a bottle opener on his key chain since we were in middle school.

"So, new girl, huh?"

I grinned. "Yup."

He quirked an eyebrow. "Where you been hiding her?"

Before I could answer, I heard a shriek followed by Mami's shrill voice yelling my name.

"Kristin!"

Quickly, I spun around and searched for the woman whose voice I could recognize in my sleep. She wasn't where I'd last seen her, and I felt a thudding in my chest when I finally spotted her. Mami stood over a wide-eyed D'Vaughn, hold-ing D'Vaughn's left hand in the air.

Oh shit.

Even from across the yard, I could see the sun glinting off of the rock weighing D'Vaughn's hand down. Even though Mami's eyes were narrowed, I felt the intensity of her glare as if it were a laser beam trained on my forehead.

"Uh-oh," murmured Raul, sounding entirely too amused for my liking. "Your ass is grass."

"Shut up," I sniped before snatching my now-open bottles of beer from his hands and hurrying over to the tables. I had to play this cool. It was the only way to fly under Mami's ire. I had to keep a cool head and act like it was no big deal.

Piece of cake.

"Where's the fire?" I asked as I slid the drinks onto the table.

"Que. Es. ¿Esto?" she gritted, giving D'Vaughn's hand a little shake.

"Es un anillo," I said carefully.

"What *kind* of ring, Kris?"

"Um." I squinted. "I'm not sure. Looks like the kind that comes out of a Cracker Jack box. Can't be more than twenty-five cents."

She flexed and I clearly pictured her kicking off one of her sandals and slapping me with it. *No big deal*, I reminded myself. We just had to get over this hump and then we could return to the easygoing atmosphere we'd enjoyed thus far.

"Okay, okay!" I laughed, holding up my hands. "An engagement ring."

Mami sucked in a breath and dropped D'Vaughn's hand as if it burned her. I took the opportunity to move in between the two of them, acting as a buffer.

"She's my...fiancée."

There was a beat of silence while my announcement was processed, but then everyone exploded. Without me realizing it, the music had been turned down and most of my family had gathered around us. Mami's mouth gaped open and eyes were wide with disbelief. She took a step back, her hands at her cheeks.

"Your *what?!*" she screeched in disbelief. *"¿Por qué estás jugando conmigo, niñita?"*

"I'm not playing," I assured her. "We're getting married." D'Vaughn slipped her hand into mine and squeezed. I glanced down to find her eyes wide and apprehensive. She worried at her bottom lip almost absently as she looked around at everyone who'd gathered around.

"How are you engaged when we've never even met her?" Mami gestured at D'Vaughn but her eyes stayed trained on me. "Until today that is, and even that was only a brief moment and not nearly enough time to get to know someone." Her lips were twisted into a frown and her brows were furrowed, but beneath her incredulity I could see that she was hurt, and that sliced at me. The last thing I'd wanted was to hurt her, but this was an unfortunate result of what I'd signed up for.

"Mami, please," I begged, lowering my voice a little. "Just think about it for a moment. I share so much with everyone all of the time. I just wanted to have this one thing to myself. I wanted her to myself for as long as I could manage it because I knew once I told everyone, the bubble of peace would pop. I won't apologize for that." I had no idea where the words had come from, but once they were out, I realized that they weren't too far from being real. If this had begun organically, I might've still gone this route.

Silence fell around us and I glanced around the room, locking eyes with Papi, who gave me a nod of approval. He and his brothers were among the last to join the crowd, but he weaved through bodies easily until he was standing just behind Mami. He wrapped his arms around her and whispered into her ear. Bit by bit I watched as she deflated right before my eyes. Taking advantage of Papi's magic, I said my lines.

"Mami, Papi. Just because you weren't there for the proposal doesn't mean we've cut you out. D'Vaughn and I want you to help us plan the wedding."

Her hanging head snapped up and her eyes immediately brightened. "Oh?"

Smiling, I nodded. Her interest was about to be tested.

"Of course. We don't have a lot of time, so we need to get on it."

"¿Qué?" Papi muttered, his face scrunched in confusion. "What does that mean?"

I took a deep breath. D'Vaughn squeezed my hand again.

"We don't want a long engagement. We both know what we want so we're thinking six weeks."

Murmurs went up as everyone reacted to my announcement. Mami frowned, stepped closer to me, and cupped my face.

"That's so soon, mija. Are you sure?"

"Six weeks?!" Kiana pushed her way through our family and propped her hands on her hips. "Are you pregnant too, bitch?"

Rhea burst out laughing and I glared at her before turning back to Kiana. "No. And fuck you for that."

"Be nice," Papi scolded.

My eyes ballooned. "Be nice?! Papi, she just asked if I was getting married because I'm pregnant and you want me to be nice?"

"Well, what do you expect us to think, Kris?" Mami snapped, throwing her hands in the air as if I was exasperating her. "You spring a fiancée on us and then say you're getting married in less than two months. Why else would you be doing this so quickly?"

My mouth hung open as I stared at her. I almost started getting pissed at the sheer ridiculousness when D'Vaughn's laugh caught me off guard. I peered down to see her wiping tears from her eyes.

"Are you okay?"

She shook her head, still laughing. "Do they think my eggs swam out of my uterus, jumped into your vagina, and somehow fertilized *your* eggs? You can't make this up."

"She has a point," Ray chirped, flicking his fingers against Kiana's shoulder. "You and Josue have been playing house so long that you forgot that some folks want to start building a life together before all of the other stuff."

Kiana slapped at Ray's hand and turned back to me. "My bad. I forgot that part."

"You forgot," I deadpanned. "You have my nibling in there and you *forgot* how biology works?"

She waved a hand in the air. "Enough about that. Let's get

back to this quickie wedding you want to plan. What are we thinking? Drive-thru? Vegas? An Elvis impersonator?"

Craning my neck, I searched for her boyfriend in the crowd. "Josue! Come get your baby mama! I think it's time to put her to bed."

Ray sucked his teeth. "Don't you think he's done that enough already?"

"Hey!"

"Enough!"

Mami and Papi both shouted over Ray, waving their hands in the air with twin looks of horror on their faces. My brother immediately burst into laughter, soon joined by several of the people standing nearby. After glaring at him, Mami turned to me and D'Vaughn.

"We will talk this week. Come by the house so we can start to plan. Also…" She pushed me out of the way, leaning down to hug D'Vaughn so tightly she rose from the chair a little. "I'm sorry for scaring you, mija. I was just caught unawares." She leaned back and kissed D'Vaughn's temple before stepping back so Papi could move in to hug her as well.

"Welcome to the family," he murmured in a voice so low I might not have heard him if I hadn't been standing a mere twelve inches away. He released her with a kiss to each cheek, a genuine smile on his face as he squeezed her shoulders briefly.

D'Vaughn nodded, quickly reaching up to brush a couple of fingers over her face below her eye. Her eyes were slightly glassy, and it was clear that she was touched by my parents' affection.

"Thank you both. So much."

"And we need to meet your family," Mami added. "Let's plan to have dinner sometime soon. They can come here or—"

"Mami," I interrupted. Just like Rhea, she could keep going if we let her, but D'Vaughn was currently abusing the fuck outta her bottom lip and I could see her leg bouncing under the table. I needed to get her alone so I could check in with her and make sure she wasn't *too* overwhelmed.

Mami held her hands up. "Okay, okay. There's just so much to do in six weeks."

I nodded. "I know. You're right. But we can't start on it tonight. It's still KiKi's moment. We'll talk next week. Prometo."

"Ven, mi amor," commanded Papi, grabbing Mami's hand and pulling her back across the yard to the cabana.

As soon as they cleared the circle of family surrounding us, several people pushed forward to congratulate us. That went on for about fifteen minutes before Mateo cranked the music back up and, as if compelled, most of them headed straight for the yard to dance. Once we were relatively alone, I crouched next to D'Vaughn's chair and placed a hand on her still bouncing knee.

"Are you okay?"

At my touch, her leg came to a halt and she gave me a thin smile.

"Oh, my bad."

My brows knitted. "It's all good. Are you good, though?"

"Um...I need to use the restroom. Can you show me where it is?" Instead of waiting for an answer, she pushed back her chair and stood.

To avoid falling back on my ass, I followed suit. She'd avoided answering my question twice, which told me that not only was she *not* okay, but she didn't want to talk about it—but this thing wouldn't work if she didn't talk to me, so we were going to have to figure it out.

"Yeah. Come on." Grabbing her hand, I led her into the house and to the bathroom that my siblings and I had grown up fighting over.

She was in and out in a few minutes, but before she could leave the hallway, I wrapped my hand around her wrist and tugged her back toward me. To my luck, she came quietly, her brows raised as I maneuvered her in front of me.

"You gon' answer me now or nah?" It wasn't hard to guess what her answer was, but I wanted to make sure we kept the communication flowing between us. For us to succeed, we had to lay everything out on the table.

I waited as she sucked in a deep breath and released it slowly through her nose.

"I'm…making it. That was a lot."

"I know."

"They're really excited."

I chuckled, because that was an understatement. *"I know."*

"And I feel like crap about it."

Ah. So there it was. Guilt was eating at her. She'd mentioned at the restaurant that she was generally a good person so I should have expected it.

"Would you have preferred they be angry?"

She shook her head. "No. Not at all."

"But…?" It definitely sounded like a "but" was in there.

"I don't know yet. I'm still working through it."

I canted my head. "Understandable. But will you let me know when you figure it out? We're in this together, and the boat won't move unless we're rowing in the same direction."

"Yes, captain."

I quirked an eyebrow and she smiled. It was playful and a little sassy and it was a marked difference from her expression when we'd come inside ten minutes earlier.

"What?" she questioned.

"What what?" I rebounded, continuing to watch her. When just looking wasn't enough, I reached to grab her other hand, needing to feel more of her skin beneath mine, loving the softness under my fingertips. Widening my stance, I leaned back against the wall and pulled her closer to me still.

"Why are you looking at me like you want to kiss me?" Even as she spoke, she stepped into my bubble until we were almost chest-to-chest. I wanted her to lean into me and press her body against mine.

Pleased, I released a slow grin and dropped my head back, resting it against the wall as I peered at her from under lowered lids. "Let me find out you can read minds," I whispered.

Nibbling on her bottom lip, she flicked her eyes from mine to my mouth and then to her left at the entrance of the hallway.

"No one is around," she observed, her voice low and pragmatic. "There's no one you need to perform for right now."

Releasing her wrists, I touched her palm, running a fingertip along the sensitive skin, sliding the pads of my fingers up her arm, gliding them over her shoulder, and cupping the side of her neck as I settled my other hand at her waist.

"Little-known fact about my family," I murmured. "There's always someone watching. Besides, when you stay ready you don't have to get ready."

I stared at her, having put the ball in her court, waiting for her to make a move. It was out there between us that I wanted to kiss her and had apparently been obvious before I'd even copped to it. My heart thumped with anticipation, hoping that we were on the same page. Then her eyes fluttered shut and her lips pursed as she moved toward me, and if that wasn't a bell ringing for me to pass "go" I didn't know what was. Bending my neck, I first pressed a soft kiss to the corner of her mouth. It was low, but she released the softest of whimpers—something I would have missed if I hadn't already been so close to her mouth. I brushed a thumb across her bottom lip before covering her mouth with my own. Slowly, in an almost hesitant move, her hands came to my waist, her fingertips brushing my shirt, just barely touching me.

But then her lips parted and she dipped her tongue inside of my mouth, curling against mine. A spark zipped through me and I grunted as if I'd been punched in the gut. Her hands clutched at my side before she grabbed the hand that was at her waist and moved it to her ass. There was no way she'd be able to convince me she couldn't read minds because all I'd wanted to do was dig my fingers into the round globes inside those shorts all afternoon. She tasted of Jarritos and spice, and there I was, once again in that space of—

"Damn, Kris! You look like you're about to whip out your strap and fuck her right here in the hallway!"

Startled, I jerked back, knocking my head against the wall as I turned to see the guest of honor standing not even five feet away from us with her hands on her hips. Groaning, I dropped my head onto D'Vaughn's shoulder. Kiana had always had the worst timing.

"What did I tell you?" I mumbled into D'Vaughn's shoulder.

She laughed, and I felt nothing but relief to hear that sound from her. One conversation and a mind-blowing kiss wouldn't fully erase her anxiety, but if it eased it enough that she was able to see the humor in what had just transpired, then I was grateful.

"Welcome to the family!" Kiana chirped as she breezed past us and entered the bathroom.

Chapter Four

D'Vaughn

First Service

The understatement of the year would be that I was shocked at how well things had gone with Kris's family. Kris had been out since she was barely a teenager, so of course everyone knew that about her, but I'd fully expected rage and disbelief to follow the announcement of our engagement. The automatic acceptance—and even joy—had made my stomach churn with guilt. It was obvious that the Zavala clan was tight-knit, accepting, and unconditionally loving. Lying to them when they were so clearly happy that Kris was getting married felt like the highest of sins. Kris, of course, didn't share in my concerns.

"The whole point is that they believe us."

She was right, of course, but that didn't eradicate the guilty feeling that settled in the pit of my gut. When Kiana had pulled me aside, I'd nearly cracked. Kris had been summoned by her father and the moment the two of them disappeared about the side of the house, Kiana had appeared at my side.

"Thank you, thank you, thank you!" she'd practically shouted into my ear as she hugged me as tight as her burgeoning belly would allow.

"Um…you're welcome? For what, exactly?"

"Thank you for loving my sister the way she deserves to be loved. All of her exes had nothing but surface level bullshit to offer her, but I'm so glad she's found someone to make her happy."

As sweet as the sentiment had been, it had immediately tanked my mood. I don't know why I thought I could pull this off. The only lying I'd ever done in my life was a lifelong lie of omission, and even that had kept me up on many a night.

"Are we going in?"

Kris's question brought me back to the present, and I chewed on the corner of my bottom lip as nerves took flight in my stomach. Immediately, Kris cupped my chin, using the pad of her thumb to pull my lip free.

"You gotta chill with that, preciosa."

Blowing out a breath, I wrenched my gaze from the front of the church I'd grown up in to the sickeningly gorgeous woman sitting on my right. I knew that the term of endearment was just a part of the ongoing game of charades we were living and didn't mean anything, but hearing her address me as preciosa made things speed up a little inside of my chest. It was all a little too loving for my intimacy-starved brain to ignore.

"Don't want you to ruin that lipstick, aight?"

I kinda sorta absolutely wanted my lipstick ruined.

By her.

I wanted Kris to kiss me the way she'd kissed on me the day before. When we sat on that porch and accidentally on purpose lost ourselves in each other's mouths. Or in that hallway after I'd had a mini freak-out in the bathroom just before her sister had interrupted us. I'd gone to sleep with my hand between my legs, my chest heaving as I tweaked my clit to the memory of her soft pink lips on mine and the way she'd pressed herself to my back as she wrapped her hands around me several times throughout the day. She hadn't been lying when she'd said the Zavalas were an affectionate bunch, and she sure as shit hadn't been exaggerating when she warned me that she would be all over me. If our rings weren't convincing enough, each and every display of affection surely had done the trick. Hell, even I had been almost convinced that Kris was so in love that she couldn't bear to spend more than a few minutes away from me.

When she'd walked me to my car at the end of the night—well, *my* night, the party continued on after I left—we'd stood under a streetlamp near my car, bathed in its orange glow. After heaving sighs of relief, we'd let the silence of the late hour settle over us, and we were left staring at each other with goofy grins on our faces at having survived—and mastered—day one of this thing, and it had been on the tip of my tongue to ask her to come home with me. Already I'd gotten caught up in the moment and wanted to see how those kisses felt when we were both naked.

But I didn't say it then because Kris wasn't some random woman I'd met eyes with over the olive bar at the grocery store, and this wasn't the early stages of a new relationship. She was my partner in this competition, and this was week one of a six-week commitment where I didn't have the luxury of exploring my attraction to a woman that I couldn't stop thinking about. Not when I had so much tied up in this. Before I could even consider taking Kris to bed, I had to make sure that things were squared away with my family, and that wouldn't happen in one day. So I blinked to clear the delicious and downright nasty thoughts of her from my mind and nodded.

"Yeah, you're right," I finally said, breaking my silence. "Let's go."

We climbed out of the car, and I straightened the skirt of my dress while Kris came around to my side and offered her hand. I looked at her, wondering if she could see just how scared shitless I was. *Could she smell the fear on me?* Surely it had to be leaking from my pores. I took her hand and she pulled me to her, stepping into the circle of personal space and using her knuckle to tip my chin up a couple of centimeters so that we were eye to eye. She didn't say anything for a moment, just stared at me as I slowly and completely imploded right in front of her.

"This isn't going to be easy," I warned, my chest hitching just a tad. "I have no idea how they're going to take things, but aside from all of that, I'm significantly emotional on a normal day. There'll probably be tears, and sobbing, and maybe a little snot. I apologize in advance." I blew out a breath, but it was a shaky, pathetic thing that proclaimed me to be just as nervous as one would expect to be if they had decided to come out to their family in the most public way possible.

At church.

On a Sunday.

Kris's lips curved up enticingly as she chuckled and I was hit with a surge of lust so strong that I suddenly felt the urge to lay myself before the altar and ask the good reverend to sprinkle holy water on me.

"Whatever happens," she began, "know that I'm right here with you and I got your back. No matter what goes down, you're not alone."

The corners of my eyes prickled, and I squeezed them shut to keep the incoming tears at bay. Yeah, this was fake, but coming out to my family was as real as it gets and I was *terrified*. Before I could descend too far into my mind, I felt Kris's hands on my face. Quickly, I grabbed her wrists, using her as an anchor to keep me grounded.

"I just—I need you to have my back, okay? We haven't had nearly enough time to get our stories together, and if I start floundering, I need you to catch me. Don't leave me out here by myself and don't let me fall, okay?"

"I'm right here with you," she repeated on a whisper that sounded significantly closer than before.

I started to crack my eyelids open, but then her lips touched mine in a gentle, affirming kiss, and naturally they fell closed again as I succumbed to her. This was different than any kiss we'd shared before. It wasn't the exploratory "practice" kiss, or like any of the dozens of chaste kisses we'd exchanged in front of her family. The way her mouth moved against mine was an extension of her keeping my feet on solid ground. It centered me in a way I'd never experienced through another human being before. I sighed into her and felt the weight of my anxiety lessen against my chest, allowing me to finally breathe easy. Greedily—gratefully—I sucked in a breath through my nose and was inundated with the cologne she wore.

Suddenly my brain was clouded with her image and mine tangled in different scenarios that were incredibly inappropriate for the parking lot of a church. Just as I felt myself leaning toward her, Kris dialed the kiss back and pulled away from me.

"Shit," she murmured, touching her forehead to mine.

My eyes were still closed and I hummed contentedly, a soft smile coming to my face.

"You can't curse at a church, Kris."

Chuckling, Kris pressed a quick kiss to my forehead, and then stepped back, putting a foot of space between us.

"Technically, we aren't at church yet, so I think it'll be alright. Vamos, preciosa. Let's head inside. We don't want to start off on the wrong foot by being late."

I sighed and then nodded because she was absolutely right. My mama did not play when it came to being in the Lord's house at the appointed hour. Giving myself a little shake, I opened my eyes to find Kris watching me intently. There was a little smirk on her face, but her brown eyes were filled with concern. She, more than anyone, understood how big of a deal today was. When she auditioned for *Instant I Do*, I'm sure the last thing she imagined she'd be doing was acting as a plus-one to a surprise coming-out party, but she'd picked up the mantle without complaint, even dressing for the occasion.

And she looked good too.

Kris wore a slim-fit charcoal-gray suit that fit her slender, toned body as if it had been tailor-made for her. The peach-colored shirt and pocket square matched my dress, which I'd paired with dark gray platform pumps and silver jewelry, and I had to admit that we looked good together. Matching had been my suggestion and Kris had readily agreed to it. It wasn't something I'd gone for in previous relationships, but it seemed exactly the type of over-the-top thing that people who would get married weeks after meeting would do. It had been a pleasant surprise when Kris said she didn't have a problem with it. When I'd picked her up that morning, Rhea had agreed and insisted on taking a picture of us before we left. Of course she was on strict instructions not to post it to Kris's social media accounts, and Kris informed me that Rhea was her one person that knew about the show. That had given me a small measure of comfort; although I had to admit that I was curious how Kris's followers would react to seeing us together.

After our first meeting, I'd gone home to do my own re-search on the online persona she said had taken her by sur-prise and now paid her well enough to replace her day job if she ever decided to quit. It hadn't taken me long to deduce that those quarter million followers were not only real, but heavily engaged with Kris's content. Each of her posts re-ceived thousands of likes and hundreds of comments, many of which trended toward telling Kris how fine she was. *As if she didn't know.*

"Shall we?"

Kris held out her hand, and after taking a deep, fortifying breath, I took it. She gave me a gentle squeeze and led us to the door of the building. We'd parked in the back of the lot—not that it made any difference. Greater Rock of Abundant Salvation Missionary Baptist Tabernacle of the Living Word was a small, family church with a parking lot to match. It didn't matter where you parked in the tiny, square lot—everyone could see you. Because of that, I had no doubt that at least six members of the congregation had witnessed Kris giving me mouth-to-mouth a few minutes earlier. It would be a miracle if my mama didn't already know I was outside kissing a girl.

Oh God.

The upside was that I was far too busy worrying about what would happen once we stepped foot inside of the building to be worried about our whole exchange being filmed by Felix. I'd noticed the van when I'd pulled into the lot, but it was the last thing on my mind. The beating in my chest sped up and I could feel the anxiety creeping in on me again. Was I *really* going to do this? Was I about to lay myself bare for the entire congregation to see and judge me? Was I going to give my mama—my family—an opportunity to turn their backs on me?

It was a miracle that I'd managed to escape the actual moment being filmed. Somehow Kevin had managed to get it approved for the cameras to stay out of the church, sticking instead to the parking lot. The caveat was that I absolutely had to let Felix inside once we headed to Mama's house after church, but I could handle that. We had just stepped under the awning and were almost to the door when Kris halted midstep and turned to face me. I saw the curious expressions of the greeters on the other side of the glass doors before my face was once again in her hands as she peered at me, that concern shining brightly and furrowing her usually smooth brow.

"Hey," she murmured, "I got you. We're gonna do this together. Take a deep breath. Breathe with me."

I nodded but couldn't speak, glad that she didn't say it was going to be okay, since I knew for a fact that it wouldn't. There was no way my Bible-thumping, prayer-warrior, and church-mother-in-training mama would accept that her oldest daughter was a lesbian. Without a doubt this was about to be the last time I'd likely see my family on a good note and fissures were slowly shooting throughout my being, ready to split and separate at the first sign of disgust in their eyes.

"D'Vaughn! *Stop it.*" Kris's firm voice brought me back from the brink and I blinked repeatedly to keep the tears at bay. "Don't give up, preciosa. The fight hasn't even started."

"I don't wanna fight," I husked. My voice was raw, preemptively stripped bare. "I just wanna live, and I want them to love me regardless of who *I* love. Is that too much to ask?"

Kris shook her head, rubbing her thumbs over my cheeks and under my eyes, searching for saline trails that I'd somehow managed to hold back. "Not at all."

"Then why does it feel like I'm begging for the world to be handed to me on a silver platter?" The cracks began in my voice as my words dodged lumps of emotion in my throat on their way out of my mouth.

Leaning forward, Kris touched her forehead to mine. "Even if you were asking for the world, you'd deserve every inch of it, and nothing that anyone inside of this building has to say can change that."

My eyes fluttered closed again as I let her words wash over me.

"Lean on me if you have to," she offered. "I'm here to support you, and if you feel like you're crumbling, let me shore you up, aight? Take what you need from me; accept my strength in addition to your own."

Releasing a shuddering breath, I shook my head. "That's too much, Kris. You barely know me, plus you didn't sign up for this."

"D'Vaughn."

Flipping open, my eyes shot to hers, startled by the admonishment in her now-gritty tone.

"I'm going to give you a pass because you don't know me well enough *yet*, but I signed up to be your fiancée. That's not just about spending bands and fucking." My brows shot toward the sky because *what*?! Who said *anything* about sex? No one, but now I was definitely thinking about it. "Being a fiancée means standing by your side through whatever. I signed up for *that*."

Was it sacrilegious to imagine screwing your fake fiancée while you were standing just a few steps away from the doors of the church? Because that's what I was now doing. Had that been her plan? Was this Kris's way of trying to distract me from spiraling out of control about a situation that hadn't yet taken place? My eyes were glued to her face, and I saw the exact moment that she realized where my mind had gone. Her lips curled into a wicked grin and she bent her head to press a tortuously slow kiss to my cheek. The way her lips barely grazed my skin was undeniably chaste, but for some reason felt illicit in a way that made my nipples pebble beneath my bra.

"Do you need some incentive?" she murmured into my ear. "Because I can give you that."

She is so freaking good at this. And just like that, my mind shifted completely away from the doom and gloom to something slick and hot and *needy*, and OMG was I *wet*?! I was. Standing less than one hundred feet away from my mama, who was only separated from us by the two sets of doors that led to the sanctuary.

Yeah, I needed to reel it in.

Properly distracted, I gave a false laugh that played at being light but was really desperation and want in disguise as I stepped out of Kris's arms and brushed my hands down the bodice of my dress.

"Your sex appeal is dangerous," I informed her. *Too dangerous.*

Sliding her teeth across her bottom lip, she reached for my hand and started for the door.

"Just know that I can back it up though."

Did I say dangerous? I meant downright treacherous because I had no doubt that there was something beneath the surface of her easy grin and warm brown eyes that would make me lose my mind—and myself. My mind, I wanted to keep firmly in my possession. My body? I wanted to give that over for her to do with as she pleased.

The double doors of the church opened outward and two women stepped forward to hold each side open.

"Good morning, D'Vaughn," greeted the younger of the two, her eyes sparkling with a knowing gleam.

"Good morning, Sister Mary." Reflexively, I searched her face, waiting for the ugliness to surface, but surprisingly, nothing came. I turned to the other woman who was old enough to be my grandmother. Her lips were pursed and eyes narrowed. Noticing her expression, Kris squeezed my hand, and I braced myself for her response.

"Young lady," she began in a prim voice full of censure, "I know you think you grown, but the next time I see you out there disrespecting the Lord's house—committing fornication and whatnot—I'mma put you over my knee."

My mouth fell open and I could hear Sister Mary stifle a chuckle behind me.

"Oh, but Mother Jacobs, this is my—"

The older woman waved her hand and raised her voice to cut me off. "Aht! I don't care 'bout none of that mess. Boyfriend, girlfriend, *whatever*. If you ain't married, you sinnin'! You hear me?"

Unsure whether I should be relieved or amused, I gave her a swift nod. "Yes, ma'am."

Mother Jacobs nodded toward the sanctuary. "Good. Now get on in there. You almost late and your mama been worried."

"Yes, ma'am," I repeated dutifully, tugging Kris behind me and entering the sanctuary.

"Well, that wasn't so bad," Kris said into my ear as I led her down the back row and up the aisle along the wall. "Though, I didn't know kissing was fornication."

"Color me surprised," I mumbled back, my eyes on my mama's large green hat a few pews ahead.

She squeezed my hand. "It's a good sign. Relish in it."

I wanted to agree with her, to nod and admit that she was right, but my heart had leaped into my throat and the blood was rushing through my ears too loudly for me to focus on anything but my mama. She kept glancing over her left shoulder at the doors to the sanctuary. She was undoubtedly looking for me, but then finally, she turned to her right. The moment she spotted me, her eyes lit up and she smiled wide, standing to her feet and scooting out of the pew, facing me just as we made it to her.

"Hey, Mama," I squeaked. Kris squeezed my hand once more, and I felt like she'd be doing that a lot throughout the day, as if I was a beach ball that kept deflating and she was my trusty air pump that refused to let me go flat.

"There you are!" she exclaimed, relief tugging her shoulders down. "You almost missed the—" She trailed off and it felt like the world switched to slow motion as I watched her eyes skirt down my body until she reached mine and Kris's joined hands. Everything sped up again as her questioning gaze jumped back up to mine, her lips first parting to ask a question and then snapping shut when she likely realized the answer.

"Mama, this is Kris."

Within seconds, Mama raked her gaze over Kris, taking in her suit, loafers, locs, piercings, and the tattoo across the front of her neck that was still visible despite her collared shirt and tie. Instead of then meeting my eyes again, Mama dropped her gaze, taking with it the sliver of hope that I'd clung to. My heart plummeted into my shoes as Mama extended her arm toward the pew.

"G'on on and have a seat. Praise and worship is about to begin."

Those fissures shifted, the cracks widening, allowing tiny streams of me to seep through. I glanced back at Kris to find her jaw tight, her eyes fierce and trained on me. She nodded and tilted her head toward the pew. Taking a shuddering breath, I leaned forward and pressed a kiss to my mama's cheek before sliding into the pew. Kris followed behind me and we both sat down. From the corner of my eye, I watched as my mama stared at us—at our hands—from the aisle. Kris had lifted our joined hands and rested them on her thigh. There was no mistaking the possessive move, and I knew my mama recognized it for what it was.

The noise in the sanctuary grew as the praise and worship singers took their place. My sister's voice sounded through the speakers, loud and joyful.

"Good morning, saints. Usually we start the service off with something upbeat to get your hearts pumping and ready to receive the word, but this morning God is telling me to go a different route. I hope y'all don't mind if we let Him move on this day that He has made." D'Niesha began to hum a soulful melody as she waited for the musicians to join in.

My breath hitched and I dropped my head, closing my eyes as I faced my lap.

How was it possible that I hurt this much when she hadn't said one word to me? Wasn't her silence better than condemnation?

"You alright?"

Squeezing my eyes tighter, I shook my head. I was a lot of things in that moment, but alright wasn't one of them. Kris ducked her head, speaking directly into my ear.

"Remember that you're not alone right now. I'm here with you. What do you need from me?"

I couldn't answer that. I didn't know how to verbalize it, and even if I did, I felt like if I parted my lips, then those fissures would bust wide open and I'd shatter into a million pieces. I hadn't even officially come out, had only showed up to church with a woman on my arm, and my mama—the one woman on the planet who I loved even more than myself—had rejected me. No, she hadn't said anything, but her polite avoidance of my gaze, refusal to acknowledge Kris, and above all, the fact that she didn't even touch me said enough.

She wouldn't even look at me.

A sob burst out of my throat and I shook my head. On top of everything, the show was over before it'd even begun. There was no way I'd be able to convince anyone I was marrying a relative stranger if they couldn't first accept me for who I was. I owed Kris a massive apology. She was losing out on the ability to win one hundred thousand dollars simply because I hadn't been brave enough to come out to my family when I first realized that it was the cheerleaders and not the football players that stole my attention under the Friday night lights.

The music surged in volume as D'Niesha tilted her head

back and sang to the rafters about God not putting more on her than she could bear despite everything she'd been through. It was a song that I'd always loved, but felt especially poignant at that moment. Chills wracked me, and my skin pebbled as if the a/c had been cut on. As Kris rubbed my back, an usher entered our row from the middle aisle and pressed several tissues into my hand. I blew my nose, but couldn't stop the onslaught of tears. I wanted my mama and she wouldn't even look at me. The doom and gloom returned with a vengeance, and I began to wonder how I was supposed to go on with things the way that they were. My mama was such a big part of my life, but if all she saw when she looked at me was a sinner, nothing of our relationship would be the same.

Kris's hand fell from my back at the same time that I lost the warmth of her thigh pressed against mine. Before I could reach for her and beg her to stay with me, I was enveloped into a familiar embrace and bombarded with the ever-present scent of Red Door that my mama had been wearing since before I was even born. Immediately, I wrapped my arms around her waist and buried my face into her shoulder.

"My baby," she spoke directly into my ear. "Release it. Holding on is bringing you so much pain. Let it go, baby."

Her words were a balm, flipping a switch that released a shudder that took over my body. I bawled. Began full-on sobbing into the shoulder pads of my mama's sensible church suit.

"I—I don't wh—want you to ha—hate me!" I blubbered.

Mama rocked me back and forth, rubbing my back in soothing circles as she clicked her tongue in my ear. "Hush! You are my greatest blessing, D'Vaughn. I had no idea who I was until I was staring down at your wrinkled face."

I sucked in a breath. "Even if I'm gay?" I whispered, almost praying she didn't hear me.

She squeezed me tighter and I felt the brim of her hat brush my hair as she shook her head. Leaning back, she cupped my face, staring at me intently.

"God makes no mistakes," she said firmly. "You've always been this way and my love for you has never wavered, so why on earth would things change now?"

I gasped and a fresh wave of sobs wracked my body. Hearing those words come out of her mouth were even more shocking than learning I'd been selected as a contestant on *Instant I Do*. Question after question flitted across my mind begging to be voiced, demanding to be answered, but I batted them back. Soon, but not now.

Now I would bask in the comfort of my mother's arms. I would let her love that first seemed stripped from me wash away the hurt as much as possible. I would sit through the service, and then, before the day came to an end, I would make sure there was a clear understanding between the two of us.

Jitter Cam 03-D'Vaughn

Oh, wow. It's interview style this time? Lucky me.

No, no. You're right. I wouldn't exactly say that I'd enjoyed the privacy, but answering questions about what happened in there is really the least I can do. I just—I have to warn you that I'm…well. I'm having a hard time right now. I don't even know what to say. I don't even know how I feel.

No. That's a lie. I'm *so damn angry* right now.

I'm thirty years old and just came out to my mama during Sunday service, but instead of her being shocked, she told me that she… She said she—she's always known.

I'm sorry. I didn't mean to start crying. I thought I'd left all my tears in the sanctuary.

Yeah, it hurts. I've struggled with this for twenty years. TWENTY YEARS! I was a ba—baby, just trying to figure out who I was. I thought I was alone.

Since I was ten years old, I lived with the fear that my mama would turn me away if she ever found out. I was stressed out of my mind. I've ruined every relationship I've ever been in because I was afraid to introduce anyone as my girlfriend.

What did you say? Am I relieved that it's out in the open now? You know what? I thought the answer would have been yes, and maybe it could be if I wasn't so angry. Like…maybe when I can sit with this and calm down some, I'll be relieved. Right now though? All I feel is regret for what could've been.

What kind of life might I have lived if she'd said something? Could I have been happily married now?

That's all I'm thinking about.

Oh, yeah. Kris was amazing. Ordinarily I'd be embarrassed, but even that is an emotion I don't have room for right now. It helps that she isn't treating me like she saw me break down into a snotty, crying mess in the middle of a church 'cause my mama hurt my feelings.

Um. I'm sorry that I don't have a concrete answer to that. I don't really know what I'm going to do now. I mean, we're heading to my mama's house for Sunday dinner, but I don't know what I'm going to do.

I just want to get past today so that I can move on with the show.

Is there any bright side to her already knowing? Hmm. I guess it will make her more likely to believe that we're getting married.

That's all I can see right now.

Chapter Five

Kris

Sunday Dinner

D'Vaughn had warned me. I'd had an inclination, but I hadn't known that it would be as…intense as it had been. When she broke down crying, I felt the most helpless I'd ever felt in my entire twenty-eight years, including when I'd watched Ray fall from a tree after he decided to rescue the family cat from the top limb without waiting for Papi. The way her mother had refused to look at her caused an instant cauldron of rage to bubble up inside of me. It was the subtlest type of rejection that could sometimes burn more than the overt stuff, evident in the way it had ripped D'Vaughn in half. That first sob that burst from her lips seemed to be the thing that snapped the older woman out of whatever hateful trance she had been in. She'd rushed down the aisle, trying to squeeze past me to get to D'Vaughn, but I was bent over tending to the daughter she'd hurt, and had no intention of moving so she could inflict more pain.

Only after she choked out, "Please," and I swung my glare up at her to be met by remorseful eyes did I release my hold on D'Vaughn. Standing up, I allowed her to squeeze past me and engulf D'Vaughn into her arms, the bouncing brim of her hat evidence that she was speaking rapidly. I watched intently, waiting to see if D'Vaughn stiffened or tried to pull away, ready to bogart my way in and get her out of here.

The main singer came down from the stage and headed straight for D'Vaughn. She eased into the row from the center aisle and placed her hand on D'Vaughn's back as she sang. Things moved pretty quickly after that. The musicians continued to play as the three other singers harmonized, but the words faded away as people all over the building began to cry out and pray aloud. The reverend took to the podium and sang a song about surrendering your heart to Christ before announcing that there was no need for him to preach when God had already had his way that morning.

It was another half hour before D'Vaughn resurfaced from underneath her mother. The two of them had gone through a box of tissues; D'Vaughn's eyes were puffy and rimmed red. It would have been fine if they were clear but that wasn't the case. They were clouded with apprehension and anger, which concerned me even as she tried to smile through it. When the service came to an end, she'd avoided meeting my eyes, worrying her lip as she led me out of the building and back to her car. It wasn't hard to deduce that she was embarrassed, but she didn't need to be. Even if she hadn't warned me that she would cry, this was a huge moment for her and would have been emotional for even the most stonehearted individual. She'd handled it admirably, especially considering the way her mother first reacted when she noticed us holding hands.

Her mother and the singer, who she informed me was her sister, had a few things to do before they could leave, and D'Vaughn had murmured that she wanted to leave without fanfare in the parking lot. After promising her mother that we'd be going to her house for dinner, D'Vaughn didn't say a word to me as we crossed the tiny lot, but I couldn't let her get in the car without doing *something*. Walking to her side instead of my own, I wrapped my arms around her, hugging her from behind as she reached for the handle on the door. Her body trembled as she took a shuddering breath, but I held my tongue, hugging her silently, not even sure if she wanted to speak.

"Don't make me cry again," she whispered hoarsely.

"I'm not trying to," I murmured into her hair, tightening my grip on her because it sounded like she needed it. "I just want you to know that I see you and I'm proud of you. It might not mean much since we just met a few days ago, but you did a brave thing and no matter the outcome, you are worthy."

She hiccupped or sobbed or something. Whatever it was, it made me spin her in my arms and frame her face with my hands. Her eyes were closed but tears slipped silently from the corners. I swiped at them without hesitation.

"Can I kiss you?"

She needed something; I just wasn't sure what it was. There was no way for me to know if my words were helping, but a kiss was tangible. At the very least I could provide a distraction from whatever waged war behind her eyes. When she nodded, I leaned in to press a quick kiss to each of her cheeks before sliding my lips over hers in a few chaste pecks. Leaning back, I watched her take a deep breath and blow it out before she opened her eyes.

"Let's go."

We climbed in the car, and I waited for her to pull out of the lot before taking her hand in mine. I didn't ask any questions when she drove to a park instead of heading straight to her mother's house. We sat in the car, neither making a move to push open the door and get out. Although my coming out was significantly less intense than D'Vaughn's had been, I had no problem understanding that she had a lot to process.

I didn't say a word, just gently squeezed her hand and linked our fingers, trying to give her strength through our connection as unobtrusively as possible. After about fifteen minutes, she shifted the car in gear and drove off. It was a short drive to what I presumed was her mother's house, and soon she was pulling into a driveway behind a compact SUV.

The doors automatically unlocked as soon as she shifted into Park, and right after that, the back door on the driver's side opened and a woman climbed inside. Before I had a chance to become alarmed, D'Vaughn introduced the woman as her best friend, Cinta. Cinta reached forward and wrapped her arms around D'Vaughn from the back seat.

"I'm so proud of you, my boo!"

D'Vaughn's eyes slid closed and she reached up to grab Cinta's arms.

"She knew, Cin. She knew this whole time." D'Vaughn's whisper was low and ragged. The tortured sound broke my heart.

"That's great, right?" Cinta asked as she shot a brief glance my way. "I mean, if she knew and never acted differently, that means she doesn't care, right?"

A frown had taken over my face before I could even process it. "Hell naw! That's not what that means at all! That's harmful as fuck."

The confusion was evident in Cinta's furrowed brow and the way she tilted her head to one side as she thought. I side-eyed her, not fathoming how she could be confused when it was as clear as glass.

"What's worse?" she finally asked. "Her assuming that you were gay and never saying anything, or her knowing for sure that you're gay and hating you for it?"

D'Vaughn shook her head emphatically. "That's not it, Cinta. I feel like they're equally bad. Hating me because of who I love, or who I have the capacity to love, or who I'm attracted to is horrible, but knowing that I'm gay, or even assuming it to be so, and never saying anything? Allowing me to struggle for years—hell, decades—noticing that I never bring any love interest around the family, and how different that is from what everyone else is doing, and never saying a word to me? That's not innocent. That's not innocuous. Not to me."

D'Vaughn's friend shook her head. "No, I'm not saying it's okay, I'm just wondering if it's worth it to be angry about that when there is no malicious intent behind that one. Could it be that she saw how hard a time you were having and wanted to wait for you to bring it up so as not to embarrass you?"

D'Vaughn curved around in her seat, her mouth set in a hard line. "You know what, Cinta? The devil doesn't need an advocate."

Eyes wide, Cinta sat back, hitting the back seat with a thud. The car was filled with silence for a few moments before Cinta took a deep breath.

"It's clear that I'm not doing a good job of expressing myself—"

"Or maybe it's just that the opinions you're sharing are unintentionally harmful and dismissive of my feelings?"

Cinta rolled her lips into her mouth and shook her head. "I'm going to shut up."

A thread of anxiety bubbled up in my gut and I cringed internally. The conversation had taken a turn, and in my experience the only thing that would follow was "accidental" bigotry and cries of being treated unfairly as an ally. I waited for the usual. For D'Vaughn to apologize and attempt to make Cinta feel better; to tell her that, no, she didn't have to shut up, even though her views weren't helpful. I was surprised when D'Vaughn merely shook her head and said, "Thank you."

And that was it. Cinta didn't say anything else, the atmosphere in the car didn't suddenly become thick with tension, and nobody started crying. It was wild and amazing.

Leaning back against the seat, D'Vaughn sighed.

"Are you coming to dinner?"

Cinta shook her head. "I'll come if you absolutely need me to be there, but I think I should sit this one out. You know how Mama Dee is about confrontations; she might take it as an ambush if all of us are in front of her."

"Sure, but what about me? She might feel ambushed, but aren't I the only victim here?"

"Okay, Vaughn. I'll come with."

D'Vaughn made an exasperated sound. "Well I don't want you to come if you don't want to."

Groaning, Cinta threw her hands into the air. "Ugh! What do you want, D'Vaughn?!"

"I don't know!" D'Vaughn cried. "I want to skip all of this and get to the part where I get to be happy and carefree! I want to plan this fake wedding and have my only concern be whether or not Kris and I are selling this well enough!"

Cinta's eyes softened and she reached between the seats to grab D'Vaughn's hand just as I stretched a hand across the center console and placed it on her knee.

"I'm sorry, my boo," Cinta began. "I'm so sorry that I can't give any of that to you. There is nothing I can do that will make any of that become a reality, but I know that on the other side of that door is your mama and she's waiting to have a conversation that is several years overdue. I know that whatever happens, you'll no longer have the burden of hiding who you are weighing you down. I know that whatever happens in that house, you'll still have people who love you, and if you come home in tears, I'll be there to wipe them away and remind you of how much I love you and how perfect I think you are exactly as you are right now, even with a snotty nose and raccoon eyes."

That hiccup sob thing happened again, and I couldn't even blame D'Vaughn because Cinta's words had me choked up as well. Living as an unapologetically queer person was tough enough just stepping outside of your front door. Knowing that you had someone in your corner who was down for you one hundred and fifty percent made a world of difference. Listening to the two of them made me appreciate my family even more.

"I love you too," D'Vaughn whispered, "even though you're making me cry."

"Good," Cinta sniffled. "Now, once and for all, do you want me to come with you?"

D'Vaughn shook her head. "No. I can handle it by myself."

I cleared my throat. "But you won't be by yourself."

"Exactly! Don't play with Kris like that! She's not just arm candy."

Tilting her head to the side, D'Vaughn eyed me. "She *is* nice to look at though."

"Especially those legs." Cinta clucked her tongue. "Those thighs look like they're about to pop out of her pants."

Ducking my head, I grinned as an unexpected surge of bashfulness washed over me. "Y'all not gon' talk about me like I'm a piece of meat."

Cinta pursed her lips. "Now she tryna act like she don't know she fine."

"Game," D'Vaughn chirped, playfulness tugging at the corners of her mouth.

I chuckled. "We going in or nah?"

Sighing, D'Vaughn shut off the car. "Only since I know 'or nah' isn't really an option."

"Not when Mama Dee knows where we live."

"Exactly. She'll pull up in a heartbeat."

We all climbed out of the car and I waited while D'Vaughn and Cinta hugged it out. After a moment, D'Vaughn laughed lightly and they parted, D'Vaughn heading my way while Cinta walked down the driveway to a sedan parked on the street. I held my hand out, she took it, and then we walked hand-in-hand up the pathway. The door swung open before we reached the porch, and D'Vaughn's mother stood there watching us.

"You get lost?"

"Really, Mama?"

The older woman stepped to the side as we entered. D'Vaughn kicked out of her heels, prompting me to toe off my shoes as well.

"Church let out 'bout an hour ago. What was I to think?"

"You coulda called."

"Hmph." She stood there, her hands on hips as she waited for us.

Finally, D'Vaughn looked up and realized her mother was still standing there.

"Oh! Um, Mama—" she reached for my hand "—this is Kris Zavala. Kris, this is my mama, Deidre Miller."

I offered my right hand. "Nice to meet you, Ms. Miller." Surprisingly, she took my hand in a solid grip and shook it twice.

"Mmhm," she murmured, still holding my hand captive. "And who exactly are you to my Vaughn?"

D'Vaughn squeezed my hand so tightly that I cringed. I had no idea what that meant. Was I not supposed to answer the question? I glanced at her, but her eyes were trained on her mother. Looking back at Ms. Miller, I pulled out the charming smile that always got me out of trouble with Tía Claudia.

Ms. Miller softened a little once I turned it on, so I took a breath and spilled the beans.

"I'm her fiancée."

"Surprise!" D'Vaughn shouted weakly, holding her left hand up and wiggling her fingers.

Ms. Miller's eyes widened and then filled with tears. She covered her mouth with one hand and reached for D'Vaughn's hand with the other.

"Fiancée?"

"Yes, ma'am. We're getting married."

Ms. Miller looked up from the ring. "My baby's getting married?"

Seemingly choked up, D'Vaughn nodded. Ms. Miller gripped her hand and took off further into the house, tugging D'Vaughn—who still had my hand in a vise grip—behind her. The older woman didn't stop moving until she reached the picture window in the living room. The blinds were pulled back and gave a clear view of the front door and yard. She lifted D'Vaughn's hand to her face.

"This is nice."

"Thank you, Mama."

Sweeping her eyes over D'Vaughn's shoulder, she met my gaze.

"Did you pick this out by yourself?"

"No, ma'am. We chose it together." I figured that would've garnered me an approving nod at least, but no such luck. From the way her face fell, you would've thought I'd just sold her favorite pet chicken to the nearest meat market.

"So, this wasn't a surprise engagement?"

With a slow shake of her head, D'Vaughn stared at her mother. "No, ma'am. We discussed it beforehand."

That wasn't exactly a lie since we *did* discuss the details with

Kevin before he pulled out three rings and matching band options for us to choose from.

Her eyes were back on D'Vaughn then, hurt shining bright in their dark brown depths. There was a thud in my gut as a pang of guilt slashed at me. Ms. Miller loosened her grip on D'Vaughn's hand, letting it fall from her grasp as she took a couple of steps backward and sank down into the easy chair next to the window. When she looked up at her eldest child, the pain was written all over her face.

"This was planned and yet you never mentioned one word of this to me. How could you keep something so important from me?"

My eyebrows shot through the roof at her audacity. D'Vaughn stiffened in front of me, her shoulders straightening as she lifted her chin.

"You wouldn't even look at me once you saw us holding hands. It didn't occur to me then, but now I see it for what it is. You already knew. I mean, why else would you react that way? Cinta and I hold hands all the time and you've never batted an eye, but this morning, your entire demeanor changed."

Her voice was steady, words sure and purposeful. She hadn't asked a question aloud but she definitely left it open for her mother to explain herself. Ms. Miller dropped her gaze to her lap and took a deep breath, and then another. After the third, she lifted her head, opened her mouth, and then quickly shot a look at me before snapping her mouth shut. They needed to talk, and it was obvious that Ms. Miller wasn't comfortable speaking in front of me. I wanted to support D'Vaughn, but it was more important for her to get the answers she deserved than it was for me to be standing next to her. Squeezing D'Vaughn's hand, I leaned over to speak into her ear.

"I'm going to go outside and let y'all speak." I started to

pull away, but she gripped my hand tightly, preventing me from getting too far. I turned back to meet her pleading eyes.

"Stay?" The *please* was silent yet I'd heard it loud and clear. Nodding, I rubbed my thumb over her wrist. Her pulse was jumping like crazy. I'd bet if she'd been sitting down, her leg would be bouncing the way it had the night before at my parents' house. She gestured to the couch.

"Can we sit down?"

Narrowing her eyes, Ms. Miller sucked her teeth. "When have you ever had to ask to make a move in this house, D'Vaughn? Don't start acting like you're a stranger in your own home all of a sudden."

I waited for D'Vaughn to sit down before sitting next to her, leaving a few inches of space between us so not to make her mother uncomfortable. My effort was rendered moot when D'Vaughn promptly scooted closer to me, eating up space until our sides were flush against each other. I, of course, had no complaint, and draped my arm behind her over the back of the couch. The way she sort of sank into my side made my entire body flush with warmth. Since we were no longer holding hands, she placed her hand on my knee as she spoke. With her eyes on her mother, she shrugged.

"I don't know, Mama. The way you looked at me this morning definitely made me feel like a stranger."

Ms. Miller blew out a labored breath. "I'm sorry, baby. I... Well, I was ashamed. I couldn't face you."

I could feel D'Vaughn's shock reverberating through our connection mirroring the pure disbelief that I felt.

"Ashamed of what? Of *me*?!"

"No! Absolutely not!" Her hard eyes and firm set of her mouth made her impassioned words believable, but I didn't really know this woman, and I wondered if D'Vaughn saw the same thing. "That was personal shame for me and no one else." She paused, her eyes flickering from D'Vaughn to her folded hands in her lap and back to D'Vaughn. "I've always prided myself on being a good mother. I might have been a terrible wife, but I was the bomb at raising you all. But if I had to find out that you were engaged...like that, then maybe I'm not as good as I thought I was."

Disgusted, I dropped my chin to my chest to hide my reaction to her words. Her ability to skirt the true issue at hand so that she could martyr herself and gain sympathy both astounded me and pissed me off. Blowing a breath through my nose, I reminded myself once again that this wasn't about me, and covered D'Vaughn's hand with my own, rubbing the soft skin with my thumb. If I had to sit and listen to her kowtow to her emotionally manipulative mother to give Ms. Miller the impression that I was a supportive fiancée, then that's what I would do.

After several moments of silence stretched on, I looked to D'Vaughn to see her jaw clenched as she stared at her lap and shook her head. The disappointment was evident in the slump of her shoulders. Lifting her hand from my leg, I linked our fingers and squeezed. I couldn't make the moment less painful, but I could remind her that she wasn't here alone at least.

Ms. Miller cleared her throat awkwardly. "Since this is the first time I'm seeing a ring, I'm going to assume this is a recent engagement."

Sighing, D'Vaughn nodded. "Yes, ma'am."

"And have you picked a date?"

"Um..." D'Vaughn slid her gaze back to me. Raising my eyebrows, I nodded. There was no point in delaying the inevitable. She'd figure it out as soon as we started planning. "We have. We were thinking in a few weeks."

Ms. Miller sat up straight. "A few weeks?!"

"Mmhm. Six to be exact."

Her jaw hit the floor, rolled back up, and then dropped back down to the floor. "A month and a half?"

"Yes, ma'am."

When she lowered her gaze to D'Vaughn's stomach before flicking it over to me and pursing her lips, I almost busted out laughing. *Not again.*

"Well, I'd ask if you were pregnant, but I guess that's not likely in this scenario."

D'Vaughn snorted. "Seriously, Mama?"

"It just seems so sudden."

"Sudden to you, maybe."

"Sudden to anybody, D'Vaughn," she huffed. "I just met her today and now you're telling me that you're marrying her in a handful of Saturdays. Who is she? I don't even know her people. What if they're racist?"

I sat back heavily, blown away by what had just come out of her mouth. *Nah. She hadn't said that. I must've imagined it.*

"Mama!" Embarrassed, D'Vaughn covered her face.

I frowned. *So I wasn't trippin'? She'd truly uttered that unmitigated ignorance?* Reaching up, I rubbed at my jaw as I shook my head. "Um… My people are Black. *I'm* Black." It was ridiculous that I even felt the need to say it. It was almost laughable.

Ms. Miller swung her gaze at me, narrowing her eyes as she gave me a thorough once-over. "With a last name like Zavala, I'm certain not everyone in your family is Black, and that means someone is racist."

"What the heck? Mama, stop it!" D'Vaughn's hands fisted and her leg started to bounce. I touched her arm, patting it a few times, hoping to calm her down before she exploded.

"It's fine," I assured D'Vaughn as I leveled Ms. Miller with a cool stare. "For the record, I want to inform you that Afro-Latinx people exist and the diaspora isn't exclusive to African-Americans. Second, assuming that someone is racist simply because their name sounds different than yours is a pretty big-oted point of view. Especially when everyone has the potential to be prejudiced and hateful." I gestured to D'Vaughn. "Un-fortunately for women like us, the bigotry oftentimes comes from people in the same community as us because they are closest to us and have the ability to hurt us unlike anyone else. My parents have done an amazing job with ensuring that the only people who have been in our lives are those who are worthy. Those people love us for who we are and don't have a shred of hate in them. Now, I'm not going to argue with you over a wrong opinion about people who you've never met. All I'll say is that D'Vaughn struggled with sharing her sexu-ality with you her entire life, which means that, while you're worried about the hate from outside sources, you might want to consider that the call was coming from inside the house."

Back straight, I sat primed and ready to rise to my feet, wait-ing for her to tell me to leave. I certainly hadn't planned on monologuing, but once she spoke ill of my family all gloves came off. To my surprise, her face drooped as she gazed at me remorsefully.

"I—I apologize. I'm just concerned at the suddenness of all of this. It's my duty as a mother to worry about the people my child attaches themselves to."

Were you concerned when you were ignoring her sexuality and pretending that you didn't know? The words were on the tip of my tongue and so eager to be spoken that I had to bite the in-side of my cheek to keep them from spilling forth. I'd already said more than enough, and I wasn't here to start shit with D'Vaughn's mother, even if the words were true. I was sup-posed to be offering support, likely in silence. So, instead of saying anything at all, I blew a long breath through my nos-trils and sat back on the sofa. D'Vaughn's hand immediately found its way back to my knee and I realized that I needed that small touch. I needed to know that she wasn't upset about what I'd said.

"Well, Kris's parents want to meet you. They suggested dinner this week and I think that's a good idea."

Pursing her lips, Ms. Miller shook her head. "It doesn't much seem like I have a choice. If they're all on board and I show a little hesitance, I'm the bad guy here."

D'Vaughn huffed out a dry laugh as she stood to her feet. Clearly she'd had enough. "You know what? I'm not going to force you to do anything you don't want to do, Mama. Maybe this was a bad idea. I probably should've taken this to my grave." Sounding dejected, she looked down at me. "Let's go, baby."

Caught off guard by the term of endearment that seemed to just roll off of her tongue, I rose just as Ms. Miller shot up from her chair.

"Now wait just a doggone minute! Sit your tail *down*. The food is almost done and you're not going anywhere until you eat. Do you hear me?"

I glanced between the both of them, taking in the twin looks of determination on each of their faces. Squeezing D'Vaughn's hand, I waited for her to look my way before I leaned toward her, lowering my voice.

"I think we should stay."

Hurt and frustration clouded her eyes. I touched her jaw, which was clenched tightly.

"Emotions are high right now. Let's just stay and give things a chance to cool down, okay?" It took a minute, but then she nodded.

"Fine." Without sparing another glance to her mother, she reclaimed her seat, staring straight ahead.

She didn't say anything, but Ms. Miller gave me a tight nod, which I took as a thank-you, and left the living room.

Once she was gone, I pulled D'Vaughn to me and pressed a kiss against her cheek.

"Were you about to go to war with your mama behind me?" I asked, a grin on my face. I hadn't forgotten the way she'd squared up in her seat.

Her lips barely moved but one of her dimples made a tiny appearance.

"I'm pissed about that comment she made and wasn't about to sit here and let her default to nonsense about people she'd never met. Your family is amazing and showed me nothing but love. They don't deserve that."

"Well, thank you for that." Sensing that she needed it, I wrapped an arm around her in a side hug.

"You're welcome," she murmured as I nuzzled her neck.

The sound of a key at the door made her straighten up, and we both looked toward the door to see her sister and a guy I recognized as the drummer from church walk through the door. The guy turned to lock the door as the woman headed straight for D'Vaughn, who was barely on her feet before they collided. They rocked back and forth as they hugged while the guy took off his jacket and hung it by the door. He entered the living room and offered me his hand.

"I'm Darren."

"What's up, man? I'm Kris." We shook. His grip was firm but not overly aggressive, which I appreciated.

D'Vaughn and her sister separated, and I was glad to see D'Vaughn's eyes were bright, and she now wore a genuine smile on her face. She reached for me, threading our fingers together.

"Kris, these are my siblings, D'Niesha and Darren. Y'all, this is Kris. My fiancée."

D'Niesha's mouth fell open while Darren's eyebrows shot up.

"Are you serious?!" D'Niesha screeched. "Oh my gosh!"

Nodding, D'Vaughn offered them a small smile. "Yep. Seriously."

D'Niesha squealed and hugged D'Vaughn again. "I had no idea you were even dating but congratulations!"

"Nobody knew, Niesha," Darren quipped, giving the younger woman a sidelong glance. "Don't give a half-assed congratulations."

Frowning, D'Niesha glared at her brother. "I didn't mean it like that." Turning to D'Vaughn, she widened her eyes. "I swear, I didn't mean it like that."

"It's all good, Niesha. You really didn't know so I didn't take it as shade."

"Thank you," she said, a smug grin on her face when she glanced back at Darren. "The food smells good and I'm starving. I'm gonna go find Mama and see if we can eat."

Once she disappeared down a hall, Darren wrapped D'Vaughn in a tight bear hug.

"Finally," he whispered into her hair. "Now I can stop pretending I don't know nothing."

My brows shot toward my hairline as D'Vaughn giggled and pushed him away.

"Boy, shut up."

"You knew too?" I thought no one but her best friend had known.

Darren shot D'Vaughn a questioning glance.

"Cinta," she replied, to which he nodded.

"Ah. Well, yeah. I definitely knew. I actually walked in on her making out with some girl in…what was that? Seventh grade?"

"Tenth grade, fool! You were in seventh."

He nodded, a grin on his face, and he reminisced. "That's right." Sliding a sly look my way, he chuckled. "I used to pretend to go out on dates in high school and Mama would make

Vaughn go as chaperone, not realizing that the date and the girl were for Vaughn."

He cracked up, clutching his stomach as he leaned back and laughed. D'Vaughn rolled her eyes but there was an amused tilt to her lips that said she found the memories amusing as well. As they laughed, D'Niesha poked her head into the living room.

"Dinner's ready."

Darren headed to the bathroom while D'Vaughn and I followed her sister into the kitchen. Several pots covered the stove and there was a stack of plates on the counter. A quick glance around the small space told me that Ms. Miller was elsewhere.

"Are we waiting for your mom?"

D'Niesha shook her head as she grabbed a plate and began to load it up with wares from the pots. "Mama's already in the dining room. I'm fixing her plate and once we all have our food then we can all join her." She finished up and left the kitchen.

D'Vaughn stepped up to the stove and grabbed a plate. When I started to do the same, she swatted my hand before grabbing a serving spoon.

"I got you, *baby*," she crooned, leaning toward me playfully. "Let me make your plate like a good wifey."

Grinning, I stepped back, posting up against the counter as I watched her. Twice now I was "baby" where I'd gone the entire day before never hearing that come out of her mouth. Logic said that it was for the sake of her family, but I couldn't help but believe that the main reason it sounded so good sliding past her lips was because she said it without thinking. D'Niesha came back a moment later, glanced between me and her sister before coming to stand next to me. Her arms were folded in front of her but then she dropped them at her side and picked at invisible lint from her skirt. After she glanced at me for the third time, I figured she had something she wanted to say.

"What's up?" I asked, drawing D'Vaughn's attention.

"So," D'Niesha began, perking up with the excitement of whatever was on the tip of her tongue, "what are your pronouns?"

"She, her…" I slid a sly gaze over to D'Vaughn, who was peering at us from over her shoulder, slotted spoon full of collard greens hanging over the plate in her hand. "…And daddy, when D'Vaughn is feeling especially nasty." My fiancée did not disappoint, sucking in an audible breath as she dropped the slotted spoon back into the tall pot and spun around quickly.

"Kris!" she hissed. "You can't talk like that in my mama's house!"

D'Niesha's mouth fell open in shock. *"Oh snap!"* she whispered. "That's true."

I bit back a laugh as D'Vaughn sat the plate onto the counter and came over to us, her hips swaying with every step. "No, Niesha. Ignore her."

"How can I ignore her when you skipped denial and went straight to scolding? You basically just confirmed it."

Fisting her hands at her hips, D'Vaughn pinned her baby sister with a firm stare. "I never said she was lying. I said ignore her. She knows better than to discuss our private time in public—" she rolled her neck to meet my gaze "—but I guess she's acting out since she's finally getting to meet the family. Is that it, babe?"

Laughing, I licked my lips. D'Vaughn wasn't just leaning into her role, she had full-fledged jumped in with both feet. This was a bona fide performance and I loved it.

"You know I love to get under your skin, preciosa."

I punctuated that with a wink and pursed my lips at her, which only served to make her narrow her eyes in response.

"You think you're so freakin' cute, don't you?"

"Nah, baby. *You* think I'm cute."

She smiled then. It was soft, small, and somehow I recognized that it was not quite a part of the game we were playing. Shaking her head, she dragged her gaze from the top of my head, running the length of my body before returning to my face without bringing her eyes to mine.

"Actually, cute doesn't do you justice. I think you're absolutely, breathtakingly gorgeous."

The room fell silent as I stared at her in surprise. D'Vaughn shifted her weight from one foot to the other, as though she was embarrassed by what she'd said, and then she turned around and snatched the plate off of the counter before stepping back up to the stove. I moved before thinking, taking determined steps until I was at her side. She didn't look up at me, not even when I gently tugged the plate out of her hand and once again settled it on the counter. It wasn't until I slid my arm around her waist and tilted her chin toward me that she finally lifted her eyes to meet mine.

She hadn't meant to admit that. The flush on her cheeks and slightly lowered brows made that clear. Regardless, I was glad she'd allowed herself to let that slip. All traces of our game had fallen away as I stared down at her, face somber and insistent.

"Kris, I—"

"Whatever you see in me," I interrupted, not giving her an opportunity to explain away what she'd admitted since I had no desire to hear her retract that, or to try and turn it into something else, "know that it's only a fraction of what I see when I look at you."

"*Kris.*"

There was a marked difference in the way my name sounded when it fell from her lips this time, and the distinction is what had me forgetting that her sister stood a few feet behind us, or that we were standing in her deeply religious mother's kitchen on a Sunday afternoon. It was the way she sighed my name as if it were a prayer she uttered before climbing into bed at night that made me press my lips to hers, in an initially soft embrace that quickly turned more insistent the moment that she slipped her tongue into my mouth. It happened so fast, and suddenly a soft moan bubbled up from between us, but I had no idea of its origin, only that I wanted to hear it again and was ready and willing to make that happen when a sound that was a cross between a squeak and a hiccup made us tear our lips away from one another.

We both turned to find D'Niesha not so silently crying with her hand slapped over her mouth. When she noticed us watching her, she shook her head quickly and waved a hand.

"Don't mind me," she choked, yanking a paper towel from the roll that was mounted under the top cabinets.

D'Vaughn stepped around me and went to her sister. "Niesha, what's wrong?"

D'Niesha shook her head again and blew her nose loudly. "Nothing. Absolutely nothing is wrong." She gestured toward me. "That was beautiful, and it just hit me that I've never seen you like this before. I've never seen you have flirty banter with someone—with anyone—let alone someone you're in a relationship with. I just—we've missed so much of your life, and it breaks my heart." Her tears started up again; this time her shoulders were shaking as she buried her face in her hands. In that position, she looked so similar to how D'Vaughn had looked hours earlier at the church that my chest got tight.

"Don't cry, sissy," D'Vaughn pleaded. "I'm so sorry."

Snapping her neck up, D'Niesha's face was scrunched into a frown as she stared at her sister. "No! Don't you dare apologize for this! You didn't feel safe sharing your whole self with us and that's not your fault. I can't speak for Mama or Darren, but I have to take responsibility for that. I know we're a few years apart, but I thought we were close growing up. I wish I knew why you didn't think you could talk to me."

"I don't know why, Niesha. I thought you might tell Mama or Daddy, and I didn't want that. I guess I was just being a coward."

My face hardened and I took a step toward them. "Don't you ever let me hear you say some shit like that again."

D'Vaughn spun around, her mouth agape. "Kris!" she whisper-yelled. "You *cannot* be cussin' in my mama's house!"

"Lo siento," I immediately said, still pinning her with my gaze, "but I meant what I said. Protecting yourself isn't cowardice. If you're around people who are notorious for being homophobic, you have to do what you have to do."

"Kris is right." We all turned to see Darren standing at the entrance of the kitchen.

D'Niesha nodded, touching D'Vaughn's arm to get her attention. "Even as a kid, you knew there was a possibility that you wouldn't be accepted. I'm not mad at you for that. I'm actually angry about the situation. You having to be alone with that knowledge of who you were at such a young age just infuriates me."

Twisting her lips to the side, D'Vaughn shrugged. "Well, if it makes you feel better, I wasn't completely alone. Cinta's parents knew."

"Seriously?!"

D'Vaughn nodded. "I told her and she told them. They were really great about it."

"Well, that's good, at least." Sighing, D'Niesha blew her nose one last time before tossing the balled-up paper into the garbage and going to the sink to wash her hands. As she dried them on a fresh paper towel, she tossed us a look over her shoulder. "We'd better get out there or Mama is gonna call the cavalry on us."

As if summoned, Ms. Miller's voice sounded.

"Are y'all eating in the kitchen today?"

D'Niesha gave us a look that said *told ya so* and motioned for D'Vaughn to finish fixing the plate she'd now twice abandoned. After adding a second scoop of greens to what she'd already had—mac & cheese, pot roast in a creamy brown gravy with potatoes, carrots and pearl onions—a generous triangle of corn bread with a golden-brown crust courtesy of the cast iron skillet it was baked in completed the meal. With two hands, she held the plate out to me.

"Here," she said, "go have a seat. I'll be right out."

Taking the plate overloaded with food that had my stomach grumbling in anticipation, I dropped a kiss on her cheek. "Thank you, preciosa, but I'll wait for you."

She gave me a look like she wanted to protest, but D'Niesha elbowed her in the side.

"Aht, aht! Hurry up and fix your food so you can walk in the dining room with your fiancée."

D'Vaughn pursed her lips but did as she was told, and soon we were walking into the dining room together. Ms. Miller sat at the round, glass-top table, her fingers steepled in front of her, her eyes zeroed in on us as we entered and sat at the table. From all of D'Vaughn's frequent scolding of what I wasn't allowed to say, I figured that there wasn't too much real talk taking place at the dinner table. The tension in the air was thick and oppressive, and once everyone took a seat and began eating, it became apparent that the conversation from earlier had ended.

It didn't sit well with me to just pretend that everything was fine, that nothing had happened, like lives hadn't changed, but when I glanced at D'Vaughn, she gave me a subtle shake of the head before returning her attention to her plate. This was just one visit and the circumstances were extreme, but if this is how it was whenever a hard topic was broached, no wonder D'Vaughn hadn't felt comfortable being free. Without a doubt, the hardest part of the next few weeks would come from the people at that table, and I was not looking forward to it.

Jitter Cam 04-D'Vaughn

Well. I guess it's safe to say that, that went better than I expected.

Was it perfect? Not at all. Not even a little bit.

Could it have been better? Absolutely.

Did I expect my siblings to jump on board and immediately root for me to win? No, but…also yes? I know that doesn't make sense; just let me cook, please.

Was I surprised by my mama's response? Honestly, no. Actually…that's not completely true. I wasn't surprised that she wasn't immediately on board with my sexuality, but I was shocked with how she came at Kris. Accusing her family of being racist? That threw me! I never knew my mama to think like that; had never known her to—

Oh gosh, what am I saying? If there was a chance that she was homophobic, then *of course* there's a chance she's a bigot. I can't—this isn't… Nobody wants to admit their mama isn't perfect, but I can't deny that I never would have expected that from her.

And Kris was just…amazing.

Having her there with me was like wearing a strap-on battery pack. For some reason, her presence gave me the boost to take on my mama without fear of disrespecting her. I think… I don't know. I love my mama, but I knew there would be some…ignorance afoot. In a way, I kinda felt like I had to protect Kris from that. Like…I had to be stronger because we were dealing with a monster she didn't know. You know what I mean?

I don't even know if I'm making sense.

She's a grown woman, and is unquestionably more confident in who she is than I've ever been; she definitely doesn't need me to protect her.

But the way she was there for me today? At church this morning, and then at my mama's? She did so much more for me than any of my exes had ever deigned to do. Kris not only supported me as I came out, but—God. Sometimes it seemed like she could see right through me and knew the exact thing to say to give me the comfort I needed. I mean…I know she had to be there for the show, and she definitely knows how to put on a believable performance, but there were a few times today that it didn't *feel* fake. I don't know. Obviously, I barely know Kris, but at those times it felt so natural to defend her in any way that I could. It felt like second nature to reciprocate her energy.

Am I buggin'? Are you allowed to give me feedback, Kevin? Tell me the truth. Does it seem like I'm reading too deeply into something that wasn't there?

Wow. Is that blank stare a yes? You're not going to answer me? Well, that's wack. And on that note, I think I'm going to wrap this up and head home.

Week Two

D'Vaughn and Kris,

Congratulations on making it to week two! Now that your families know you're getting married, it's time to start planning your wedding! Listed below are the tasks you must complete within the next seven days. Remember, you have to include your loved ones on every decision you make.

Good luck!
—Kevin

1. Book venues for the ceremony and reception

2. Secure a caterer for reception

Chapter Six

Kris

A Setup

The hard part was over and the game was on. The three-by-five index card that was delivered first thing Sunday morning gave us our first tasks—outside of breaking the news to our families—and Kevin had already told us that we had to get right on it. To D'Vaughn's dismay, the show had already preselected the three venues that we were to choose from. Of course, we had to let our families believe that we found these places on our own, which was sure to be a large part of this week's conflict.

"It's going to be a fight," D'Vaughn told me as we stood outside of the first location, waiting for our respective parents to arrive. Felix stood fifteen feet away with his camera in tow, and D'Vaughn and I were both mic'd. "Mama is going to want us to get married at Abundant Salvation."

"Nah," I countered. "It won't be a fight at all. This isn't her wedding and she isn't paying for it." Twisting my neck, I met her gaze. "So, we'll let her know that, while we appreciate her input, the ultimate decision will be ours."

The way one of her eyebrows rose as she pursed her lips said she absolutely didn't believe that would work.

"That sounds good coming out of your mouth, but we'll see how it goes in real life."

I chuckled and fanned a hand out in a wide arch in front of me. "Is this not real life?"

Grinning, she shook her head as she turned to face the parking lot. Ms. Miller's champagne-colored Chevy Malibu had pulled into a spot a few feet away from where we stood on the sidewalk. I tried not to let latent anger from Sunday get the best of me.

"Absolutely not. In fact it's—"

Casting a glance over at her mother's car, I stepped closer to D'Vaughn, getting into her personal space and extending my neck so that I was speaking directly into her ear.

"For the next few weeks, this *is* real life, preciosa. You gotta remember that and act accordingly, aight?" I needed her to be in this like I was in this, and if she was constantly reminding herself that this was "for television" that wouldn't happen. She might not have come on the show for the same reason as me, but she wouldn't even be able to acknowledge that the potential was there if she didn't relax some.

As if processing what I'd said, she nodded slowly.

I started to pull away, but the slamming of car doors said that her mother was now within eyesight, if not yet close enough to hear what we were saying. Although I could now hear the sound of Ms. Miller's voice, I had no idea what she was saying, so instead of immediately pulling away from D'Vaughn, I leaned in closer and nuzzled her neck. She immediately stiffened, and in response, I placed one hand on her lower back and the other on her belly to keep her from stepping away from me.

"It's okay," I murmured in a soothing voice, "they know you're gay, remember? They know we're engaged. It's *okay*."

A shuddering breath went through her, and she visibly relaxed in my hold, giving me a single nod before tilting her head to the side as if to give me more access to her neck. The movement made me smile. I understood that this was hard for her. She'd gone her entire life concealing this part of herself from her family, and the instinct to hide or play off my affection in front of them wouldn't just disappear because everyone now knew the truth. Having her back meant that I didn't penalize her for that. Instead of punishing her, I would help her work through it; I would do as she asked and push her when it was evident that she wanted to run. I would prop her up and keep her from falling.

Maybe D'Vaughn had known exactly how this would play out and was more calculated than I had given her credit for, because unlike an organically acquired fiancée, my feelings were less likely to get hurt by her pulling away from me. I'd been anticipating this from day one, so to me, it was just a part of the show. As if it was simply another task that Kevin had given us that had to be completed in the face of our loved ones. Thinking of it that way made it easy to move past her hang-ups and be outwardly affectionate with her.

Lifting my chin, I captured her earlobe between my lips and tugged playfully, keeping the pressure light. She shrieked and jumped out of my embrace as if it had been a rabid dog that had latched onto her. With her hand to her ear, she gave me a wide-eyed look.

"Did you just *bite* me?"

Shaking my head, I took a step toward her. "Nah. It was a love bite. Nothing too serious."

She narrowed her eyes at me. "I'm failing to see how that's different from what I said."

Grinning, I shoved my hands into the pockets of my khakis and shrugged. "What you want me to say, my love?"

Ms. Miller and D'Niesha walked over to us and I turned to

give them both a one-armed hug before shooting D'Vaughn a grin. "You shouldn't taste so good."

D'Vaughn's mouth fell open, and I fought not to laugh at the shocked expression on her face. D'Niesha held her hand up.

"Um, if y'all needed a minute, you could've just let us know and we would've waited in the car." Her little quip was enough to shake D'Vaughn out of her stupor.

"Hush, Niesha," she scolded as she bumped her sister out of the way with her hip before wrapping her arms around her mother in a tight embrace and giving the older woman a loving kiss on the cheek. "I promise that it's not what it sounded like, Mama," she hurriedly explained. "Kris just bit me on the ear is all."

"My statement still stands," I said with another shrug, smiling widely at the way D'Vaughn's face flushed as she tried to redefine what her mother and sister had walked up on. It was fun, teasing her like this, especially when she was such a good sport about it.

Narrowing her eyes at me, she shook her head. "You always wanna misbehave in public. I'mma stop taking you places."

Crossing my arms over my chest, I turned to her mother, who was watching the two of us in amusement, a soft smile on her face as her eyes volleyed between us. "Ms. Miller, *please* tell your daughter to stop being such a spoilsport."

The woman giggled and gave her eldest child a knowing look. "You'd better cherish the silly moments, D'Vaughn."

Heaving an exasperated sigh, D'Vaughn threw her hands up in the air. "How did you manage to steal my mama's loyalty so quickly?"

"Oh hush, girl!" Ms. Miller exclaimed. "I'm always on your side. I want to see you happy, and since Kris seems to make that happen—at least as far as I've seen—I'm going to advocate for her. If that starts to change, *then* you should be worried."

Both D'Vaughn and D'Niesha were staring silently at their mother, pure astonishment on each of their faces, but she ignored them both in lieu of turning to face the building. "Now, tell me about this place you picked, since you wouldn't even consider the church even though we just redid the sanctuary."

D'Vaughn quickly shot me a look and I nodded my acknowledgment. She'd already warned me how her mother might react to the venues, so I was more than prepared to handle the blowback. I began to rattle off the information.

"The Starlight Palace is the premier one-stop shop for weddings and receptions in the Greater Houston area." Since I was essentially parroting the bullet points that had been included with our tasks for the week, I waved a hand in front of us as if I was Vanna White.

The Starlight Palace was a nondescript anchor in a mostly unoccupied shopping strip. Half of the signs on the marquee were faded, and there was grass growing straight through the asphalt in several places across the parking lot. Standing outside felt like we were in some dystopian-era video game where zombies randomly appear out of nowhere and run headfirst to attack you. I didn't like that feeling. The place already gave me bad vibes and we hadn't even stepped foot inside yet. I hadn't been expecting the show to pick the venues, but I supposed it made sense since they were not only covering the costs, but also wanted to guarantee good television.

"Hold up!" D'Niesha called. "Um, who is that and why is he filming us?"

I looked over my shoulder to see that D'Niesha was pointing to Felix, who'd been standing off to the side with his camera on his shoulder, trained on us. I'd forgotten that he was there. Raising my eyebrows, I turned back to D'Vaughn who quickly took over, giving her sister the story we had agreed to use.

As close to the truth as possible.

"Oh, Kris is big-famous on the socials. She's filming content for her fifty-leven million followers."

D'Niesha's eyes swung over to me. "You're not exploiting my sister, are you?"

"OMG, Niesha." D'Vaughn covered her face as I jerked back in surprise.

"What?! Hel—ahem. I mean, of course not. I never even post her."

Apparently, that was the wrong thing to say because her eyes narrowed into tight slits.

"You're social media famous and you *never* post the woman you're about to marry in five weeks? That sounds highly suspicious." She looked back and forth between me and her sister. "Whose idea was this?"

D'Vaughn sighed. "It was mine, Niesha. So you can back down now."

"Nah, not yet. Not until I know that you didn't suggest this after being made to feel like you weren't good enough to be posted." She turned back to me. "Are your followers hostile to anyone who isn't family? Does your brand depend on you appearing single?"

"Leave them alone, Niesha," Ms. Miller scolded. "Vaughn hasn't implied anything like that is going on."

D'Niesha shook her head. "No, Mama, because I refuse to see my sister get taken for a fool behind a pretty face and nice tatt—"

"D'Niesha," D'Vaughn snapped, cutting the other woman off sharply. "I appreciate your concern, but this is *not* what you're making it out to be. *I* requested that Kris keep me off of her pages because I don't want to get caught up in a viral moment that could possibly affect my job in a negative way. Even if I don't go viral, if Kris happened to post an opinion that isn't shared by the directors of my school, it could have less than stellar consequences for me. You, of all people, know how much my career means to me. Kris knows as well, and because she loves and respects me, she in turn honors my decision, even if it goes against what she would prefer."

"Hey," I interjected, facing D'Niesha and using the soothing and melodic voice that I usually reserved for calming unruly preteens. "I love that you've got your sister's back. It makes me feel good to know that she has you in her corner going hard on her behalf."

D'Niesha smirked. "I'm glad you feel that way, because since y'all robbed me of the opportunity to grill you before you even got to the engagement stage, you're going to be getting more of it as I get to know you. Your bad." She smirked, not at all resembling the sweet woman with the powerful voice who sang the building down at their church on Sunday.

Ms. Miller just shook her head. D'Vaughn's groan made me chuckle. She rolled her eyes toward her sister.

"I swear you get on my nerves sometimes."

"And that's fine. But you'll also never be able to say that I'm not your rider, and that's more important to me."

As D'Vaughn giggled and pulled her sister into a hug, I shared a smile with their mother. From the way she was mostly quiet during the confrontation, it was clear that she was used to this. Glancing at my watch, I noted that my parents were about ten minutes late. As I pulled out my phone, ready to call and check their ETA, I heard the familiar rumbling of an SUV. I looked up to see Papi's Tahoe turn into the parking lot at no less than forty miles an hour.

"Oh my," Ms. Miller murmured as the Zavala clan climbed out of the three-row vehicle. "That's some entourage."

Apparently, Rhea, Ray, Kiana, and Josue had all opted to tag along with Mami and Papi. Their presence was unexpected but not unwelcome. Honestly, the more the merrier when it came to the show. Kevin was probably hiding in some room inside the building behind us doing a fist pump to the number of people we had with us today.

"Sorry we're late, mija," Mami began as soon as she stepped onto the sidewalk. "Your father decided to ignore the directions and go *the way he knew*." She frowned. "As you can see, he didn't know as much as he thought he did."

Papi rolled his eyes, pocketing his keys. "We made it here, didn't we?"

"¡Dios mio! We're late, Reynaldo!"

"They're not even inside yet, mi amor."

I smirked when Mami instantly softened at his endearment. No matter what she was fussing about, as soon as he spoke sweetly to her, she forgot the issue and forgave him. Granted, he never did anything worth being angry about for more than ten minutes, but it was a blessing to grow up in a home where my parents rarely held grudges. Papi looped an arm around Mami's waist and kissed her cheek and then her lips. Once she started giggling like a schoolgirl, Ray cleared his throat.

"Ahem! There are children present."

"¡Cállate!" She slapped his arm before walking toward me and enveloping me in a hug. "Perdoname," she whispered into my ear.

"It's fine, Mami."

Leaning back, she met my eyes. "Are you sure? I know this is a big moment for you."

I nodded, a slight twinge of guilt hitting me in the chest at her earnest expression. She was genuinely upset at being late. Smiling, I nodded again. "Lo prometo."

Seemingly relieved, she smiled. "Good. Now where is my future daughter-in-law?" Releasing me, she pulled D'Vaughn into a tight hug, rocking her from side to side as if it hadn't only been three days since she'd first met her.

"D'Vaughn!" she exclaimed loudly. "You look so good, mijita!"

I shook my head, groaning good-naturedly at the over-the-top display, but movement in my peripheral stole my attention. I turned to my left to see that Ms. Miller's face had fallen. She looked completely devastated as she watched her daughter and my mother embrace. I didn't think twice, moving quickly but not fast enough to draw anyone's attention away from Mami and D'Vaughn until I was standing before her, using my body to block her expression from the others.

"What's wrong?" I asked, my brows knitted with concern.

Blinking, she shook her head and looked off to the side, but I didn't miss the way she swiped at a few tears that had started to fall.

"It's fine."

"It's not fine if you're crying. Please talk to me. It would break D'Vaughn's heart if she knew you were upset about something and I didn't do anything about it." It didn't matter that I had only met her less than a week ago; I already knew that the love D'Vaughn had for her mother could likely move mountains.

Ms. Miller sighed so heavily I wouldn't have been surprised to see two boulders perched on her shoulders. When she met my gaze, I could see the pain and regret shining in her eyes.

"Well…seeing her with your mother affected me more than I expected it to. Realizing that my baby didn't think she could talk to me, learning about you and…all of this, it's been a hard pill to swallow, but knowing that it hasn't been the same with your family—seeing that she's built a relationship with your mother in a way that I haven't even fathomed—it cuts me deep. She's built an entire life that I had no knowledge of."

Shit. That was beyond what I expected her to say, but it made total sense. I couldn't fully assuage her guilt—and wouldn't even if I could because, in my opinion, she deserved to feel it—but I felt confident that I could remove at least one of those worries from her plate. First, I hugged her tightly, taking a chance that she would jerk away from me, but all she did was clutch me in return. Then I pulled back and gripped her shoulders, looking her in the eye.

"Let me ease your mind, Ms. Miller. D'Vaughn just met my family on Saturday."

The older woman's eyebrows crinkled, and then she looked from me to the subjects of our conversation who were now fawning over Kiana and her protruding belly.

"You're kidding!"

Smiling, I shook my head. "Not at all. My mom just fell in love with her instantly."

Returning my smile, Ms. Miller's still slightly watery eyes sparkled. "As she should," she declared proudly. "My baby is incredibly lovable."

"I would have to agree with that one."

Sighing, she grabbed my forearm and squeezed. "Thank you," she whispered.

"You're most welcome, Ms. Miller."

Clicking her tongue against the roof of her mouth, she stole another glance over at the group. "Well, now it just feels silly for you to be so formal with me after I've heard D'Vaughn call your mother by her first name."

I waved a hand. "Don't worry about it."

Unconvinced, she eyed me, her lips pursed, but she didn't say anything else. All I could do was laugh.

"How about we stick with Ms. Miller for now, and when the time feels right, we discuss something else?"

"That sounds like a plan," she agreed with a nod.

"Good. Now let's introduce you to my family so we can

get inside. Thank God I told everyone to be here a half hour early."

We walked over to the group to find Kiana and D'Niesha having an animated conversation while everyone else looked on. Apparently they knew each other from the magnet high school for performing arts that they'd both attended.

"Oh, Mama!" D'Vaughn exclaimed as soon as she caught sight of us. "I am so sorry; I didn't mean to abandon you like that."

Mami stepped forward, her hand at D'Vaughn's back, a sheepish smile on her face. "It's my fault entirely. I sort of swallowed her up and brought her over here. I take full responsibility. I'm Kayla." She extended a hand, which Ms. Miller took graciously.

"I'm Deidre, and it's no problem." Glancing down at their joined hands, she gave me an amused look before turning her attention back to Mami. "You know, I was just telling your daughter that she didn't have to be so formal and call me Ms. Miller, and now you're shaking my hand. I see she gets it honestly."

Mami let off a stuttered laugh and pulled her hand back to prop it on her hip.

"You know what's funny? I'm usually a hugger, but *Reynaldo* insisted that I shake your hand. He said it would be too much to hug you the first time we met." Cutting her eyes at Papi, she clucked her tongue. "It's what I get for listening to him, eh?"

Papi chuckled lightly. "What do you want me to say, mi amor? Me equivoqué. Perdóname."

Mami smiled sweetly at him. "That's a start." Turning back to Ms. Miller, she spread her arms. "Shall we hug?"

Ms. Miller nodded. "We're going to be family soon; it's only right."

With a squeal of laughter, the two embraced, rocking from side to side the way Mami had with D'Vaughn. When they separated, I could see that much of the uncertainty in Ms. Miller's eyes had disappeared, replaced with a spark of happiness that made me grin widely.

"Aww," D'Vaughn murmured, coming to my side and resting her head on my shoulder, "look at them!"

"They look like fast friends."

"*I know!* I love it!"

"It's a good sign."

D'Vaughn lifted her head and looked at me. "You think so?"

I nodded, sliding an arm around her waist and pulling her closer to my side, using our proximity to speak directly into her ear. "The next few weeks will go by much more smoothly if they are on the same side. With them as friends, they'll probably want to take over planning of the wedding, which pretty much eliminates the possibility of anyone else questioning whether this is real or not. It's foolproof."

She didn't say anything for a moment, and I tilted my head to find her staring off in the distance, chewing on her bottom lip contemplatively.

"What's on your mind?"

Shaking her head, she stepped away from me, putting a few inches of space between us. It was a negligible amount of space, but for some reason it felt significant.

"Nothing important," she answered.

It would have been a fine response, but her voice was flatter than usual. Or, at least flatter than I was used to hearing. I eyed her in confusion, wanting to press the issue, sure that something was suddenly off, but not sure if I was just imagining things since we'd really only known each other for less than a week. It was possible that I was seeing something that wasn't there, even though that's not what it felt like. I watched as she walked over to our siblings without giving me a second glance before trailing behind her.

What the hell had happened to make her mood shift so quickly?

When I reached the group, I dapped up Ray, Josue, and Rhea and then hugged Kiana from the side.

"What are you guys doing here?" I asked Kiana after rubbing her belly and murmuring a greeting to my nibling.

She gestured to Josue, who stood next to Ray with his eyes on us. "We're taking notes."

My eyes widened and I looked back and forth between the two of them. "Wait! Are you serious?!"

Quickly, she started shaking her head as he held up a hand and dragged his fingers across his neck.

"You're the only one getting married right now," confirmed Kiana, "so you can calm down. We're taking notes for *future* reference. Just...so when we get to that point, we'll already have an idea of what we like and don't like. That's all. Cool your boxers. Thanks."

Wiping a hand across my forehead, I shook off imaginary sweat and released an audible breath. "Girl, you really had me going for a minute."

Kiana rolled her eyes and rubbed her belly. "That's what you get for jumping to conclusions before I get to finish my sentence."

Rhea frowned. "Nah, KiKi. There was definitely a period there."

With her hands on her hips, Kiana arched an eyebrow. "See, that's where you're wrong, because there hasn't been a period *here* in a long time."

Josue started choking on air while Ray pretended to gag. Rhea and I busted out laughing, drawing everyone's attention to us.

"You wild, girl," I told her, catching my breath as I made

my way back over to D'Vaughn. "Are we ready to go in?" I asked, grabbing her hand and linking our fingers. She wouldn't look at me for some reason, but at least she didn't pull away from me.

"Yep," she replied shortly. "It looks like the gang's all here."

Something was definitely off with her, but instead of calling her out on it in front of everyone, I nodded and led the way inside of the building. We all stopped right inside of the door, looking around at the completely empty room. Straight ahead was a grand staircase that led to a second-level mezzanine. On either side of the staircase were open areas that were oddly empty. Just...wide-open spaces that looked as if they *should* have held tables and chairs, but for some reason didn't. The floor underneath our feet was covered in a low-pile, cream-colored carpet with swirls of blue and green that repeated in a headache-inducing pattern from wall to wall.

"Hello?" I called out, taking a step forward. D'Vaughn, who now had a tight grip on my hand, tugged me backward. I looked at her in question and she immediately shook her head. "We have an appointment," I reminded her. "C'mon. They're probably in the back or something." I tilted my head for her to follow before taking another couple of steps forward.

Then I stopped in my tracks.

The floor felt...squishy. Peering down at my feet, I bounced on my toes a couple of times, gasping when I noticed little bubbles of liquid rise to the surface of the carpet around my shoes. With my eyes to the ground, I walked a little further, noticing the same thing. *Holy shit!* The entire carpet near the door was soaked!

"Be careful, y'all!" I called over my shoulder. "The floor is wet."

"Uh-uhn!" protested Ray. "This looks like the set of a horror movie in here!"

"Don't say that!" Mami scolded, slapping his arm. "Give it a chance, mijo. It might be nice."

Scoffing, Ray shook his head. "Sure thing, Mami. I'll give it a chance, and then the next thing I know, I'm being sucked into the walls."

"¡Ay Dios mío!" Mami whispered harshly before making the sign of the cross.

I started to roll my eyes, but then a low uttering caught my attention. Glancing over my shoulder, I noticed Ms. Miller praying under her breath. She lifted her hands into the air as she walked to the right side of the room. Mami took one look at her and dug into her purse to pull out her rosary and begin reciting the Lord's Prayer as she went to the left. My eyes ballooned and I spun to see if D'Vaughn was seeing this. Her and D'Niesha were exchanging a look that I couldn't decipher, but neither of them seemed particularly surprised.

"Look what you started," Papi muttered to Ray, who busted out laughing.

Raising his hands into the air as if that would prove his innocence, Ray shook his head. "I had no idea that they would start praying. You can't blame me for that."

"Yeah, doofus, we can." Kiana rolled her eyes. "You're the one who said the walls would start eating people."

Ray pointed to the dingy, cream floor-length curtains that hung from the ceiling in intervals that didn't make sense, especially since there were no windows on either side of this venue. It was in the center of a building, with storefronts on either side of it.

"Are you going to tell me that those curtains don't look like they can wrap around you of their own volition?!"

Covering her ears with her hands, Kiana started singing a loud melody. "I can't hear you!" she shouted.

Papi sighed. Rhea glared at both of our youngest siblings

before settling on Ray and hooking a thumb in Kiana's direction.

"*She* has pregnancy hormones. What's your excuse?"

Rolling his eyes to the ceiling, Ray heaved a loud sigh of frustration. "Fine!" he snapped. "Don't come running to me when you see some weird shit in here! Ghosts, monsters that wanna fuck you with their tentacles, little clowns on tricycles trying to lure you down unrealistically long hallways. I don't care, leave me out of it!" He threw his hands into the air.

Slowly, I turned to face D'Vaughn, dreading the look on her face. I was used to my dramatic siblings and their theatrics. D'Vaughn's family seemed significantly less outrageous by comparison. Her eyes were wide, mouth slightly parted.

"Um," I began hesitantly, "welcome to the family."

Instantly, she burst into giggles, bringing me a measure of relief.

"That was intense, but hilarious," she commented after catching her breath. "I can only imagine what it was like to grow up with them. Ray is a character all by himself." There was no judgment in her tone, just pure observation. That she could see my zany family and roll with it was another point for us and made me like her even more.

I grinned and shook my head. "No lie, Ray is a one-man show on a regular basis."

"I can believe that, no convincing necessary."

"Yeah, so, um…" As I tried to think of the next step in this seeming failure of a first outing, the sound of a heavy door slamming near the staircase shocked the hell out of me, making me nearly jump out of my skin. "*Fuck!*" I breathed, too startled to even speak louder.

The room fell silent as every single one of us looked toward the source of the sound. Low thuds made their way to my ears and my heart started pounding. D'Vaughn squeezed my hand tightly and I pushed up onto my toes, ready to take off toward the door if necessary, but then a woman appeared from behind the staircase and I deflated. All of the nervous energy flew out of me in a whoosh, and I wanted to punch Ray for getting me all riled up with his talk of horror movies.

"Hi, everyone! So sorry I'm late!" Holding a zippered binder in one hand, the woman waved as she approached us.

Mami and Ms. Miller made their way back to the center of the room just as she reached us. She was smiling widely, wearing a knee-length, forest-green sweater-dress and slouchy black booties, her kinky afro like a halo around her head. She looked pleasant enough, but now I was suspicious of how long it took her to come out and greet us. *What the hell did the show have up its sleeve?*

"We've been waiting for quite a while," Ms. Miller stated, her voice remarkably even, without a hint at the ten minutes of praying she'd just completed.

The woman bowed her head in acknowledgment, the smile never leaving her face. "Yes. Again, I do apologize about that. Shall we move forward with the tour?" Although her expression hadn't changed, there was an undeniable sharpness to her words that rubbed me the wrong way. *She was the one who was late, so why was she being short with us?* Clearly, *this* is what the show had up its sleeve. This was so bizarre that it was undoubtedly manufactured. I glanced at D'Vaughn to see that, although there was a slight furrow in her brow, her face was otherwise blank. Was that because she was unaffected by this, or did it have anything to do with whatever happened outside?

Mami's eyebrows shot toward her hairline and it was clear that she'd heard the same thing that I did. Slowly, she craned her neck to face Papi, who was giving her a warning look. After being with her for more than thirty years, he knew exactly the type of things that set her off.

"We're here for the girls, Kayla."

Thankfully, his reminder seemed to work. The hard set of her jaw didn't loosen, but Mami didn't say another word, instead, folding her arms across her chest and staring at me pointedly. If it weren't for the show, I would have told the rude woman to kiss my ass as I walked out. Hell, if I didn't know that there were cameras watching my every move, I would have hightailed it out of there as soon as I noticed the soaked carpet, which was probably what D'Vaughn had in mind when she stopped at the door. But we were there for a reason, and since Kevin was likely watching this happen in 4K, I swallowed my irritation and nodded at the woman.

"Yeah, let's move forward with the tour."

The woman's smile slipped a little, almost as if she was disappointed by my answer. "No problem," she said tightly. "I'll just go grab the brochures and we can go on up." Without waiting for me to respond, she spun on her heel, her booties squeaking on the wet carpet, and all but stomped off.

"Where did y'all find this place again?" Ms. Miller asked.

"Kris got a recommendation from social media."

My jaw dropped and I turned to D'Vaughn. It was almost comical how quickly she placed the blame on me, throwing me under the bus.

"Whoever recommended this facility to you is not a friend!" Mami whisper-yelled. "That is an enemy and you need to cut them from your life!"

Sighing, I rubbed a hand down my face before shooting my father another pleading look. At this rate I'd be able to cut a '90s R&B album by the end of the night. I understood Mami's position, but we couldn't just leave. As grateful as I was that her complaints were about the facility and *not* my fake relationship, D'Vaughn and I had an obligation to fulfill, and part of that obligation meant seeing this visit through.

Thankfully, Papi was able to decipher my expression as quickly as always. Grabbing Mami's hand, he pulled her off to the side to speak with her privately. The moment they stepped away, my siblings started talking and I took their distraction to my advantage, using the noise to cover up my voice as I checked in with D'Vaughn.

"What's the problem?"

She turned her narrowed eyes on me.

"What do you mean?"

"Your entire demeanor changed outside. You're closed off right now, and I'm trying to figure out what happened and how we can get back to the place where you fake love me again."

I watched her eyes widen and her lips part before she dropped her gaze to the floor and shook her head. When she lifted her head, there was a sheepish smile on her face.

"I'm sorry. I'm—I was tripping over something in my head, but I didn't mean to take that out on you."

I peered at her. Although she was looking at me, she wasn't meeting my eyes, looking just to the left of my face and probably focused on the row of earrings in my ear. I couldn't put my finger on it, but something about her answer rang false. Like chewing bubble gum with silver caps on my teeth. The motion is there, but I'm missing out on the full experience. D'Vaughn had given me an answer and she'd apologized, but I wasn't satisfied. Because I had no reason to feel that way, and didn't feel comfortable pushing for more with so many people who didn't know the truth about us around, I hugged her to my side and dropped a kiss on her temple.

"As long as we're good, I'm not trippin'. We good?"

She nodded. "We're good."

The whole conversation hadn't taken more than a few minutes and by the time I looked away from her, my parents were returning. I have no idea what was said between them, but I felt a sense of relief when Papi gave me a nod. Mami said nothing, just stood there looking as if she'd swallowed a lemon. It was tough, but it would do for the rest of this visit at least. I definitely owed my old man a beer when this was all said and done.

Actually, I owed him more than a beer. It was another fifteen-minute wait before the woman returned and Mami didn't say a peep while we waited. When the venue representative finally reappeared, the half-assed tour did little to improve our visit. After carefully climbing the wide, stone steps, hoping that the wet soles of our shoes wouldn't cause anyone to slip and break a limb, I asked about an elevator. The answer I received was a brusque "Don't have one." She hadn't even looked up from the folder in her hand.

D'Vaughn had squeezed my hand, and when I looked at her, she reached up and rubbed her thumb across my eyebrows, smoothing the wrinkles from the deep frown that I hadn't even realized I wore.

"Let's just make it through this," she whispered into my ear.

I nodded. That was the plan. It was only supposed to be about an hour, with a tour and then a discussion of offerings and bridal packages. That damn woman gave us a twenty-minute walk-through and then told us we could meet her in her office if we had any questions, before somehow managing to jog down those steps in those little black booties. We all stood there speechless, watching the cloud of smoke that trailed behind her. The silence was broken when Rhea burst out laughing.

"I feel like we're in the Twilight Zone," she announced, pulling off her fitted cap to scratch her scalp.

"That's a good way to describe it," agreed Ms. Miller.

"What's this place called again?" D'Niesha asked as we descended the stairs to the main level.

"The Starlight Palace," offered D'Vaughn flatly. After our talk, I was confident that her tone was now due to disappointment in the venue and not from whatever had flipped the switch on her mood earlier.

Ray snorted. "They need to rename it the Midnight Dungeon, because it's drafty, there are bugs everywhere, and the windows at the front of the building are so covered in grime that we can't even tell that it's only five thirty outside. It feels like it's eight at night in here."

Everyone started laughing. He hadn't told a lie. This place was filthy and likely needed to be condemned. The fact that the show selected this place had me on high alert. Obviously we weren't meant to pick this place, but what was the point in bringing our families here? All we got out of this was a good laugh and maybe a few stories to tell down the line.

I turned to my parents, who'd thus far managed to remain silent throughout the entire tour and package discussions.

"Mami. Papi. What do you think?"

They looked at each other before Papi nodded toward me. Mami took a breath and gave me a self-satisfied smile.

"I think you need to show us your second choice."

Jitter Cam 05-Kris

I think our first family task was a success. I mean, the venue itself was a hot ass mess, but our families got along and even banded together when shenanigans were afoot. That's a win, right?

Man, I thought for sure that somebody was going to call us out when the Starlight Palace rep had a full attitude. I expected them to take a look at the cameraman, look at the chick, and say 'Oh *hell* naw!' But that didn't happen and now my mind is kind of blown.

Looking forward, there is no possible way that the other locations can be worse than this one so I'm cautiously excited about what's to come. One of them has to be marginally decent, at least.

On another note, D'Vaughn did pretty well with the PDAs in front of her family. I could tell it was a struggle for her, but she says she wants to move past it and she's putting in the work to do that. I'm proud of her for that.

I can admit that I'm enjoying this too. I like holding her hand and pulling her close to me so I can whisper in her ear, and it doesn't even matter what I say 'cause she's gonna react every single time. She does this little shudder and bites her lip, sometimes she closes her eyes and just stands there like she's letting my words—my voice—wash over her. That shit is such a turn-on. On top of that? I really, *really* like kissing her. I don't have to go into detail about that, do I?

Funnily enough, although she'll try and move away if I'm standing too close to her, she never pulls away from a kiss. We can be standing directly in front of her family, but if we make eye contact and the vibe is there, she's gonna close her eyes and gimme those lips.

Yeah, being out is a process, but she can't fight our chemistry.

Speaking of D'Vaughn's family, it was a happy coincidence that our sisters know each other. I mean, it's pure perfection! Not only do they know each other, but they were friends in high school. They sang side-by-side in the choir and performed in plays together. That's a built-in bond that brings our families together, giving us even more credibility, even though D'Vaughn and I didn't know each other at the time. It's just another point in our favor, proving to me that we're meant to win this thing.

Alright, well we're headed to the next venue. Fingers crossed that this one doesn't have water damage, at least.

Chapter Seven

Wires Crossed

The second location was only marginally better than the first. Starlight Palace wasn't a hard act to follow, but The Moxi Event Center managed to struggle. While it was similarly in a strip of businesses, The Moxi thankfully was in an active location, with busy neighboring storefronts and a parking lot that didn't double as a garden. There were also people present when our crew walked in who were not only expecting us, but even had pamphlets ready to pass out. Unfortunately, that's where the positive points ended.

For starters, I wasn't expecting the decor to match the name of the venue. The lobby and waiting area were painted an eye-gouging gold-and-hot-pink combination with matching furniture that made me want to punch a plant and kick a pillow. It made me think of drinking Pepto-Bismol out of a golden chalice. It made me nauseous and gave me a headache. The only upside of that was Kris noticing my pinched expression and tucking me into her side, as she reminded me that my face was likely on camera and would be remembered exactly as it was.

Honestly, the fact that she stayed by my side, touching me

in some way, was the only thing that made the visit tolerable. Every member of the staff seemed to be a teenager from a local high school. The tour guide was just a baby girl in her awards day dress who read off the information from the pamphlet but knew nothing beyond what had been printed. At one point, Mama asked her if the ministers they worked with were ordained, and the poor baby searched those three sheets of paper back and front before I told her not to worry about it.

"That wasn't so bad," Mama offered as everyone exited the building and headed toward the parking lot. D'Niesha snorted, earning a narrowed glare from Mama before she continued. "I just mean that it was an improvement over the last place."

"It's not hard to be better than a place called the Midnight Dungeon," Josue quipped, his eyes on his phone as he typed furiously.

"Yo, what?!"

"Baby, no!"

"Bruh, were you even there?"

Laughter rang out, with just about everyone cracking up and Kris, Kiana, and Rhea shouting at him.

"I made that up, bro," Ray laughed. "That's not the real name of that place."

Eyes wide, Josue looked around at everyone before swinging his eyes to Kiana, who was laughing harder than everyone else.

"That's what you get for not paying attention," she teased. "Coming along was your idea in the first place."

Josue made a face before slipping his phone into his pocket. "Both of those places were wack, baby. I peeped that and checked out." He shrugged as if it was no big deal, nonchalant as always. His laid-back manner seemed to be the perfect complement to Kiana's high energy.

Kiana cringed and shot me and Kris an apologetic look

before nodding at her boyfriend. "No, you're right though. They *were* busted. Sorry, y'all."

I shook my head. "No need to apologize for telling the truth. Both venues have been less than desirable."

Kris's warm hand settled on my waist as she stepped closer to me and I instantly had to fight the instinct to lean against her.

"If the last place is anything like the first, we might just have to make that Vegas thing happen."

I gave her a sharp look because *what the heck*, but then she winked at me, the playful smile on her lips simultaneously informing me that she was playing the role she'd been assigned. This was one of those times when she was clearly giving good television, but I wasn't even worried about that because that wink and smile made me want to fist her hair in my hands and pull her face to meet mine. The inclination was so strong that my fingers flexed and my lips puckered. Swallowing hard, I blinked and averted my eyes, sucking my lip into my mouth to stave off the intense yearning.

Sure, a kiss right then would have been fine—encouraged even—but I couldn't make that move. It didn't matter that everyone around us, with the exception of Rhea, thought that we were engaged. If Kris somehow read my mind and came to me, I'd be helpless to deny her, but just the thought of initiating any type of romantic affection in front of my mother stopped me cold. No one from Kris's family would have batted an eye, but I wasn't stupid enough to believe that Deidre Miller was suddenly 100% on board with this thing just because she seemed to be Team Kris. Decades of pretending not to see me didn't disappear with the snap of my fingers, despite how easy Thanos made it seem, and that niggling fear of being found out gripped me tight enough that I had already taken a step away from Kris before I could even process that I was moving.

It was a small—tiny, even—movement but it felt gargantuan, and I couldn't even look at her face because I knew that even if no one else noticed, Kris would. She would have realized that I'd put space between us, and she would hopefully understand why—but I couldn't take the risk of glancing at her face to be certain, because there was the faintest of possibilities that it might've offended her and I didn't have room for that guilt on top of all of the other baggage I was carrying around. Releasing a harrowed breath, I took a second, imperceptible step away from her.

Arms snaked around my waist and I was tugged back against Kris's chest, startling me in the worstbest way.

"Where do you think you're going?" she asked directly into my ear, her voice low and playful to mirror the outward appearance of her actions.

It was a wonder I was able to hear anything from the way my heart pounded in my chest and the blood rushed in my ears. Her arms surrounded me in a hold loose enough that I could just step away without friction, but tight enough that I understood the message.

"You know I'm not letting you get too far from me, preciosa. I'll drag you right back and tongue you down in front of everybody. Keep playing with me."

From the timbre of her voice, she'd intended it to be a threat, but all I heard was the promise of a good time.

"Don't talk about it, be about it," I murmured, my eyes on her fingers that were splayed across my stomach.

Kris's response was to lift a hand and cup my chin, tilting my face to the side. Craning my neck, I made the awkward position not-so-awkward and stared at her expectantly. That selfsame grin that had gotten me into this position in the first place beamed down at me, making things heat and tingle beneath the surface of my skin. When her mouth met mine, I was surprisingly disappointed that she opted for keeping her lips closed. We were surrounded by our families, so I understood why she'd done it, but I was too-quickly becoming infatuated with the taste of her tongue and the way it felt sliding against my own. The desire that was ever-present since I'd first laid eyes on her began to make itself known, but before it could fully materialize and start to do wonky things to my body, Kris pulled back.

Before she could speak, I pursed my lips and pouted. "You said something about tonguing me down, but I see that was a lie."

Chuckling, she shook her head. "Nah. I know how you can get and I'm not tryna give these people a free show."

Bucking my eyes, I leaned away from her.

"How *I* get? What does that even mean?"

She sucked her teeth. "You know. You be getting all nasty and tryna take my clothes off and stuff."

"Hwhat?!" I cackled, throwing my head back as I howled with laughter. "What are you even saying right now?"

"I mean, I like it, but baby—" she dropped her hands from my waist to my hips "—at least wait until we get home."

"Please wait until you get home," Kayla urged. "If we have to cough up bail money, I want it to be for something juicier than public indecency."

Mouth open, I gaped at her as Kris busted out laughing. Shooting a quick glance at my mama, I noticed that her hands were on her cheeks and her eyes were wide.

"What's juicier than having sex in public, Mami?" Ray queried. "Inquiring minds want to know."

"No they don't," Reynaldo grumbled. "And it's getting late." Lifting his wrist, he checked his watch before turning to me and Kris. "Do you have other venues?"

There was a low, pleading note in his voice that I identified with. Neither of the two places we'd seen thus far were a location that I could see myself getting married, even if the wedding in question was a fake one.

"We have one more location to check out," Kris answered, "but our appointment isn't until tomorrow. Will you be able to make it?"

"Of course."

Kris grinned and clapped her hands together. "Buen. Alright, people. Thanks for showing up for us. We're gonna call it a night, but you're all invited to check out the next place with us tomorrow."

"Is it just one place?" Mama asked, attention switching from Kris to me.

"Yes, ma'am," I answered. "We only had three initial locations to choose from. We'd hoped that we wouldn't have to search long."

Mama nodded. "Well, I'll be here."

"Me too," chirped D'Niesha.

Everyone else made a similar announcement, bringing a smile to my face. It seemed like we had a good group of supporters which would take us a long way in the competition.

"If everyone will return tomorrow, why don't we all go to dinner after the final location?"

At Kayla's suggestion, Mama nodded again.

"That's a good idea. Hopefully it'll be a celebratory dinner." To me, she added, "I'll see if Darren can come as well."

"Sounds good, Mama."

She hugged me which sparked a full round of hugs and goodbyes from the entire group. As cars cranked up, Kris and I held hands as we waved them off. Once everyone had driven away, we started to follow suit, only to be stopped by another task. At the request of Kevin via Felix, we needed to stand between our two cars and talk for a moment. Since I was parked under a light and Kris had parked on a different side of the lot against a fence underneath a cluster of trees, I waited while she went to get her car and pulled into the spot next to me. After she stepped out of the car, we turned to Felix and waited for further instructions. Leaning his head to the side, he peeked around the camera so that we could see his face and pointed toward the space between our two vehicles.

"Can I get you both to move over here and each lean against your own cars? And just talk naturally; it doesn't even matter what you say. I just want a few minutes of this because the sun is going down and the lighting is damn-near perfect, so if you'll indulge me a little, I'd greatly appreciate it."

He wasn't asking for much, and it wouldn't have mattered either way since we'd each signed a contract. We did as he suggested, and I had to admit that it was a good look. Posted up as we were reminded me of dating in high school, when there weren't many places we could go after a certain hour but we just wanted to be around each other, so we'd stand in the parking lot of the mall and talk for hours underneath that big yellow-orange light. I felt that same sort of juvenile giddiness in my belly as I watched Kris lick her lips and brush a hand down the front of her face, my fingers itching with the desire to reach out and touch her. With every moment that we spent together, I learned more about her and continually found myself surprised. Although I had to admit that the most surprising thing of all was that I was able to formulate coherent sentences when around her.

"That went better than I expected," Kris admitted.

Releasing a heavy sigh, I nodded. "Same here. The locations were downright tragic, but that only seemed to bring everyone together for our benefit. It was pretty amazing."

"Right!" she laughed. "I hadn't seen that one coming."

"I hadn't seen these terrible venues coming, but I guess I should have."

"Hell yeah. I watched the first season of the show; they never make it easy on folks."

"Wait." I held a hand up, tilting my head to the side as I squinted at her. "You knew it would be like this and you still auditioned? You must like a challenge."

Laughing harder, she shook her head. "Correction, I love a challenge."

"So you came on the show to flex your competitive skills?"

Her laughter faded into a muted grin as she stared at me.

"You know why I came on the show, D'Vaughn. You just want to act like you don't for some reason."

Suddenly, I felt like we had been transported into a room with no window or doors, where the air was vacuumed out of it. My chest heaved as I returned her gaze, wishing I could look away but her intense brown eyes preventing me from doing so. Of course, I knew the reason she'd come on the show. Well, I knew what she told everyone that first night, and I'd strategically avoided mentioning it since then for all of the reasons I initially didn't want to be matched with her and also because I was an s-word that rhymed with *bared*. Just as I'd predicated, Kris had the type of personality that could make a girl lose her head quickly.

I swallowed down a lump in my throat as Kris pushed off of her car.

"I'm just wondering," she murmured as she took measured steps toward me, "why is that."

When she touched my car, placing a hand on either side of my head as she licked her lips and waited for my response, I wondered what exactly that li'l play-prayer I'd said during my first Jitter Cam had gotten me into. Kris was walking sex and the wetness between my thighs demanded to see her in action.

"The camera…" I whispered, trying to remind myself as much as her.

"Fuck that camera," she said nonchalantly, her plush lips curved up enticingly. "Answer my question."

"Um…what was the question again?" I may or may not have been distracted by her face being so close to mine and just wanted to see those lips moving again.

"Why you playin' with me?"

Finally giving in to my body's incessant demand to touch her, I shook my head as I settled my hands at her waist.

"I'm not. Your mouth made me lose my train of thought."

Her grin widened and she leaned closer to me, moving from her hands to her elbows but still managing to leave a foot of space between our bodies.

"I asked why you keep pretending that you don't know why I came on the show."

"Oh yeah," I murmured, rubbing my hands up and down her sides. "It's not that I'm pretending that I don't know… I just don't know what I'm supposed to do with that information."

"What do you mean?"

"Exactly what I said. You came on the show to find the love of your life. Okay. I know that. Now what?"

"Now you let me do my thing."

I laughed. "Let you? Kris, how could I stop you from doing anything? Outside of our families and close friends, no one knows about our engagement. You're kind of free to do whatever you want, as long as you're discreet. I mean, the contract didn't say anything about us dating anyone and we don't even see each other outside of these scheduled tasks. The ring comes off and you're free to find whatever you're looking for without me hindering you."

It was safer to let her know up-front that I would be cool

with her searching, instead of being blindsided like I'd been in the past. I'd been that foolish girl who thought I was in a committed relationship only to find out that my girlfriend was prowling for someone who didn't tuck away their terms of endearment when around their family. This situation wasn't exactly parallel, but try as I might to deny it, I was already feeling way more than I should for Kris and there was no way it didn't end badly for me. If the cameras weren't around, I was certain that she would have turned back the first time I stepped away from her, when my mama climbed out of her car earlier.

For a moment she didn't say anything, just stared at me with her brows furrowed as if she didn't understand what I'd said. Maybe she hadn't expected my response, but I couldn't fathom answering any other way. How ridiculous would I look trying to lay claim to a fake fiancée? Even with all of our chemistry and the way her lips fit so well against mine, she wasn't *truly* mine, despite the secret whispering in the back of my mind that said she could be if I wanted her to. I knew better than that optimistic voice. A woman like Kris had to have a certain kind of woman on her arm and I wasn't anything like that woman. I mean, not even half an hour earlier, I'd been prepared to run across the parking lot just to put some space between us because I didn't want my mama to see me being hugged up with another woman.

No. I felt fairly confident that the woman Kris would fall in love with would be someone who was bold and secure in who she was. Not someone like me who saved my more outgoing self for the bedroom.

"*Okay,*" Felix drawled, his voice breaking through the awkward silence that had fallen over us. "That's all I need."

Grateful for an excuse to peel myself away from Kris's piercing stare, I turned to him and smiled.

"You were right. That was only a few minutes."

His eyebrows rose and he flicked his gaze from me to Kris, who lowered her arms from my car and went back to leaning against her own.

"Yeah. It seems like that was actually too much time."

"Shiiid," Kris drawled, "you ain't lyin'."

After passing a narrowed look between the two of them, I pulled out my phone to check the time.

"That wasn't even ten minutes. What are you talking about?"

Kris shook her head. "That was an inside thing between me and my mans right here. Don't worry about it." She held out a hand to her left and Felix slapped it.

"On that note, I'll see you two tomorrow." He shot Kris a look. "Good luck."

Kris snorted and did a reverse nod. "'Preciate you, big dawg."

He walked off toward a van, shoulders shaking as he chuckled. Turning to Kris, the question on my lips died when I saw her once again standing next to my car. This time, she looped an arm around my waist and pulled me next to her as she opened the driver's door. She released me immediately after and shoved a hand in her pocket as she gripped the door with her other hand.

"C'mon. It's getting late and we both have to get up early."

I frowned, not liking how dry she suddenly seemed.

"Okay…"

Feeling totally confused, I climbed into the car and looked up at her.

"I'll see you tomorrow?"

"Of course," she answered smoothly, smiling down at me.

She leaned into the car and dropped a kiss onto my cheek before stepping back and closing the door. I watched her open her own door and slide into the seat before the engine revved and she pulled the strap of the seat belt across her chest.

"Let's go," she mouthed before pantomiming driving.

The silly move was cute, and I was unable to keep from grinning at the sight. It wasn't until I turned onto the street and watched her drive off in the opposite direction that confused feeling returned. I wasn't an expert on Kris, but I knew my feelings, and I was certain that something had happened. I just needed to figure out what.

Chapter Eight

Kris

Do-Over

"She said *what*?"

Rolling my eyes, I flopped back on the couch and stared up at the ceiling while Rhea cracked up. She hadn't been home when I'd arrived, so I'd jumped in the shower. Emerging from my bedroom refreshed, but no less confused about my conversation with D'Vaughn, I found my sister in the kitchen digging into a plate of smothered chicken. After dapping me up, she pushed a container bearing the name of a soul food spot near Raul and Ray's apartment that we frequented toward me. While I ate, she gave me her feedback on the outing and told me about the family's conversation on the way home. As I'd suspected, they absolutely loved D'Vaughn. Mami had sung her praises the entire drive, with the only negative talk being at the venues' expense. It was what I'd wanted to hear, but after the conversation D'Vaughn and I'd had, the news was a little bittersweet. Sighing heavily, I waited until we cleared away our empty containers and moved into the living room to fill Rhea in.

Although she was silent the majority of the time, her face was so damn expressive that I had to lie back across the seat cushions just so I wouldn't have to watch her reactions. When I got to D'Vaughn's bizarre response to me telling her she needed to let me love her, Rhea shot to her feet. The sudden movement startled me into sitting up.

"You heard me."

"Nah." She shook her head. "You gotta say that again because I know damn well you're fucking with me right now."

Groaning, I dragged both of my hands down my face. I wish this was a joke. I'd been so thrown off when D'Vaughn had said that shit that I hadn't even known how to respond. *What the hell did you say to someone who had missed the point completely?*

"I told her that she needed to let me find the love of my life and she told me that all I had to do was take off my ring and be discreet when I went out scouting."

Rhea clutched at her stomach, wheezing. "I know you fucking lyin', bro. Ain't no damn way."

Without taking my eyes from the ceiling, I reached blindly for a decorative pillow and pressed it against my face. Where the fuck had our wires gotten so crossed that D'Vaughn thought that I was telling her that I wanted her to move out of the way while I searched for somebody to love?

"You told her you came on the show to find love, and then said she needed to let you do what you came to do, and she said 'none of your other bitches even know about me so do what you gon' do'. I'm crying!"

Without removing the pillow, I lifted my middle finger into the air and waved it around in hopes that Rhea would follow the directive and go fuck herself.

"I'm so glad I could provide your post-dinner amusement. Truly honored."

"Whew, shit!" She slapped my feet off of the couch before dropping down beside me. "Don't be mad at me. You know this is all your fault."

At that, I shot upright, face pinched into a disbelieving scowl.

"How is this my fault?!"

"Because you're used to only having to lick your lips and blink your pretty little eyes to get what you want. Women usually take a look at your tatts and your locs, and fall at your feet. And once you start speaking Spanish, it's over. They be eating right out of your hand."

I frowned harder, wanting to dispute her claims but knowing that anything I said would just be bullshit because she wasn't lying. Unfortunately.

"You're tryna handle ole girl like you handle all those women that you claim you don't want. And you know I wasn't with this love-of-my-life shit from the beginning, but now I gotta ask, how do you expect to get something different if you're pulling the same old tricks?"

"I'm not pulling tricks. I'm just—" I broke off, not having an answer to what was probably a rhetorical question to begin with.

Rhea leveled me with a knowing look. "You're just what, Kris?"

"I'm just…being overly affectionate and hoping for the best," I offered lamely.

"Uh-huh. And what will that get you?" She held up a hand and ticked off a single, solitary finger. "*Maybe* pussy. Anything else?"

With a sigh, I shook my head. That method hadn't gotten me anywhere before and it likely wouldn't get me anywhere now.

"Okay, so what do I do?"

"Pshh!" She mushed me. "I can't tell your ass what to do."

I bounced off the cushions and came right back to her.

"You *always* tell me what to do. It's one of your driving forces in life."

Pursing her lips, she looked off into the void and chuckled before shrugging.

"Yeah, you're right. Well, the first thing you need to do is be up-front with her."

"Done. ¿Qué más?" I'd been telling D'Vaughn what my aim was since the night we met. That was easy.

Narrowing her eyes, Rhea stared at me. "Done, huh?"

"Yeah, bro. That's lightweight. Done and done. What's next."

Rhea shook her head. "Nah, man. Do that first and then come talk to me."

"It's basically done already!" I exclaimed, throwing my hands into the air.

"Básicamente no es completamente. Just finish it all the way and then come talk to me."

"Man, whatever." Annoyed, I pushed off of the couch and went to my room.

If she wasn't going to help me then there was nothing else to be said. If we both knew what I was looking for, how much more transparent could I be? I grumbled the entire time that I slipped out of my clothes and jumped under the covers. When I finally closed my eyes, the image of D'Vaughn danced beneath my eyelids. She was so close, but whenever I would reach for her she would shimmy away. It felt like more than a metaphor and I slept restlessly with that heavy on my mind.

The next afternoon, I was determined to do things differently. We were working with a limited amount of time and I had to get the ball rolling before we got to the end of this thing and said our goodbyes. As we'd done the day before, D'Vaughn and I met at the venue before everyone else. When I spotted her car, I parked and walked over, knocking on the passenger window to make my presence known. After I heard the unmistakable sound of the locks disengaging, I opened the door and climbed inside.

"Hey."

"Hi, Kris."

She gave me a quick glance before doing an immediate double take, raking her gaze over me as her nostrils flared slightly. Grinning, I grabbed the back of the seat behind her. I might have rushed home after work for a quick shower so I could change, and I might have spritzed on a couple squirts of cologne and dressed with her in mind. If I was gonna pull the trigger on getting her to be the love of my life, it didn't hurt to have the clip fully loaded. I might not have intended to lean on my looks, but I'd be a fool not to at least use them to my advantage. At the very least, I knew D'Vaughn liked how I looked, so I'd selected a pair of dark-wash denim jeans and a gray short-sleeved T-shirt. Gray-and-black Air Max were on my feet, and I'd left my hair free since she seemed to like it when I wore it that way, if her constantly fingering the strands meant anything.

"You wore that to work?"

I shook my head. "I wore a tracksuit to work, but went home and changed before coming this way."

"Oh, okay."

She returned her gaze to the phone in her hand, straight dismissing me in a way she'd never done before. That stung and I had to admit that my feelings were hurt a little bit. Maybe Rhea's know-it-all ass had a point. Reaching across the console, I grabbed D'Vaughn's hand in mine, linking our fingers and resting them on my thigh. She gave me a questioning look.

"I think we had a misunderstanding yesterday."

Her brows furrowed. "Why do you think that?"

"Because I'm pretty confident that you wouldn't have told

me to take my ring off and 'be discreet' if you'd known that I was talking about you."

Her lips parted as if she were about to say something, then quickly snapped shut as she looked out of the windshield at the parking lot. When she still hadn't said anything after a minute passed, I squeezed her hand.

"Tell me what you're thinking." Her silence was unnerving.

"I…I don't know what to say."

"You don't have to say anything if you don't want to." I meant that, but I'd be lying if I said her response didn't burst my bubble a little bit. "I'm not trying to put any pressure on you," I assured her, in case that was a concern. "You already knew my goal; I just wanted you to know that you were the person I had in mind."

"Am I though?"

"What do you mean?"

She tugged her hand out of my grasp and flexed her fingers in her lap.

"I'm just trying to get a clear understanding of what you're saying. You already knew, well before you were paired up with anyone, that you were looking for love on the show. Now here we are and you're telling me that person is me. You're staring at me and waiting for a response, but I truly don't know what to give you. Am I supposed to be excited or something? *Yay, I was the chosen one!*"

"What? I ain't asking for all of that."

"But you *do* want me to be excited, no? You've reached the point in your life where you're ready to settle down and I just happened to be in the right place at the right time. From where I'm sitting, it could have been Margo in this spot, or shoot, even Tanisha, and you would be telling them the same thing. So once again, I'm trying to figure out how I'm supposed to respond to this."

Her logic had me thrown.

"It couldn't have been either of them because it was never supposed to be either of them. Yeah, I'm ready to have something serious, but I'm not so desperate that any ole body would do."

"That's not desperation. You'd be figuring it out regardless of who's on the other side."

"But it's *you* on the other side."

"But if it wasn't me, you'd still be trying to make someone your future something-serious. I'm not a Lego. You can't just put me into a slot because I fit."

Oh. *Oh.* It hit me then what her argument was. She didn't want to feel like she was just filling a role. To her, I would have "fallen for" whoever I'd been paired up with, so anything I did was taken with a grain of salt. That also meant that she didn't believe that I was being authentic with any of the affection I showed her. *How the hell was I supposed to convince her that I was being serious and that it was her specifically that made me feel the way I did?*

Ah, hell. Rhea was fucking right again.

"Get out of the car," I instructed, reaching for the handle on the passenger door.

Blinking rapidly, D'Vaughn turned to me. "Huh?"

Pushing open the door, I stepped out and looked back at her. "Get out of the car."

While I waited for her to do as I said, I rounded the trunk of her car and grabbed the door as she pushed it open, reaching in to offer her my hand. She allowed me to help her out of the car but gave me a curious look, her brows furrowed and lips twisted to the side. Once she stood in front of me, I grabbed her hands and made sure that we had full eye contact before I spoke.

"I like you, D'Vaughn. I know that we have to show a

level of familiarity for those around us, but I think that you can agree that it's been easy to do." I paused, waiting for her to nod or verbally agree. When she dipped her chin twice, I continued. "That type of chemistry isn't easy to fake for me, but it's come natural with you and that's because it's not all fake. I'm attracted to you physically, but beyond that, I really vibe with your energy. I think that if we let it, something real could happen between us. Obviously, I'm down with that. The question is, are you?"

She gaped at me. "I wasn't expecting this. I'm not sure. Um…" She started to chew on her bottom lip but stopped as soon as I lifted my hand. "Can I think about it?"

"Of course. I meant it when I said I wasn't trying to pressure you. I'm an all-in type of person, but I understand that everyone doesn't share that mentality. Think about it and let me know. I'm going to keep doing what I've been doing, and if you decide that you don't want to take it there, then let me know and I can reel it in as much as possible. At least in a way that won't affect the show. No hard feelings, no drama, none of that. Aight?"

She nodded. "Okay. That sounds good. Thank you for being up-front with me. I definitely took it wrong yesterday."

Blowing out a relieved breath, I nodded. "That was damn sure."

I chuckled, taking note of the familiar van parked in a far corner of the parking lot. I hadn't noticed it when I'd first arrived, but I wondered if Felix had been recording us this whole time.

"Did you see Felix?" I pointed at the van.

D'Vaughn glanced over her shoulder and then nodded.

"Oh yeah. He was here when I arrived. Got me mic'd and everything." She pushed her twistout back behind her ear and pointed to the tiny ball in her ear.

My stomach twisted. For some reason I'd thought that we were having a private moment alone. Finding out that our conversation had definitely been recorded made me want to kick myself. I should have checked before I'd started speaking.

"I hope none of this ends up on the show."

Quirking an eyebrow, D'Vaughn gave me a look. "Now, you oughta know better."

Sighing, I shook my head. "You're right."

In the grand scheme of things it didn't matter. By the time this aired, we'd hopefully have moved well past this moment, and there was always the chance that it wouldn't make it to the final edit of the episode. In the corner of my eye, I saw Ms. Miller's car pull into the lot, followed shortly by Papi's SUV.

It was showtime.

Unlike the other two locations, this venue was a freestanding building, with no other businesses on either side and a private parking lot. The façade of the building was gorgeous, with four wide columns spread out along the front, serving as a backdrop to an opulent polished stone fountain, both of which gave the venue a palatial look that the Starlight Palace had failed to achieve. The inside was even more impressive than the outside.

The first thing that caught my eye once I stepped inside of the glass doors were the two fish tanks on either side of a mini replica of the fountain out front. Instead of water, the fountain inside was filled with lush greenery and vibrant flowers. There was a fresh, clean scent in the air that seemed like it came from the terrarium and gave me the feeling of having a picnic in the park.

"Oh! Look!" gasped Mami, her arm outstretched as she pointed at the arrangement in front of us.

I hadn't noticed it at first glance because I'd been trying to take in so much at once, but in the center of the garden fountain was a chalkboard banner with our names scrawled across in loopy handwriting.

Welcome D'Vaughn & Kris!

As we marveled over the sign, a person appeared from behind the fountain, smiling serenely at us. They wore a sheer, pink duster over a sleeveless, cream slip dress and pale pink mules on their feet.

"Good afternoon, all. Welcome to The Majestic. I'm Airyn."

They smiled, and I swear I saw a glint of sparkle from their blindingly white teeth. Not only did the building radiate prestige, but so did Airyn. If this was real and I had to pay for this thing out of my own pocket, I would have turned on my heel right then. There was no way this place was affordable to the average working woman.

"I love those shoes, Airyn," Ms. Miller gushed as she stared at Airyn's feet.

Their smile widened and they tipped their head.

"Thank you, darling. They're one of my favorite pair."

"Lord, I would love to wear a pair like that to the wedding," she added wistfully.

"Oh? Are you one of my guests of honor tonight? Kris, perhaps?"

Shaking her head, Ms. Miller giggled. "Oh no. I'm the mother of the bride." She stopped short and cast an uncertain glance at me. "Or rather…one of the brides. Do you identify as a bride or groom? I'm sorry. I'm still learning."

"Bride and groom are not genders, Mama," offered D'Vaughn gently. "They're just labels."

"It's okay, Ms. Miller." I smiled to show her that I wasn't offended. "The language can be confusing."

"It's not *that* confusing," murmured Ray.

Kiana was already elbowing him in the side before I shot

him a censoring look. I didn't need him adding on to an already precarious situation. Ms. Miller was making an effort, which was more than D'Vaughn had expected, but the bare minimum that she deserved. It was easy to judge from the outside looking in because me, Ray, and Rhea had been blessed with parents that never made loving or accepting us feel like anything other than regular parenting, but we do others in our community a disservice when we forget to give them grace.

"If I may interject," Airyn smoothly inserted, aiming their attention at D'Vaughn's mother. "It sounds like you are trying to fit your daughter's situation into the traditional marriage box. Perhaps if you think of it in terms of two souls joining together instead of a man and woman, it may help you."

"Ooh," whispered Mami, "I like that."

I nodded in agreement and spent the next hour repeating the movement over and over. The Majestic was heads and tails above both Starlight Palace and The Moxi, with Airyn's gentle elegance the icing on the cake. The rooms were breathtaking, with each one staged in preparation for an event the following day. From the chandeliers to the finishings on the floor, it was clear that time and effort had gone into this venue. By the time we made it to the conference room to talk pricing and packages, I was sold. A quick glance at D'Vaughn told me she felt the same way, if the stars in her eyes were any indication. After signing the contract and paying a deposit that was conveniently the exact amount as the check we'd received on Sunday, our band of merry wedding planners spilled out onto the paved circular driveway in front of the building.

I could see the excitement on their faces as soon as we cleared the fountain and I spoke quickly to head off any conversation. Slipping an arm around D'Vaughn's waist, I smiled at our family.

"I know you guys probably want to discuss things, but save

it for the restaurant. We want to treat you all in celebration of us making the first big decision of our wedding, so we made reservations for dinner." Pulling out my phone, I glanced at the screen. "And if we don't leave now, we'll likely be late."

The mention of food got them moving. After texting out the address to the location that had been arranged by the show, we all piled into our respective vehicles and made the twenty-minute trek to a popular steakhouse on the west side. When we arrived, I gave my name to the hostess and we were immediately shown to a private dining room with an oblong table that sat at least fifteen people. The lighting was dim and intimate, and on the table were three glass cylinders that served as centerpieces. There was no doubt in my mind that I was going to miss the extravagant pleasures I'd been exposed to when these next few weeks were over.

Two servers came in as soon as we were seated, placing baskets of warm bread in front of us, laying fabric napkins over our laps, and taking our drink orders.

"Ooh," murmured D'Niesha. "This is fancy!" Leaning across Ms. Miller, she tapped D'Vaughn on the thigh. "You marrying into money, or nah?" I bit back a laugh at her whispered question. *If she only knew who was bankrolling this meal.*

Gasping, D'Vaughn covered her face. "Oh my gosh. Niesha, shut up!"

Ms. Miller shook her head. "Don't be so tacky, little girl."

D'Niesha pursed her lips. "So, you're telling me it didn't cross your mind? Really, Mama?"

Flattening her lips into a thin line, Ms. Miller didn't say a word, but her youngest daughter must have taken it as an admission, because she snapped her fingers and sat back in her chair with a smug grin.

"That's what's I thought."

"Anyway," D'Vaughn said a little louder, pulling everyone's attention toward her. "What do y'all think of The Majestic?"

"It was amazing!" Kiana gushed. Beside her, Josue nodded emphatically.

"Yes, but those prices." Papi whistled.

He had a point. The Majestic was more than Starlight and Moxi combined.

I shook my head. "You don't have to worry about that. *We're* paying for this." I hooked a thumb at myself and D'Vaughn to emphasize my point.

You would have thought I'd just called him by his first name from the scandalized look he gave me.

"¡Primero muerto!"

Groaning, I leaned my head back. "Papi—"

"No. I give on a lot of things, but this, I won't budge on. No child of mine is paying for their own wedding."

Mami reached for his hand, which was fisted on the table. "Rey. Mi amor."

I'd expected this to happen. Had been waiting on it, actually, but it still didn't make it any less difficult to hear. It warmed my heart that my father wanted to pay for my wedding. It meant so much to me that it meant so much to him, but knowing that there was absolutely no way that he could do the *one* thing he didn't want to budge on was a hard pill to swallow. I didn't know how to explain to him that he couldn't just write a check or swipe a card—not when he had to be present at every point in the planning process.

Silence fell across the table. I sat there, my jaw clenched, not wanting to disappoint him but not seeing any other way, when D'Vaughn laid a hand over mine, prying my fingers out of the fist I hadn't even realized I was holding, and linking our fingers together. I looked at her, but her eyes were on my father.

"Reynaldo," she began, her voice soothing and amicable.

She waited for Papi to look at her, and when he did, the sight of his eyes red-rimmed and glossy brought a stab of pain to my chest. I felt tears build and I tried to blink them back.

"Right now, we are only paying deposits to secure our reservations. If it's okay with you, Kris and I will continue covering these, but after the wedding, you can pay the final balances, if you'd like."

Startled, I swiveled my neck to face her once again, but her eyes were still on my father. His light brown eyes swung from D'Vaughn to me.

"You're not going to pay ninety percent of the cost and send me a bill for one dollar, are you?"

"Absolutely not," D'Vaughn answered, even though he was looking at me. "I promise you that I will hand deliver every single bill we receive that is related to the cost of this wedding." I sat there mute, in awe of how she'd come up with a solution for something that had the potential to blow this entire thing to pieces.

"Except for your dress," interjected Ms. Miller. She cleared her throat and lifted her chin. "I'm paying for your dress."

D'Vaughn nodded and quickly swiped at an errant tear that fell from her right eye. "Yes, ma'am." Turning back to my father, she met his gaze. "Is that okay with you?"

"Yes. Gracias, mija." His voice was infused with a satisfied sort of gratitude that made my chest swell with affection for D'Vaughn. In retrospect, it was a small thing, but the way she had immediately worked to make sure his interests were served just showed me how well she fit with my family.

Pushing back his chair, he stood to his feet and walked over to us. Standing between mine and D'Vaughn's chairs, he leaned down to kiss first D'Vaughn's cheek and then mine. Afterward, he stared at me for a moment.

"You know that I only want the best for you, yes?"

Throat thick with emotion, I nodded quickly. "Lo se, pero you do so much already, Papi."

He cupped my cheek and smiled. "And yet I always feel that I could do more."

This guy.

I slid out of my seat and walked right into the arms that he'd already spread in anticipation of my next move.

"I love you, Papi," I whispered.

"¿Cuánto?" he asked as he patted my back, something he hadn't asked since I was a teenager.

"Con todo el mundo."

"And still, I love you more."

Burying my face in his shoulder, I wept. There was no way to stop it. He tightened his hold on me, murmuring comfort in Spanish. As he went from patting to rubbing my back, I felt another pair of arms encircle me from the side and cracked my eyes to find Mami had joined us. Her cheeks were wet but the smile on her face said that they were the result of happy tears. Moments later, I heard the sound of several chairs scraping against the carpet and then my siblings all piled onto our family group hug.

"Well?" I heard a muffled voice ask. "Get up there."

"This is a family moment, Mama."

"Ain't you about to be family?"

"Mama, please."

D'Vaughn's voice was low, but even with mi gente surrounding me, I heard her as clearly as if she was standing in front of me. I started to move, shifting my body back and forth until they got the message and began to loosen up. When my limbs were free, I sat in my abandoned seat, scooted the chair over to hers, and grabbed the backs of her knees.

"Let this be the last time you mention my family and don't include yourself, aight?"

Her eyes widened and I opened my mouth to reiterate when Papi clapped me on the shoulder. I looked up to catch his approving nod before he returned to the other side of the table and reclaimed his seat. Turning back to D'Vaughn, I raised my eyebrows.

"You gon' answer me or nah?"

She blew a soft breath through her nose and cast a quick glance around the room before bringing her eyes right back to me.

"What do you want me to say, Kris?"

I observed her. Her leg was bouncing in my grasp and her shoulders were tense, so something was up, but I couldn't fathom what would make her react that way. My confusion only fueled my determination to get to know her better outside of what was required for the show. Squeezing her legs, I leaned closer to her.

"I want you to say that if I pull you into the next family group hug, you'll come willingly."

Her shoulders fell marginally, but enough for me to know that my answer was better than whatever she'd been expecting.

"That's it?"

"Yeah. Can you do that for me?"

She nodded, a soft smile making its way onto her face.

"I think I can manage that."

Jitter Cam 06-D'Vaughn

This week has had its challenges so far, but I think we're doing pretty well. I thought we would crack when we got to the Starlight Palace, but surprisingly, it seemed to bring our families closer together. I never would have seen that coming. I don't think I'll ever be able to forget Mama and Kayla walking around the room like it was Sunday morning prayer before service began. You really can't make this stuff up.

That moment before dinner, when Reynaldo insisted on paying for the wedding, was so special. It's clear that bond he and Kris share is deeply rooted, and it was so touching to witness. And then to see the whole family surround them in a group hug? Ugh! My heart!

I really love everything about the Zavalas. They are so accepting, and loving, and hilarious. I couldn't have picked a better family to marry into if the task had been mine alone. More than anything, the way they interact with my family means so much to me. Anyone standing on the outside looking in wouldn't be able to tell that these two groups of people just met, and that is saying something.

On the flip side: this sucks.

No, I'm serious. Honestly, it all seems too good to be true right now. Things are just flowing in a way that would be perfect if this were real, but it's not so it isn't. Everyone is buying this whole charade a little too eagerly for my liking. Like dang…was I so lonely that you have no problem believing I'm marrying the first person I introduce you to? It's what I want, of course, but I can't say it doesn't sting. Like…no one is even questioning this! Not one person.

Maybe I'm being irrational, who knows? Well, I know, but I don't care. Obviously, I'm going to keep acting the part and I want them to believe me, just know that I'm side-eying them at every turn.

I know my propensity for honesty was my biggest selling point in my audition, but it backfired on me because they're eating these lies up hook, line and sinker. I don't know… I wonder if they—my mama especially—was so stunned by me coming out that she just…agreed with everything else. It's just a thought. Hmm. That wouldn't explain Darren, though. Gah! Now I'm going to be up all night thinking about this!

Anyways. I'm looking forward to the tasks next week. Despite the craziness, it was kind of fun, but I'm one-hundred and seventy-five percent sure that had to do with Kris and less the actual tasks.

She's…great. And so nice to look at.

Huh? Did you hear that? I think my mama is calling me. Gotta go. Bye!

Week Three

D'Vaughn and Kris,

You've advanced to week three. Congratulations! This week your task is for what some might call the most important part of the wedding day. There is only one, so make it count.

—Kevin

1. Order custom wedding attire

Chapter Nine

D'Vaughn

Change Clothes & Go

"They want you to order a custom gown *three weeks* before your wedding?!"

Cinta's incredulous screech perfectly reflected my shock. I should have known that things were going too well. Kris and I were doing a pretty good job of appearing to be in love—too good of a job, if you asked me—and our families didn't seem to suspect anything. After last week's venue shenanigans worked out in our favor, I was feeling pretty confident that we'd make it to the end of the road. The postcard I'd received no more than twenty minutes earlier promptly knocked me right back into a position of humility.

"I couldn't believe it either," I murmured, dropping my head back against the couch and covering my face with my hands.

"This is a setup."

I didn't argue because she was absolutely right. What other reason could it be to make such an outrageous demand? Also, it was becoming rather clear that the show had a trick up their sleeve every single week. First, that travesty that was the Starlight Palace, and now this.

"Apparently, y'all are doing too good of a job with this and need to shake things up."

"Girl, you pulled the words right out of my head."

"Hmm."

Cinta's thoughtful hum made me drop my hands and peer over at her. She was staring off into the distance, her brows furrowed. I recognized that look.

"What are you thinking about over there?" I asked.

"I'm just thinking about how I already have your measurements…"

Sitting up straight, I swiveled on the sofa to face her, heart rate increasing. "I know you aren't saying what it sounds like you're saying."

My best friend of twenty years cocked her head to the side and smirked at me. "Except you know damn well that what I'm saying is *exactly* what I'm saying."

"Cinta," I whispered, my eyes welling, "are you being serious right now?"

She fixed me with a no-nonsense look. "What have I always told you?"

"That I'm the great non-romantic love of your life and whoever I marry has to understand that they are obligated to share me."

Rolling her eyes to the ceiling, she poked her lips out. "Huh. Well, yes. That too. And depending on how things progress with Ms. Thick Thighs Save Lives, I'll be having a little talky-talk with her soon. *But* that isn't what I was talking about. What *else* have I always told you?"

"That you'll end me abruptly like my name was *Girlfriends* if I walk to the altar wearing anything but a wedding gown made by your two hands."

Clasping her hands in front of her, Cinta quirked an eyebrow at me. "Okay, so…"

I groaned. "So, it's not the same! We're not even getting married. We just have to make it to the altar and we win."

Frowning, she stuck a knuckle in her ear and shook, making her glasses slide down to the end of her nose. "Maybe I'm missing something because you just said 'walk to the altar' and 'make it to the altar' as if they mean different things. Baby girl, those two phrases aren't just kin, they're twins. Identical in fact. Same mama, same daddy, same amniotic sac."

I busted out laughing. "Come on with the rhymes then, Cinta!"

"No, heifer! Don't try to change the subject. Just be real with me. If you don't want me to make your dress, say that. All of these excuses are pointless. We're grown. Speak your mind." She stared at me expectantly, not even giving me the courtesy of staring at the wall so that I wouldn't feel so pressured by all of this.

Releasing a shuddering breath, I dropped my gaze to my hands in my lap. "I'm scared, friend."

"What are you scared of, my boo?"

"I've always imagined myself wearing your dress when I got married, and I'm scared that wearing it now, only to get to the altar and not do the thing, will jinx it."

Cinta reared back. "Jinx what?!" she asked incredulously. "The dress?"

I nodded solemnly. *Among other things.* "Yeah, and then I won't be able to wear it again when it's the real time and I'll be ass out."

She stared at me a moment before chuckling and sitting back against the sofa. "D'Vaughn, I almost just slapped the taste out of your mouth for saying that ridiculous shit."

Pursing my lips, I frowned at her. "And then we would've been two tussling heifers because I ain't going out like that."

"I can't believe you said that you'd be ass out as if I'd let that happen!"

"I'm not saying you'd let it happen—"

"Okay, then how would it happen if *I* didn't *let* it happen? Because I've never let your camera-shy tail leave out the door unless you were suited and booted from the time you asked me if I wanted to be your best friend during recess in the fourth grade, so what's really the truth, D'Vaughn?"

My view of her shrank as I squinted and wrinkled my nose. "Why did you have to dive deep into the historical facts though?"

Scoffing, Cinta stood up and started clapping her hands. "Because you got me fucked up! Now, stop playing with my emotions, Smokey, and let's get to the root of the problem here."

I covered my face with my hands as I flopped back against the couch. "It would be amazing if Kris and I made it to the ceremony and I wore your dress. Millions of people would see it and your business would explode."

Propping her hands on her hips, Cinta nodded. "All true things. But?"

The desire to cry was a strong one and I pouted to hold back the urge. Cinta wasn't going to let this go unless I gave her an answer that made sense.

"But if I wear a *Cinta Crowder Original* for a wedding that is broadcast on prime-time television and don't get picked at the end, then that is just more humiliation to heap on. I don't think I'd recover. In fact, I'd probably never date again."

"Whew, shit. I didn't know we were going to take a nose-dive right into a nineteen-nineties-era dramedy. Good Lord, there is a lot to unpack in that little meltdown. Future dating, humiliation, picking. Where do I start?"

Grabbing my hands in her own, she tugged until I lifted

my head and looked at her. I really didn't want to look at her. I was on the cusp of having *a moment*, and I wanted to sit in that and be emotional for a while.

"What is it?"

"Well, for starters, do you *want* to be picked?"

Shrugging, I scrunched my nose. "I don't know. Maybe?"

"That's not a good answer," she deadpanned. "Try again. And be honest this time. Thanks."

I sighed. "Fine. Well…yes, I think. It would be nice to be chosen for once."

Her face fell as she caught my meaning.

"Aww, my baby!" She pulled me into her bosom, hugging me tightly. "You deserve all of the love in the world, you know that, right? You always have."

"I know. I also know that I wasn't ready to receive it back then."

Cinta leaned back, her eyes full of interest as she stared at me, an indicator for me to keep going.

"As fake as this whole thing is, the past few weeks have really made me open my eyes to some things. The way my relationships failed had less to do with me being closeted and everything to do with who I am—who I was—as a person. I've spent so much time over the years decrying the women who didn't have my back and instead turned their backs on me, when the truth is that I wasn't capable of being a good partner because I was too focused on hiding who I was. Hell, I couldn't even treat myself the way I deserved with how much time I spent looking over my shoulder."

"*Shit,*" she breathed. "Well. Okay then. Damn."

Giggling, I nodded. "Yeah. The realization hit me like that also."

"What brought that about?"

Thinking back on the trip to the Starlight Palace, I shook

my head. "Just a stupid misunderstanding that could've gotten blown way out of proportion if Kris hadn't nipped it in the bud."

"*Ah.* Speaking of Kris, why don't you tell me more about this mound of humiliation you're suffering under?"

My mouth fell open as I gasped. "Uh-uhn!" I yelled. "Why would you segue like that?!"

She jerked her neck back at my loud tone. "Ma'am, calm down. You are the one who said you would be even *more* humiliated if Kris didn't pick you, which implies that there is already some humiliation lurking around. You connected the two, so I'm just following your example."

Nibbling on my bottom lip, I dropped my eyes to the coffee table. Even though Cinta knew just about all of my secrets—dirty and clean—I hadn't meant to reveal so much with that slip of the tongue. It was embarrassing enough without her knowing the details.

"I'd rather not say."

Her eyebrows rose. "Really? Well, can I guess?"

"Absolutely not!" I practically shouted, sitting up straight with both hands held out toward her. Knowing Cinta, she probably already knew and had just been waiting for me to say something. I'd rather we just pretended not to know that the other person knows we know they know and keep on trucking.

Surprisingly, Cinta shrugged. "No biggie. Now what's this nonsense about not dating again?"

I released several slow blinks, staring at her blankly. Was she really going to move on as if I hadn't just avoided answering a question? Is that how things were going to go?

Her brows were raised as she gave me an expectant look, but if she wasn't going to give me the correct response, then I sure as hell wasn't going to just *move on*. After a full minute of us staring at each other in silence, she cut her eyes to the side, cringing slightly as she twisted on the couch and retrieved the sketchbook she'd abandoned when I'd come running to tell her about my tasks for the week.

"Okay," she drawled awkwardly, as if I was the one being weird.

The fact that she wasn't pressing me for the information that I didn't want to share was grating on my nerves. How could she be so calm about me withholding a secret from her? We told each other everything! This was a big deal and she was chillin' like it wasn't.

"I like Kris!" I finally blurted.

She didn't even look up, her hands moving slowly with purpose, dragging the graphite pencil back and forth across the page in sweeping arcs. "Duh, girl. You came home from that first get-together and spent two hours telling me about her tattoos."

My face heated from the memory. I'd been immediately enamored with her, just on looks and the sound of her voice, but when she said she wanted to find love on the show, I'd been a goner.

"No. Like...*I like her*, like her. As in...I could see myself falling in love with her."

That finally caught her attention. Lowering the graphite pencil, she slid her gaze over to me.

"Y'all fucked?!"

"What? No! How did you get that from what I said?"

"It's only been five-to-ten business days, D'Vaughn. The exchanging of bodily fluids and distribution of orgasms has a way of making time seem inconsequential." Tilting her head, she quirked an eyebrow. "So what is it, because I know something happened?"

"Not everyone is a horndog, ma'am. All we've done is kiss."

She opened her mouth, but I shook my head. "But that isn't the point. I'm not falling for her because of a few kisses, even if they were *so freaking amazing.*"

"Uh-huh. Then why?"

I flopped back against the couch, sighing dreamily at the memory. "She said that she wants to fall in love with me and that I need to let it happen."

The pencil stopped moving and Cinta swung her gaze over to me.

"Okay, that is sweet as hell."

"I know, right!" I gushed, cheesing like a fool.

"What did you say when she said that?"

Slapping a hand against my chest, I leaned forward and coughed a few times. "Huh? Uh...that's not important."

Sliding the sketchbook back onto the table, Cinta turned to me and folded her legs in front of her, clasping her hands in her lap as she stared at me.

"Well, that was definitely a lie. Let's try again, shall we? Without all of the fanfare this time, if you don't mind."

I stared straight ahead, nibbling on my bottom lip as I tried to think of a way to get out of this. Cinta cleared her throat dramatically.

"I'll ask again, what did you say when Kris said you needed to let her fall in love with you?"

Cringing, I ducked my head. "Well, at first I misunderstood her and I kind of told her that I wouldn't stand in her way if she decided to go cruising for women as long as she was discreet."

Cinta looked as if she'd swallowed a fishbone. "Okay. And after she cleared it up? What'd you say once you knew what she was talking about?"

I sighed. "Before I answer this, I just want to point out that

she said she was looking for love on the first night, before anyone was paired up."

"Mmhm. What'd you say?"

"I told her that I wasn't a Lego and that she couldn't just
put me in a spot because she felt like it."

A deep, mournful sound like a whale crying out in the dead
of night burst from Cinta's mouth, startling me and making
me jump. I stared at her in shock. Reaching behind her, Cinta
grabbed one of the cushions off of the couch and smacked me
across the head with it. I howled with laughter and fell back.

"I can't believe you're over here crying about not being
picked when this woman is literally picking you at every stage!
You told her to go troll for pussy while you turned the other
cheek and she turned around and explained herself further.
Then you told her that she was a desperate hoe who'd take any
ole body as a wife, and all she did was come for you harder!
Baby. Vaughn. My love. My boo. Where are your wires going?
Why aren't they syncing to the correct sources? How are you
missing this when it's right in front of your face?"

"I'm not—"

"You are!" she interrupted. "Kris is telling you how she feels
and you're pulling out a thesaurus and searching for alternate
meanings. Stop that! Give her a chance and take her words
at face value. You can't tell me that you believe you deserve
love and affection when you keep pushing it away like this."

Eyes wide, I shook my head. "That's not—I'm not." I
snapped my mouth shut. Is that what I was doing? Was I
pushing Kris away?

Cinta grabbed my hand and squeezed.

"I'm not telling you to jump headfirst into a real relationship
with Kris, I'm just suggesting that you get out of your head.
Take things for what they are, not what they have the potential to be or what they might be like if x equaled y squared.

This isn't algebra and you don't have to solve for x. You can just live and let love do its thing."

I heard her loud and clear, receiving her input and putting real thought into it.

Days later, I was still thinking about Cinta's words when me, Mama, and D'Niesha walked into a bridal shop in search of the perfect gown. Before the seamstress could create something from scratch, she wanted me to try on different silhouettes to see what looked best on my body. Although it would take longer, I didn't mind and hoped the longer appointment would give me the opportunity to run into Kris. We hadn't spoken since Sunday, and that was only a brief conversation to discuss the week's task.

As with much of everything the past few weeks, the shop had been pre-selected for us. It was owned by Dory and Francisco, a husband-and-wife team, and on the other side of the bank of dressing rooms was a tuxedo shop where Kris was scheduled to have a fitting for her suit. She said everyone but her mother and Kiana would be with her, and from the sounds of things, it was bound to be an eventful appointment.

My own appointment left much to be desired. Dory was impersonal and didn't speak much, only humming every so often when I would emerge from behind the velvet curtain. I went through three different dresses before she actually formed a whole word with at least four letters. Mama and Niesha commented after every style, but there was something different when I pushed back the curtain and stepped out onto the raised platform for the ninth time. The energy in the room felt different but I didn't get a chance to examine why before I was being poked and prodded.

"Lovely," Dory murmured, shocking me into really taking a good look at the dress in the mirrors before me.

It was a nice dress. Beautiful even. The front plunged down

halfway to my belly button, with the top holding my boobs like the hands on the infamous Janet Jackson *Rolling Stone* cover. The mermaid silhouette didn't just hug my curves, it made love to them; kissing, and licking, and caressing before flaring out at my calves as it fell to the ground. The dress was sexy with a capital S-E-X, but it was too much. I felt too exposed with far too much of me on display. It wasn't my style at all.

When Dory finished settling the veil over my face, I lifted my head and opened my eyes. I expected to see my mama standing behind me but instead my gaze landed on someone I'd only met once, and hadn't seen in weeks. Gasping, I whipped around to face her. She looked good. *Really good.* She wore a sleeveless top that plunged almost as low as the dress I wore, with a pair of vintage-inspired, denim bell-bottoms with several rips across her thighs. Her microbraids were gone and in their place were thick Havana twists that hung down to her waist.

"Tanisha?!" I exclaimed, half-surprised to see her, and half-confused by her presence.

She released a husky giggle and spread her hands on either side of her. "That's my name, don't wear it out." Trailing her eyes from the top of the veil on my head, to the bottom of the floor-length gown, she lifted an eyebrow. "Well, in this dress, I just might let you."

My face heated from the unbridled suggestiveness to her tone, and I swept my gaze around the room in search of my mother and sister. I didn't have to search too far. As soon as Dory stepped away to jot down notes onto a little book, Mama was at my side, straightening the gown at my feet, and D'Niesha was behind me, smoothing the veil around my shoulders. My heart pounded. *Had they heard the suggestive way that Tanisha had spoken to me?*

"Mama. Niesha." I gestured toward Tanisha. "This is Tanisha. A…" I paused, searching for the right word to use, and when I could think of nothing fitting, settled on, "friend," I finished lamely.

I didn't really know how to describe her—never considered that it would ever be necessary. Honestly, I didn't think I'd ever see her again, except for when the season finale aired and all of the contestants were contractually obligated to be present. We'd only met once, and I hadn't seen her since. But there was nothing else that really would fit, and I couldn't very well tell them that I know her from the show because I'd signed a contract that spelled out in legal and layman's terms that I wasn't allowed to mention it to them.

Niesha peeked around me, a smirk on her lips. "A friend," she teased. *"Right."* She dragged the last word, letting me know that she didn't believe that descriptor for a second.

Tanisha laughed, and I brought my hands up to my heated face. "Niesha!"

Why did she have to say it like that? Oh my gosh. How embarrassing. Mama didn't say a word, just kept her head bowed while she worked at my dress.

Tanisha didn't seem to mind. "Nice to meet you both."

Finally, Mama hummed in response, but it was so dry and unlike her that I was startled. It was almost rude, and Mama was *never* rude. I looked down at her curiously, but she still wasn't facing me. Raising my eyes from her, I met Tanisha's golden-brown eyes.

"What are you doing here?"

She grinned widely. "I heard you were getting married and had to come see it for myself. I see they weren't lying, because you look amazing." She gave me another once-over, appreciation for what she saw shining clearly in her eyes.

There was something about the way she was looking at me

that made me feel guilty. There was too much interest in her eyes. She was too open with it, and with the way my feelings were increasingly growing for Kris with every day that passed, it felt wrong. It didn't matter that this was all fake; that's not how my heart felt, and because of that, I wasn't happy to see Tanisha give me the same looks she'd given me at the party weeks ago. I wasn't in the same place that I was in then.

"Shouldn't you be planning for your own wedding?" I asked pointedly, ignoring the way D'Niesha yanked on my gown in surprise.

Tanisha fluttered her eyelashes, and I didn't like the look of the secret smile she wore. She shook her head. "No. It didn't work out. We broke up."

My eyes widened in shock. We were only in the third week. The *middle* of the third week at that. How could they have broken up already? *What the hell happened?*

"I'm sorry to hear that." And I meant it. Even if I knew the relationship itself wasn't real, I knew that everyone who'd been at that party wanted to make it to the final stage of *Instant I Do*. Hearing that Tanisha and Margo weren't going to make it to the altar was more than a little sad.

Tanisha shrugged, seemingly unaffected. "It is what it is. We weren't compatible anyway."

I kissed my teeth. "Don't say that."

She quirked an eyebrow at me. "Why not? I know *exactly* who I should've been with, and it wasn't her."

No longer able to pretend that Tanisha wasn't there, Mama's head snapped up as she gave me a sharp look. I bit my lip, hoping that Tanisha didn't say more than she should. After passing her gaze from me to Tanisha, Mama tapped D'Niesha on the arm.

"I'm going to go find the seamstress to see if she can take in the dress a little bit. Come with me."

My sister's narrowed eyes bounced from me to Tanisha and then back to me. I could see that she wanted to protest; she definitely wanted to say something to—or about—Tanisha, but Mama grabbed her arm and pulled her out of the dressing area. As soon as they disappeared through the curtain, I slapped my hands on my hips.

"Okay, seriously. What are you doing here?"

Giggling, Tanisha shook her head. "I already told you. A little birdie told me that you would be here trying on gowns today, and I wanted to come see you, so here I am."

A little birdie? I hope she wasn't implying that one of the producers had something to do with this. I had no idea who she'd been working with, but I couldn't see Kevin orchestrating something questionable like this. I waved away her excuse, not wanting to dig into her declaration that she wanted to see me.

"Okay, but what happened between you and Margo? It's only been a couple of weeks."

Tanisha shrugged. "I already told you that too. We weren't compatible. There was no way to convince our families that we were going to be together. Hell, it was hard enough trying to convince one another. We couldn't sell it, and nobody believed us, and so we were knocked out last week."

My mouth fell open. "You were knocked out in the second week? Dang!"

Tanisha shrugged again and looked off to the side, but I saw the way her lips tightened into a flat line. She couldn't feign complete nonchalance.

"Well, Margo found it to be a difficult task pretending to be in love with me, or even attracted to me. So, shortly after introducing her to my family, they took me aside and told me that there was no way in hell they would let me marry her.

At the end of the night, instead of having me record a Jitter Cam, Rebecca called it a wrap."

I gasped, bringing my hands to my mouth. That was an awful way to have the rug pulled from under you. It's one thing for people to not believe that you would even get married—it's another for your supposed fiancée to not even be able to pretend that they wanted to be with you. And no matter how nonplussed Tanisha seemed to be, there was no way she wouldn't feel the sting of that. Stepping forward, I grabbed her hand in mine and squeezed.

"I'm so sorry."

She shook her head, as if ridding herself of the momentary emotions brought on by reminiscing, and gave me a sexy leer. Flipping our hands, she threaded her fingers through mine and rubbed her thumb across my wrist.

"Like I said, it is what it is. More importantly, now that it's over with her, I can come to you and let you know that not only am I still very interested in you, but I would love to pursue something with you."

That uncomfortable feeling came back with a vengeance, settling into my gut heavy enough to make me a little nauseous. I might've been overly flattered by her attention and bold words at the party, but right now, hearing them made me sick. Slowly, I slipped my hand from her grasp and backed up a couple of steps.

"I still have a fiancée, you know."

Quirking an eyebrow, Tanisha gave me an uncaring look as she swept her hand in an arc. "I know. Obviously. But when that's over in however many weeks, I was thinking that you and I could maybe go out somewhere." She grinned, and it was a wicked, suggestive thing that under different circumstances might've had me penciling her into my schedule expeditiously. "Or stay in. Maybe pretend to watch Netflix while

we do the opposite of chill. Something like that. I would really, really like to get to know you better."

"Um…" I tried to think of something to say that would
throw her off of this trail she was on, something that would
let her know that *I* was no longer interested, but my words
failed me. Flicking my eyes over her shoulder, I wondered
if anyone would come in and save me. *Where was my family?*

"Oh my God!" groaned Tanisha. "I don't believe it."

My eyes widened as my gaze snapped back to her. Her face
was twisted into disbelief with an inexplicable dose of sadness.

"What?" I asked frantically. "What is it?"

She chuckled dryly as she shook her head. "It's barely been
three weeks and you're already falling for the tattooed butch,
aren't you?"

My face heated. *How had she clocked that so quickly?* "Her
name is Kris," I offered lamely, conveniently ignoring the
question.

Tanisha rolled her eyes and slapped her hands onto her hips.
"Of fucking course," she mumbled. "You know what? I'm not
even mad."

"Hmm?" I wasn't even sure what exactly she was talking
about, and I was too embarrassed to say the words outright.

"You already know how I feel about you," Tanisha said
pushing a handful of her twists over her shoulder. "If I only
had six weeks with you, I would spend the time trying to
make you fall in love with me too."

Blinking rapidly, I shook my head a little and took a couple
of steps back. "That's… What? I don't think that's what's happening here." Technically. *Right?* I mean, Kris wasn't *trying*
to get me to fall in love with her. She just wanted me not to
interfere while she allowed herself to fall. So she said.

Tanisha stared at me in silence, the contemplative look in

her eyes making my palms sweat a little bit. After a minute, a slow smile came across her face.

"Oh, this is going to be amazing TV."

At that, I frowned. "Tanisha, you lost me here."

She shook her head. "Don't worry about it, babe. I'll get out of your hair now. I'm sure your mother and sister are standing outside of the curtain, waiting on me to leave."

As soon as the words left her mouth, Mama and Niesha reentered the room with Dory in tow. Tanisha turned to me with a wink.

"Told ya." She turned around to face my family. "It was really lovely to meet you both. Hopefully this won't be the last time."

With flat eyes, Mama offered Tanisha a bland smile that barely lifted the corners of her lips. *What in the world was up with her?* My mama was usually so friendly and welcoming to everyone we met that, although she wasn't being outright rude, I was completely taken aback.

Thankfully, Tanisha didn't seem to notice a thing, moving closer to the platform to give me a hug, the odd angle putting her face right into the exposed valley of my breasts. Wiggling her fingers at Mama and D'Niesha, she swished out of the shop. I watched her departure until Mama's sharp clearing of her throat quickly brought my attention to her. She had me pinned with a disapproving frown that made my brows knit in response. As Dory wrapped measuring tape around my hips, I narrowed my eyes at the woman who'd birthed me.

"What was that about, Mama? You were less than welcoming with Tanisha."

Mama pursed her lips. "I don't like her."

"Mmhm!" D'Niesha added, nodding as she headed for a plush settee and took a seat.

Gasping, I brought a hand to my chest, bouncing my disbelieving gaze between the two of them. "You just met her! How can you already not like her?"

D'Niesha crossed her legs. "For starters, she was flirting her behind off!"

"Flirting with who?!"

Mama clucked her teeth. "I know I make beautiful children, but the way she was looking at you was highly inappropriate. She practically undressed you with her eyes."

Slapping my hands on my cheeks, I shook my head, my face heating even as the accusation boosted my ego. "Mama, please!"

"Don't *'Mama, please!'* me! You should've told her to stop looking at you like that! It was completely disrespectful to Kris!"

The short train of amusement I rode at her blustering came to a screeching halt. It took the force of God himself to keep me from rolling my eyes. Of all the reasons to be offended, that was so insignificant that it didn't even warrant a line on my to-do list.

"Seriously, Mama?" D'Niesha asked, exasperation bringing her voice down an octave. "Kris is cool and all, but she isn't here, so how about focusing on Vaughn?"

My eyes nearly popped out of my head, but I bit my tongue so quickly that I felt the unmistakable taste of copper. It never ceased to amaze me how Niesha had the ability to say things to Mama that neither me nor Darren could ever get away with, simply because she was the baby of us all. It was evident in how Mama only shot her a confused look instead of reaching for a belt.

"What are you talking about, li'l girl?"

Niesha shook her head. "You gotta let that patriarchal mess go, Mama."

Mama fisted her hands at her hips and turned completely

to face my baby sister. "Now you ain't making a lick of sense. How is it patriarchal when they're two women?"

I raised my eyes to the ceiling, silently praying for the sky to open up and swallow me whole.

"It's all about a sense of ownership," Niesha answered, sitting up straight and facing us with her hands on her knees. "Patriarchy says that wives are the property of their husbands. It's why men won't bat an eye when women tell them to stop harassing them, but quickly back off when they say they're married or have a boyfriend. She belongs to that man and they don't want to be disrespectful to him, completely disregarding the woman as her own person who is worthy of respect on her own. Claiming that Tanisha's overt flirting was disrespectful to Kris instead of even *considering* Vaughn and her feelings is along that same vein."

Mama jerked her neck back, blinking as if she'd been slapped. Her mouth opened, closed, and then she frowned. When she turned to face me, remorse shone bright in her brown eyes, and my chest squeezed tightly.

"I'm sorry, baby," she uttered so sincerely that tears sprung to my eyes. She waved a hand around. "All of this is new to me, and I know that's no excuse, but I have a few decades to… unlearn some things. Just know that I'm trying to do better."

"Mama—" I broke off, choking back a sob. I'd had so many dreams over the course of my life about having conversations like this with her and now that they were happening, I couldn't handle it.

She was on me in a moment, wrapping me in her arms tightly before leaning back to wipe away the wet trails on my cheeks. "No, my baby. Don't cry. Mama is gonna get it together."

I squeezed my eyes shut and nodded. It was in her effort; in acknowledging that she was wrong and vowing to do better. And while I was happy to hear it now, it was bittersweet that I had to shove us into this place. There was a war inside of me between being grateful and being resentful.

"You ain't done yet, woman?"

At Kris's teasing question, I looked up to see her coming through the curtained door that separated the private dressing area from a short hall that connected to the other dressing areas. The moment that she caught sight of my tearstained face, the smile she wore melted immediately. Her eyes narrowed and she swept a quick glance around the room, silently reading the scene as she made her way toward me.

"How are y'all fine people doing today?" she asked. "Good to see y'all."

After placing a hand on Mama's back and pressing a quick kiss to her cheek, Kris grabbed my hand and smoothly pulled me out of my mama's arms without waiting for a response. Her hands encircled my wrists, sliding up my arms and over my shoulders to cup my face as she gave me an intent once-over. As she touched her thumbs to the damp trails on my face, her frown deepened.

"What's wrong, baby?"

My voice was already thick with emotion from the exchange between me and my mama, but the sincere concern in Kris's eyes did me in. Sucking in a long breath through my nose, I shook my head.

"Nothing. These are good tears." Mostly. Technically.

Tilting her head to the side, Kris eyed me. "You sure?"

"I know that's right!" yelled Niesha, punctuating each word with a loud snap, a wide grin on her face. "You better check on your woman!"

Kris didn't even crack a smile as she stared at me, waiting for an answer to her question.

"I'm fine. Better than fine, in fact. I'm good; really good. *Lo prometo.*"

At my Spanish, she offered me the small grin that I'd been aiming for. Slowly, I watched as she visibly relaxed, her jaw loosening and the lines of her shoulders softening. Before she released me, she leaned in and kissed me softly, not even caring that my mama and sister were *right there* watching us. When she ended the kiss, she took a step back and allowed her eyes to take a journey, roving me from head to toe.

"You look beautiful, mi amor."

I started to bite my lip, but the way she immediately narrowed her eyes made me stop, a giggle bursting from my lips.

"Thank you, baby," I responded softly.

The dress was nice, though it wasn't my favorite—but from the way Kris licked her lips as she eyed me, I felt like I was dressed in a gown fit for Cinderella after her fairy godmother got a hold of her. We weren't alone, but suddenly the moment felt incredibly intimate. The expression on her face, the heat in her eyes, my body's response. It all felt like a private moment that no one else should have been witnessing.

"Well, shoot," breathed Niesha. "Suddenly, I'm feeling a little voyeuristic."

"Oh my gosh!" I squeaked, covering my face with my hands.

Mama chuckled, and I fought to ignore how thick and wet the sound was as she walked over to swat at Niesha's arm.

"Cut it out! You're embarrassing your sister."

Kris flicked her gaze over to Mama and came back to me. The questions were front and center, and I shook my head.

"Later."

She stared at me for a moment and I thought she would

press the issue, but then she nodded, and I released a breath grateful for the reprieve.

"I'mma hold you to that."

Her voice was light, but for some reason those words held a sense of foreboding that hit me in the gut.

Jitter Cam 07-D'Vaughn

Seeing myself in those dresses really made this thing seem real. Like…wow! I mean, sure I know that I really have a fake fiancée and we're getting fake married, but standing on that pedestal and looking in that three-way mirror? Wearing a white wedding gown and veil? It just hit me in the chest.

I've always wanted to get married. My exes might not believe that—since I always refused to come out—but being somebody's wife has been on my vision board for the past ten years. One day I want to be that friend that is so obnoxious with her sickeningly sweet marriage. The girl who's always unnecessarily using her left hand for everything, or saying 'Ooh, I don't know. Lemme ask *my wife* about that.'

So, when I saw myself in those gowns, it felt like…I don't know. Kismet, maybe? Like, even though this is as real as K. Michelle's butt, it just felt right. Don't look at me like that, Kevin. You know I see your tall self back there. I know it sounds crazy, hell, it *is* crazy, but it felt like I was doing the right thing. I'm on the right path for my life.

And when that feeling hit me, it was so…great, so magnificent that I started to cry. I couldn't help it; but Mama thought I was crying for a whole other reason, which made her emotional as well and then I felt guilty for deceiving her like this. But then I wondered if I should even feel guilty if I'm doing the right thing.

Oh gosh! Speaking of feeling guilty; I cannot believe that Tanisha stopped by! Seeing her was the shocker of a lifetime, but her behavior wasn't at all.

And...uh, about that.

I'm so used to pretending not to notice those little instances—you know, the touches and looks—when I'm around my mama that I played it off immediately, but the truth is that Tanisha was *absolutely* flirting with me! I'm not even surprised that Mama and Niesha picked up on that because apparently Tanisha wouldn't know the word *subtle* if it stood under a spotlight and tap-danced in front of her.

Kevin, stop looking at me like that. I'm 100% certain you're supposed to be an unbiased party. Make sure you don't edit this part out so they can hear how you're talking to me. He sounds like my daddy, y'all.

I didn't even say anything! OH EM GEE! I was *not* leading her on! I'm not a cheater! Yes, it would be cheating because—fake or not—everyone who matters to me thinks that I'm engaged right now. The respect they have for me matters. Maybe it shouldn't. Maybe I shouldn't care about other people's opinions of me, but that's not who I am. These are my family. My church family. My friends. I've known them my entire life, and when this is over, they'll still be there. It's bad enough that this will make them question any future relationship and woman that I bring around. I don't want them to have doubts about my fidelity on top of that. I mean, who in their right mind would cheat on Kris?

Kevin! You're fired! Why would you ask me that? Of course I like Kris! That's not a question. I'm not discussing my feelings for her with you. I said I like her, that's enough. Anyways, I hope we make it to the final week because I'd really love to see her in a tux. I know she's gonna look—mm!

You know what? On that note, let me go on home. Kris

and I are going to have dinner together and discuss strategy at my place since we can't be seen in public outside of the events scheduled for us. I'm not cooking. We're ordering takeout. Ooh, wait! I wonder if it's too late to ask if she can bring some of her dad's chili con carne! That stuff is amazingly addictive.

Okay. I'm going for real. My final thought is that I'm looking forward to next week. I have no idea what our tasks might be and that makes me nervous, but with our family around us, I know that we can get through anything.

Chapter Ten

Kris

When I Dip You Dip

When D'Vaughn opened her door that evening, she wore high-waisted leggings that came up past her belly button, a fitted crop top, and her hair was gathered into a puffy bun on top of her head. I quickly realized that I hadn't seen her dressed so casually in the few weeks that I'd known her, and that I'd apparently been missing out. D'Vaughn's body was mouthwatering and my fingers itched to dance across her skin while I put my lips on her.

Not for the first time, I wondered if tonight was a mistake.

"You know we could've just had this conversation over the phone, right?" she said, as if she hadn't asked me to bring over a very specific dish.

She turned on her heel after closing the door behind me, giving me an uninterrupted view of her jiggling cheeks moving freely in those leggings as she headed for the sofa. Internally, I let off a groan. I'd only insisted on coming over because I was feeling a way after the state I'd found her in at the fitting, but I hadn't expected D'Vaughn's curves to be displayed like this. She'd insisted that everything was fine, but I hadn't been able to shake the feeling that something was off. Now, we were at her spot, and she was looking how she was looking not even a week after I'd declared that I was going to keep sex out of this thing.

It was going to be a long night.

"Yeah," I agreed, "but we can't get good video over the phone." And I couldn't see her, or touch her, or kiss her over the phone either.

Dropping down onto the sofa, she folded one leg underneath her and snapped her fingers. "I forgot about the dang cameras."

Grinning, I handed her the plastic bag I'd brought with me, and crouched down to set up the mini tripod on her coffee table. I knew that she had the camera she'd been assigned, but I was already so used to carrying one around with me that I grabbed mine without thinking. "Yeah, I figured that. We eatin' or talkin' first?"

"Talking first. I don't want to accidentally belch midsentence."

Grinning, I finished turning on the small device. "You ready?" I glanced over my shoulder to see her lips pursed in a pout as she cradled the stacked containers inside the bag.

"If I have to be."

I chuckled. "Stop playing, girl. You already know what's up. Besides, this is the easy part." We didn't have to record every moment of our lives, but we were required to submit at least two hours of video every week, not including our filmed tasks.

Nodding, D'Vaughn sighed. Stretching forward, she placed the opened bag on the table, out of view of the camera, and sat back. "You're right. Go ahead."

With the press of a button, I started the camera and took a seat next to D'Vaughn.

"So, why don't you tell me what I walked in on between you and your mother earlier?"

"It was nothing big," she assured me, shaking her head. "Tanisha stopped by the shop for a quick minute, and Mama had an attitude about it. Niesha called Mama to the carpet, and then we hugged it out."

As she recounted the entire story, I could feel my forehead wrinkle. When she finished, I could barely see through my narrowed eyes.

"Tanisha? The same Tanisha from the show?"

Smiling at some memory I wasn't privy to, D'Vaughn nodded. "Yeah, that's her."

I remembered her well. I also remembered how she'd spent the majority of the night with her hand on D'Vaughn's thigh as she whispered in her ear. Hearing her name brought a bristly, grassy feeling to the pit of my stomach, and I didn't like it one bit. Canting my head to the side, I asked, "What was she doing at the shop? How did she even know you'd be there?"

"You know what?" D'Vaughn's brows furrowed as if she'd just thought about it. "I don't even know! She said a little birdie told her, but I never got a real answer."

Seemingly tickled about the idea, she laughed. I didn't join in because I didn't see what was so funny. There was no way it was a coincidence that the woman who'd shown D'Vaughn the most attention during the meet-and-greet just so happened to show up at her dress fitting. I'd watched *Instant I Do* before, and bringing in ex–love interests to stir up drama was their MO. But if anything, I would've expected one of D'Vaughn's unsympathetic-ass ex-girlfriends to pop up. Not a chick from the show who she clearly had some sort of chemistry with.

After a moment, she realized that I was sitting there somber-faced, and abruptly cut her amusement short.

"What a minute. What is this face for?"

"This is my thinking face."

"Oh yeah? What are you thinking about?"

"About how fucking suspect it is that she popped up while you were trying to find a dress to marry me in. Something isn't adding up."

Sitting back against the sofa, D'Vaughn considered me, a contemplative look gracing her features. *"Oh,"* she murmured, her lips curving up in dark satisfaction. "I like this. I like it a lot."

Despite me trying to hold on to my mug, her tone brought a smile to my face. It was low and sensual and made me think of things that didn't require clothing. I licked my lips slowly in an attempt to erase my expression and possibly bring my scowl back.

"You like what, preciosa?"

"This…jealousy." She gestured at me. "This whole possessive thing you have going on."

Raising to her knees, she lifted a leg to straddle my lap. Instead of sitting down, she hovered over me, using her grip on the back of the sofa for leverage as she leaned in to nuzzle at my neck. I was stunned into silence by her bold move. It was technically PG, but still not anything I would have expected from the ever-bashful and constantly blushing D'Vaughn.

Fuck me. Without even knowing the decision I'd made to keep things nonsexual between us, she was making this difficult as hell.

"Yeah," she drawled softly into my ear, "I'm liking this quite a bit."

Unable to help myself, I palmed her thighs and squeezed, letting my eyes drift closed as I inhaled her earthy scent, a mixture of Egyptian musk and shea butter that tugged at me like an invisible version of the hook from *Showtime at the Apollo*. I didn't like the accusation that I was jealous, but possessive was one that I would own without hesitation. D'Vaughn was mine. She would continue to be mine for the next three weeks, and if I played my cards right, she'd be mine for a long time after that. The reemergence of Tanisha didn't sit well with me, and something told me that this wouldn't be the last time we'd have the displeasure of her presence.

The wet rasp of D'Vaughn's tongue slicked against my neck, bringing my thoughts running back to her. Licking my lips, I asked, "What else do you like, preciosa?"

"I like how you taste."

Señor ten piedad. I thought I'd had a thing for the reserved D'Vaughn, but this unapologetically horny D'Vaughn had my body heated and vibrating with want.

"What a coincidence," I murmured. "I like how you taste too." Fuck! That was the wrong thing to say, but the words just tumbled out of my mouth before I could catch them. I should've been telling her to cool her jets.

Curving her neck, she pressed an openmouthed kiss to my neck before whispering, "Show me."

Digging my hand into her bun, I lifted her head from my neck and brought it to mine, crashing our lips together in a fierce, passionate kiss. She was ready for me, meeting me half-way, receiving my tongue stroke for stroke. When she spread her legs even further and sat in my lap, settling her weight onto one of my thighs, the moan she released filled me up. I wanted, I needed, I had to have *moremoremore*, and then she rocked her hips against me and I groaned, and suddenly those images of us doing things without clothes were so close to being reality that my breath hitched. As soon as the realization hit me, alarms blared in my head. I tried like hell to fight through the fog of lust to heed their warning.

Was it wise to take things further when D'Vaughn couldn't even fathom that my feelings for her could be real?

Wouldn't sex give her an excuse to dismiss the validity of my feelings in the future?

What if it's so good that I wanna marry her for real, but she just wants the check?

That last question pulled me up short, and I broke the kiss abruptly, dropping my head onto the back of the couch as I sucked in air. From our conversation the week before, that was too real of a possibility to ignore. Once I was in, I was in—I'd told her as much—but sex likely wasn't the best act to engage in with her already being unsure if she could trust my intentions. D'Vaughn didn't stop her momentum, attacking my neck with the same fervency that she'd just shown my mouth. Licking and sucking along my jaw until she reached my earlobe, which she then traced with her tongue. The sensation that ran through my body visibly shook me. My toes might've even curled in my sneakers. I felt her cheeks lift against my neck as she grinned.

"What are you doing, preciosa?" I rasped, needing the distraction of a conversation to help me get my bearings.

"Ouch," she husked, giggling softly. "If you have to ask, I must be doing a terrible job."

The bedroom voice she was using had a steady percussion happening between my legs.

"I have to ask because things are moving kind of fast and I want to make sure we're on the same page."

She stiffened and leaned back to look at me. I tried to keep my expression open and amicable, but apparently, she didn't like what she saw because she quickly climbed off of me and scooted a sofa cushion away.

"Telling me that I'm the one you were talking about when you said you were looking for love isn't moving fast, but doing...*this* is?" She sliced her hand in the air between us, the sharp move matching the suddenly sharp lines on her usually round face.

I blew out a silent breath and turned to her.

"What exactly is *this* supposed to be?" If she couldn't even say the words, then what was the damn point?

"You know what?" She broke off on a mirthless chuckle, shaking her head as she stared at something past my head. Huffing, she shot to her feet and stomped across the room and down the hall.

Pursing my lips, I quickly shot off a text to Rhea, telling her not to wait up, then followed after D'Vaughn, catching her just before she walked into one of the bedrooms.

"Why you running? What's the problem?"

She'd pushed open the door of her bedroom and flicked on the light before turning to face me, her arms folded under her breasts, drawing my eyes right to the juiciness underneath her top. She blew a breath out through her nose, bringing my eyes to her face. The carousel of emotions that flitted across those warm brown irises worried me. After opening and closing her mouth a couple of times, she finally shook her head.

"I'm sorry. I know the way I flipped was...unexpected. I was just trying to make something happen and...I know better. Just ignore me."

Frowning, I leaned against the doorjamb and shoved my hands into my pockets. That was bullshit and I wasn't gonna let it fly. I knew what she was trying to do, but I wanted her to own up to it. If D'Vaughn couldn't admit that she wanted to take this beyond the cameras and the assigned tasks, then I wouldn't let her take us beyond clothes and orgasms.

"What were you trying to make happen, D'Vaughn?"

Her eyes snapped up from whatever she'd found interesting on the floor and she glared at me. I fought the grin that threatened to overtake my face. After we'd settled on an official nickname, she caught a mad attitude whenever I used her real name.

"It really doesn't matter."

Blinking slowly, I gave her a blank look. "If that were true, I wouldn't have asked. C'mon, man. Just tell me so we can get it over with."

She took a subtle step back as her brows shot up. "Get it over with? Get *what* over with?"

Canting my head to the side, I quirked a brow and stared at her. She was trying to deflect by making what I'd said a bigger deal than it was, but I refused to let it happen. Shrugging my shoulders, I pushed off of the door and took a step toward her. Meeting her eyes, I pinned her with my gaze, attempting to show her that I was here to listen to her wants—her desires. With every step I took, she echoed, moving further into the room until we were halfway toward the bed.

Her ass hit the footboard before the rest of her realized there was nowhere else to go. Leaving my hands in my pockets, I leaned forward, running my nose along the jut of her chin and down her neck, before reversing until I reached the shell of her ear. Once there, I inhaled her scent, the soft notes of that body butter making my stomach clench.

"You gotta talk to me," I said directly into her ear. "Tell me what you want." Straightening, I cocked my head to the side and waited. As she'd so graciously reminded me, I'd already expressed what I wanted from her. Now, it was her turn to be frank.

Her eyes had darkened to a deep, dark brown reminiscent of molten chocolate, and her unrestrained nipples had pebbled to visible points, once again calling my attention to her chest. Anticipation of possibly having those luscious nipples in my mouth made me lick my lips.

"I want more than what we have right now," she admitted. "I don't know if it's the right next step, but I want it."

"You know what I told you," I uttered in a low voice. She was on the right road but in the wrong lane. If she wanted to catch her exit, she needed to move quickly. "If you mean it, then say that shit with your chest. I'm not gonna guess—"

"I want to fuck you. Right now."

Shit.

I swallowed the rest of my words as my excitement had my chest heaving and my rationality disappearing behind my lust. It wasn't the conversation we were supposed to be having, but I'd wanted for a distraction and one had landed right in my lap. Besides, there was always pillow talk.

The heat that engulfed me at her declaration was like a fire under my feet, and I started toward her. Clocking my movements, she moved briskly, meeting me halfway, wrapping her arms around my shoulders as our mouths clashed together in flurry of want and need and hunger. Instantly, I reached for her ass, slipping my hands underneath the thin material of her leggings and gripping her cheeks tightly, pulling her body close to mine. It wasn't enough. There were too many layers of clothing separating us; too much space that didn't need to be there.

Once again, D'Vaughn proved how in-sync we were when she clutched the hem of my shirt and quickly raised it up my body. Only when the material reached my armpits did I break our connection, lifting my arms so that she could yank the shirt over my head and toss it behind her. Before I could reach for her, she crossed her arms at her waist and tugged the tank top that had been torturing me all night up, releasing her bountiful breasts right into my hands.

Bending my knees, I hefted the round globes up and sucked one nipple into my mouth while rolling the other between my thumb and forefinger. A soft whimper fell from her lips and she trailed her hands down my shoulders and over my rib cage, delicately dancing along the lines of my tattoos, leaving heat everywhere that she touched.

"Kris," she breathed, "get on the bed, baby."

Instead of moving around her and getting on the bed first, I gently pushed her backward and lifted her legs to scoot her toward the center of the mattress. I climbed over her, kissing up her stomach, through the valley of her breasts, and along her neck until I reached her lips. She dug her fingers into my locs and tugged. Pushing up on my hands, I peered down at her through heavily-lidded eyes.

"Why did you get in this bed with all of these clothes on?"

Smirking, I glanced down my body. I still wore my sports bra and jogging pants.

"If you want me naked, preciosa, just say that."

Those chocolate orbs glinted at me. She pushed up on her elbows and held my gaze. "I want to feel your skin sliding against mine. Take off your clothes."

My heart pounded in my chest and a connected vein pulsed between my legs. It was in her even, unwavering tone. The matter-of-fact way she gave voice to her wants. It shook me.

I scrambled to the edge of the bed and pushed down my pants and boxer briefs, kicking them to the side as I ripped my bra off and dropped it mercilessly to the ground. Wearing nothing but the skin I was born in, I crawled back toward the sexy woman who had managed to penetrate even my slumbering thoughts. Her bottom lip was firmly secured between her teeth as she tracked my movements with a hungry gaze. Before correcting that, I reached for the waistband of her leggings, rolling them and her cotton thong down and off of her body, flinging them over my shoulder to join the growing pile of abandoned clothing. Kneeling above her, I took in every dip and curve of her body, unsure of where to start because I wanted to be in so many places at once and briefly wishing I'd been born with more than one set of hands.

While I was trying to decide, D'Vaughn lifted her hips,

wrapping her legs around my waist and pulling me down to lie flush against her. I braced myself on my forearms to keep our heads from crashing together, but that didn't stop her. Seamlessly—almost as if we'd practiced the move—she rose to meet me, wrapping her arms around my back and once again bringing her mouth to mine.

The moment our lips met I opened for her, welcoming her probing tongue as if it had always been a part of me. She moaned, and an answering groan from me met her through the seams of our hungry kiss. My brain once again cried for *moremoremore* and I was helpless but to deliver. Reaching down, I tapped her thigh, waiting for her to lower it to the bed before I rolled us until I was on my back. The delicious feel of her weight on me made me sit up, wrapping my arms around her waist as she rocked against me.

She needed it too.

I could tell by how her hips searched for pressure, friction. Gripping her thighs, I maneuvered us until she was almost sideways across my lap. It didn't take her long to figure out what I was trying to do. When I spread my legs, she slid a knee between them, settling her pussy right above mine, and when she ground down, a guttural sound fell from my lips. D'Vaughn bent her neck, parting her lips to catch it, swallowing the sounds she elicited from me even as she worked her hips to bring forth more.

"Baby," I moaned, running my hands up and down her back. I didn't know what I wanted to say but whispering her name like a prayer seemed like a good start.

Breaking our kiss, she shook her head and latched onto my neck. "Uh uhn."

"Te sientes tan bien, cariño."

"Mmhm." She hummed the satisfied sound in the back of

her throat as she licked across my collarbone and sank her teeth into the taut flesh of my jaw, pulling a sharp cry from me.

I was a mess. The usually reserved and sometimes shy D'Vaughn that I had gotten used to had disappeared and left this vixen in her wake. I'd gone into this thinking I would have to constantly coax her into telling me what she wanted, and instead was having my mind blown. Between her steadily rocking hips, her lips on my neck, and her fingers alternating between plucking and twisting my nipples, I was on sensory overload.

But then she kicked it up a notch.

With one hand, she grabbed the back of my neck, sinking her fingers into the locs at my nape as she curled her other hand over my right titty. She tilted my head forward and tugged my hair until I opened my eyes. The fire in her eyes was so intense, it was almost like looking at another person. Unbidden, a whimper fell from my lips before I could even think to suppress it.

"I want to watch you cum."

Then she dropped a kiss onto my parted lips before pulling back to watch my face intently as she ground against me. My brows knitted as I felt heat start a determined path up my toes heading straight for my core. She went from massaging my breast to pinching my nipple and the *painpleasurepain* was an unexpected jumpstart to my already building climax. I bucked against her and sucked my lips into my mouth, trying to drop my head back but unable to due to the grip she had on my neck.

"Don't you fucking dare hold out on me," she gritted, a line of sweat appearing along her top lip. "If I make you cum, I deserve to hear every single sound you make."

Lids low, face scrunched, I splayed my hands across her back and stared directly into her eyes as my orgasm washed over me, bringing with it unintelligible grunts and odd Spanglish that I wouldn't have been able to decipher if my life depended on it.

Releasing my nipple, she wrapped both arms around my neck and I met her midway as she surged toward me, our lips crashing into each other once more as she seized in my lap, her own release taking over. This kiss was less coordinated and more frenzied than any we'd shared previously as we rode out our tandem releases. As we came down, the kiss became less frantic and I laid us on our sides, pulling D'Vaughn's thigh over my hip and holding it there with a firm grip as we breathed each other's air while our heart rates slowed to a normal pace.

As I roved her face, a thought occurred to me. In hindsight, I should've known that D'Vaughn was with the shits when she said *she* wanted to fuck *me*. It didn't click for me then, but she'd let me know exactly how this was going to go down. Suddenly, she gasped, pushing up on one arm and staring down at me.

"What is it?"

"The camera! We didn't turn it off!"

My eyes widened as I realized that she was right, but then I burst into laughter.

"Well, there ain't shit we can do about it now." The way the cameras were configured, we couldn't even review the videos, let alone delete anything.

D'Vaughn shook her head, her lips curling up into a sexy smirk. "Go turn it off. They don't need to hear what I'm about to do to you next."

Jitter Cam 08-Kris

I should've known you would ask about the sex. Can I say 'no comment'? Fine. All I'll say about it is that it happened and it was amazing.

You have the fucking audio so that's all you're getting out of me.

But uh…I also want to tell you that seeing D'Vaughn in that dress didn't have anything to do with it, but that'd be a lie. I know it's not the one she'll be wearing if we make it to the end, since it has to be a custom dress, but *damn*. She looked so fucking breathtaking in that gown.

Which reminds me. I don't know why Tanisha popped up all of a sudden, but I don't like it. She's wanted D'Vaughn from the get-go and I know D'Vaughn was interested in her at first too. I don't want her to fuck anything up, ya know? I mean, yeah, I want to make it to the end, but I'm also invested in seeing where this thing can go between me and D'Vaughn.

The only positive from this is that her presence is just radicalizing D'Vaughn's family. She said they were up in arms, calling Tanisha disrespectful and shit like that. That's great. Them being defensive on our behalf means that they're in our corner and they're rooting for us to win. And if they're rooting for us, then we're doing a good job.

We're taking this thing day by day, week by week, so that's all I can ask for right now. And now, we'll see what next week holds.

Week Four

D'Vaughn & Kris,

Congratulations on making it to week four! Your tasks this week are small, but have a mighty impact on your big day! Have your friends and family help you make your decisions, and let's see what you come away with!

Good luck,
—Kevin

1. Order flowers for the wedding and reception

2. Secure a DJ

Chapter Eleven

D'Vaughn

Brotherly Love

Days later, Kris and I met at a local club to audition DJs for the reception. Since Darren was a musician, it was a no-brainer to bring him with me, but I was surprised to see Ray in tow when Darren and I stepped inside of the relatively empty building. Kris stood as soon as I came into sight, spreading her arms so that I could walk right into them. I wasn't sure what sort of greeting to expect from her after our night together, but I was pleasantly surprised when, after hugging me, she gripped my chin between her thumb and the side of her finger, meeting my lips with hers. She kept it brief, but the firm press of her mouth slanted over mine was intentional enough to impart that not only was I her woman, but she didn't care who knew it. When she pulled back, I might've held my eyes closed for a few seconds and taken a moment to bask in the feeling of her arm at my waist, the weight of it sure and warm.

"Hey," I breathed, sounding giddy even to my own ears as I thought of how those lips felt on other parts of my body.

"Hey," she intoned teasingly. Then she shot me a wink that made those parts tighten and throb.

Sliding her gaze over to my brother, she reached out a hand. "What's up, Darren?"

Darren slapped her hand with his own before they both snapped. "Hey, Kris. What's good?"

Kris grinned. "Besides your sister?"

"Girl, what!" Ray busted out laughing, which caused Darren to join in.

"Kris," I scolded. Or tried to. My cheeks were hot, but I couldn't remove the grin that popped up at her words. She was, of course, unfazed by my tone, and all she did was lean in and drop a soft kiss on my jaw.

"What?" she asked, as if she had no idea why everyone was cracking up.

I shook my head as she then gestured to Ray, who had stood to his feet.

"This is my baby brother, Raymond."

Ray moved toward us, his eyes narrowing as he gave Darren a lengthy once-over. When he extended his hand, there was a slick grin on his face that gave me pause. *What was he up to?*

"Hello, daddy, I mean Darren. Nice to meet you."

Stunned, my mouth fell right open.

"Oh, shit," Kris mumbled, shaking her head. "C'mon, man. That's my future brother-in-law."

Darren's brows shot toward the ceiling, but surprisingly, all he did was laugh as he shook Ray's hand.

"Nice to meet you, Raymond." He tried to retract his hand, but Ray held it in a tight grip.

"Please, call me Ray," he murmured. "Or baby. Or just call me. Please." Pursing his lips at my brother, he winked and released Darren's hand.

Unperturbed, Darren let off a good-natured laugh and shot me a look that asked if Ray was serious. Cringing, I nodded, because even though I'd only known him for a few weeks, this was right up the alley of his personality.

"Ignore him," Kris instructed, "and follow me. We're gonna sit over near the booth so we can talk to the DJ during their set and ask them any questions." She linked her fingers through mine and led us to a section near the DJ booth.

The chairs were low and wide, like fancy futons, which provided space for a few people to sit down, but weren't comfortable enough for anyone to camp out on for longer than half an hour. An oblong table sat right in front of the chairs, and had three sheets of paper on it. I picked up one sheet and saw that it was essentially a media kit for one of the DJs that would be auditioning. After reading it, I passed it to Darren. He read it over and nodded. I watched his face carefully for any ticks or signs that he didn't like what he saw, but he didn't make any off expressions, so hopefully that was a good sign.

"Which one of you is into music?" he asked once we were all settled.

"That would be me," sang Ray as he pointed to himself. "I DJ occasionally, so I told Kris that I'd help her find the right person."

I gave him a surprised glance. "I didn't know that you were a DJ!" Turning to Kris, I asked, "Why can't he just DJ the reception? We don't even have to listen to anyone else."

Both Kris and Ray began shaking their heads before I could even get my first words out.

"Absolutely not," Kris said, dragging her hand across her neck.

"Out of the question," agreed Ray. "I don't do family events as a rule. All it takes is one person to start requesting weird stuff or complaining about my set and then I want to fight. Besides, I can't be the DJ because I'll be the best man and I have to give a speech."

Kris rolled her eyes. "You're not the best man."

Ray curled his lip, glaring at Kris. "Fine. I'm the best man's understudy."

"You're a groomsman. Period."

Sighing heavily, Ray rolled his shoulders back as if trying to shake off the setback. "Fine! Whatever."

Not paying Ray any more attention, Kris grabbed my hand again, linking our fingers, and tugged me toward her. She didn't have to work hard; I wanted to be closer to her and found myself leaning in her direction by default.

"I missed you," she whispered, reaching up and fingering a couple of my mini twists.

My mind understood that there was likely a microphone attached to her person, and what she was saying was for the benefit of the cameras dotted around the room, but those words hit me in the chest and warmed me right through.

"I missed you too," I responded, surprised to realize that I also meant it.

After Kris secured her tux and Kevin green-lit Cinta making my custom gown, he then reached out to us the morning after the fittings and instructed us to do additional fittings for our wedding party as well. The following visits had taken up the rest of the week and there hadn't been time—or a reason—for us to see each other again. We'd been in each other's presence so often over the past few weeks that going the last couple of days without seeing her face made me realize that I really, *really* enjoyed looking at her. And being around her. And kissing her.

The grin that lit Kris's face was a mixture of pleasure and satisfaction. It was a little smug, as if she could see the thoughts swirling around in my head, but happy. Genuine.

"So, why didn't you call me?"

My cheeks plumped and I wondered if I was ever not smiling when I stared at this woman.

"Because I knew I would see you soon. I'd much rather look at your face while I hear your voice." Her knuckles brushed my cheek, and I might have leaned into her touch a little bit. Just a few centimeters. Nothing too outrageous.

"Shiiid. Say the word and I can make that happen anytime."

And I believed her when she said that, which is why I'd held off on calling her each and every time the urge hit me over the past couple of days. Biting my lip, I nodded.

"Noted."

The first DJ stepped up to the booth and set up his equipment, which consisted solely of a slim laptop. After a few moments, he switched on a microphone and called out to us.

"How y'all doing?"

"We're good!" Kris yelled back.

"Thanks for coming," I called, cupping my hands around my mouth so that my words would carry. It sounded so loud in the large space that I giggled nervously afterward. For a moment, I'd forgotten that we were in a relatively empty club.

"No problem. No problem. I'm gonna play a little ten-minute set for y'all based on the answers to your questionnaire. Feel free to come ask me questions or request a song. Otherwise, let's rock out."

"Love and Happiness" by Al Green sounded through the speakers and my brows furrowed. Although it was a classic, I wouldn't exactly call it appropriate for a wedding reception. Personally, I wouldn't want to hear that love could sometimes make you do the wrong thing, especially not after just pledging my life to someone. I glanced at my brother to see a frown on his face as his head bobbed, his eyes on nothing in particular. He was in the zone, processing the music. This was why I'd wanted him with me. A few more songs cycled on that had catchy melodies but had shady or downright depressing lyrics. When he played "Pretty Wings" by Maxwell, I tuned out, mentally scratching him off of my list.

Ray leaned forward, his eyes on Darren. "Did you have another question about the music? Your first question seemed like a two-parter."

Darren nodded. "Oh, yeah. I was going to suggest we bounce ideas around for a proposed playlist." He gestured to the DJ who was wrapping up his set and stepping aside so a woman in a backwards fitted cap could get into position. "Listening to this guy, it's clear he needs a list of songs *not* to play."

I nodded, glad I wasn't the only one who noticed it.

Ray laughed. "So you're also into music?"

"He is," I inserted, immensely proud of my brother and always ready to spout off about his varied talents. "Darren's a musician."

"*A musician?* Really now?" Ray's eyes flared with renewed interest. "Tell me more."

"Well, foremost, I'm a percussionist. I also play the piano, guitar, and I sing a little."

"Hmm." That sly grin from before reappeared onto Ray's face. "What about wind instruments? Do you...blow pipes?"

Slapping a hand over my mouth, I tried to muffle the scream that immediately bubbled out of me.

"Ray, what the fuck?!" Kris didn't even try to hide it, exploding with laughter as she shouted at her brother.

Darren was such a good sport, laughing along and seemingly not even upset.

"Okay, that's enough, Ray," I said, holding up a hand. "Leave my brother alone."

"Please, Ray," added Kris. "The man was kind enough to curve you silently but you're doing the most, acting like nobody ever paid you any atten—"

The song smoothly transitioned into the popular Xeno song "Drown Me" and I laughed as Kris stopped talking midsentence and jumped onto her feet.

"Aye! That's my shit!"

Rocking a little in my seat, I nodded. *This* was wedding reception music. This got people on the dance floor and was liable to get someone pregnant at the end of the night. My giggle faded as I watched Kris rock her hips from side to side, her hands in the air as she rapped along to the lyrics. The carefree way she moved, unconcerned with whether or not anyone was watching her, pulled at me. I felt like that when I was around her—she made it impossible not to—incapable of worrying about anything but how grounded I felt when her fingers dug into my waist or her nose brushed the sensitive skin below my ear.

Darren nudged me, pulling me out of my thoughts. I turned to him, my brows lifted in question. He leaned toward me, a smile on his face as he lowered his voice.

"I like this look on you."

"What look?" Confused, I smiled at his expression and waited for him to elaborate.

"This." He gestured at my face. "This…madly-in-love thing you have going on. I worried, you know."

Frowning, I ignored the very immediate thumping in my chest that cropped up when he said the *l*-word. "Worried for what?"

He shrugged. "Worried if I'd ever see you get to love someone out loud. To *be* loved out loud. Unapologetically."

My heart wrenched and I felt tears prick my eyes.

"Bubba…" Out slipped the nickname I'd had for him since I was a toddler teetering around on unsteady legs as I peered into the bassinet at the new baby in the house.

He swung an arm over my shoulder and tugged me toward him. His lips brushed my temple before he released me.

"Nah, I'm just saying. I hated not saying anything, ya know? And I felt like shit every time me or Niesha went out on a date and you only went places with Cinta—as far as Mama knew. But seeing you now? The way you are with Kris; the way she treats you, the way you look at her. I love that."

I released a shuddering breath, my heart panging. Although he was two years younger than me, Darren had always acted as if he was my big brother. We were just kids when he learned I was gay, and after that, he went out of his way to protect me. At the time I appreciated it, but looking back, it breaks my heart that he felt like he had to do that. We were *babies*. We should have been having the time of our lives back then, but instead we had the inherent knowledge that there were things in the world that would do us harm if they could see all of us.

Wiping away the tears his words had wrought from me, I laughed lightly as I shook my head. "Would you believe me if I told you that I wasn't in love, but the sex was good?" It was only partially a joke. Darren hadn't spent much time around us since that first Sunday dinner, and I was invested in his answer. *Did he see the same things that Mama and Niesha seemed to see?*

Tossing his head back, Darren let out a bark of laughter, clearly amused by my question. Instinctively, I looked over at Kris, my breath catching in my chest when I found her eyes on me. She was still dancing even though a different song was on now, but she started slowly moving toward us. With each step she took in my direction, I felt my breaths deepen and my internal temperature rise. My nostrils flared, and I felt a little light-headed. I was no stranger to attraction; had felt it hundreds of times over my life with more than a dozen of those times happening around the woman I now watched. This wasn't that.

Not simply.

It wasn't that cut and dry, but it also wasn't wholly complicated either. It was a thing that I could at least admit that I was terrified of putting name to. It might've rhymed with glove and had one less letter. A thing that I'd believed I'd experienced a time or two in the past, only to realize in a heartbreaking fashion that it wasn't what I'd thought it was. So now, it was a thing I planned to ignore until the next few weeks were up, because names gave things life, and what did I gain from naming *this* thing?

Darren swiped under one of his eyes and squeezed my shoulder. "Not a chance."

Kris reached us, and I watched her, still arrested in her gaze, as she stopped in front of me, bent at the waist, and grasped my chin. My eyes fluttered closed then, because I knew that whatever I received from her in that moment was a gift that I wanted to first experience by touch. I didn't want to see it coming. I wanted to be surprised. Kris didn't hesitate, pressing her lips to my forehead and then the tip of my nose before brushing them against my lips in a soft caress that pulled a contented sigh from the back of my throat. It was all rather chaste, and sweet, and completely nonsexual.

And it ruined me.

Yeah, I thought, thinking over Darren's answer to my question. If I were being honest, I hadn't believed it either.

Jitter Cam 09-D'Vaughn

I have no idea where y'all found these DJs but this was an interesting task. That first guy apparently doesn't listen to the lyrics of any song at all because why would he think that some of those songs were appropriate?

DJ High-Fee though? She was amazing! She started off her set on the right foot and stayed there until the end. I almost asked her to keep going, but Darren insisted that we hear all three of them. She's my choice though.

Um…can we talk about Ray turning his horny up to level ten when he met my brother?! I did not have that happening on my insta-wedding bingo card! And Darren was so kind about it! He just laughed it off and remained cool. Actually, this just reminded me that I need to go pop up at his house later because I haven't had a chance to hang out with him good since the show has started. We've always been really close, and I want to make sure that he knows that hasn't changed. He was fine today, but still. That's my Bubba and I miss him.

This was fun, but it sucks that we're doing all of this work for nothing. I mean, even if we make it to the wedding, we won't get to experience this part. If we win, that's it. That's the end. Who do I have to talk to to request that we still get to have a reception? That's the real question. I mean, The Majestic had some mouthwatering meal options. It's pretty evil to make us pick out six full courses and not let us get to eat them. I'm gonna start a campaign to petition for the reception. Did y'all hear DJ High-Fee? I want to dance to her set while eating chicken cordon bleu and sipping champagne.

Kevin! I need to talk to you!

Chapter Twelve

D'Vaughn

Flower Child

It was no surprise to anyone that the two people who agreed to go with Kris and I to choose the flowers were our mothers. So far, the only task they'd passed on was selecting the DJ. Kayla insisted that she wouldn't be any help because she had no idea what music we liked these days, and I think Mama only bowed out because of how Darren perked up when I started talking about it at Sunday dinner. I'd always planned to bring him along, but I guess Mama hadn't known that and wanted to push his involvement.

The florist was on the north side of town, closer to Kris's hometown than any of the other places we'd been visiting thus far, so Mama and I decided to carpool. When we arrived, Kayla was already there and inside looking at arrangements. We met Kris on the sidewalk in front of the storefront and she led us inside.

"D'Vaughn, hi!" greeted the bubbly florist whose green apron was embroidered with Jae in the top right corner. "Welcome to Blissful Blooms!"

Her exuberance was contagious, and I suddenly felt a little excited about the evening's task.

"Thank you!"

"I've been chatting with Kris and Mrs. Zavala here while my assistant finishes pulling all of your pieces together. Why don't you all follow me to the back and we can take a look?"

Jae led us to a room that was filled with several colorful groupings of flowers. There was an empty table in the center of the room and a counter that ran the length of the room. The table was surrounded by chairs, and the walls held several images of wedding paraphernalia like dresses, venues, tuxedos, and hairstyles. Under each photo was an arrangement.

"Please, have a seat," she instructed, waiting for us to do so before bringing the first arrangement to the table.

Mama gasped. "Oh my. These are beautiful!"

"I agree. Que hermosa!" Kayla exclaimed, lifting the arrangement with both hands as if it were a newborn whose neck still needed to be supported.

It was a mixture of blue roses, baby's breath, lilies, and white daisies. Jae then brought a tray containing a couple of each flower from the arrangement over to the table and began explaining their significance. Kris plucked a lily from the tray and brought it to her nose, inhaling deeply. As she exhaled, she caught my eye and smiled. Before I knew it, she was standing in front of me, tucking the stem behind my ear, arranging the flower so that it sat perfectly alongside my twistout. Taking a step back, she cupped my chin and nodded.

"Beautiful as always."

"Aww!"

Heat engulfed me as Mama, Kayla, and Jae all turned their eyes on us. Kris always knew the right thing to say, and do, when we were within earshot of an audience. It made perfect sense that she was so successful as a content creator on social media. Everything always seemed authentic, even when— *especially when*—it wasn't. *This* moment was definitely for the cameras. I understood that. But the look in her eyes and the words falling from her lips were so reminiscent of that night at my apartment that my brain felt a little cloudy. I didn't want to second-guess her, but I wondered how I was supposed to know when she was "on" and when she wasn't if there was no real difference between the two.

As I thought too hard about things that I had no control over, things that didn't matter at that moment, Kris leaned in and kissed my neck.

"Kris," I halfheartedly scolded, cherishing her closeness but annoyed with myself for the directions my thoughts had gone. "We're supposed to be picking arrangements for the wedding. You're holding up the process."

"It's not my fault that you distract me from work. What am I supposed to do? Ignore you?"

Biting back a pleased grin, I opened my mouth to suggest that she do exactly that, but she immediately shook her head, stepping closer and wrapping her arms around my waist.

"Ain't happening, so you might as well toss that thought right out of the window."

How exactly was I supposed to argue when she was on me like this, her body pressed against mine, her arms around me, and her scent pervading my senses? *Why was I even worried about arguing when I could just sink into her arms and accept her kisses?*

"Oh, um. Excuse me, Jae. Can you show me the mother-of-the-bride flowers? Those are somewhere else, right?" Mama's voice was a mixture of airy nonchalance and urgency. I couldn't see her, but I imagined that she was making her way to the door and probably trying to drag the poor woman with her.

"Huh?" Jae sounded so confused. "No. Everything is right—"

"Ah, yes!" Kayla added. "I would like to see those special

flowers as well. Why don't you show those to us while we give these two a minute to look at what you've already brought in?"

"Well—"

Whatever Jae was going to say was cut off sharply as all three voices disappeared through the door, which closed loudly behind them.

"That wasn't obvious at all," I laughed.

"Mmhm," Kris hummed, her face in my neck, nose running along my skin bringing goose bumps to the surface. I shivered in her arms.

"You're too good at this," I murmured absently, wishing my heart would get the memo that sex didn't equal love, that this was all fake, and that I needed to stop falling into her eyes like a lovesick puppy. Everyone was gone, leaving nothing behind but hidden cameras and the mics that Kris and I wore, yet she was performing as if we were in front of a studio audience.

"At what?" she questioned, lifting her head to look at me. A small smile played on her lips even though she looked genuinely confused.

"Pretending to be in love with me."

Because wasn't that what this was? She'd been playing the part of a woman so enamored that she couldn't keep her hands to herself for weeks. Even if I wanted to believe things had changed for her like she insisted she'd wanted—like they had for me—she was doing many of the same things that she'd been doing before we'd even gotten to know each other. All I had to do was recall the baby shower, and I was reminded that this was acting. It was for a show. The only time I'd seen her "off" was right before we'd slept together, when she'd failed to conceal her jealousy behind Tanisha's pop-up. The uncertainty I'd seen in her eyes showed me that she wasn't as confident as she tried to appear, and to that, I could relate.

The smile slowly melted away as she stared at me. Unable

to read her expression, I was once again annoyed with my-self. *Why did I say that?* We were having a good time and I ruined it with my overactive brain. Finally, Kris shook her head softly. Then she lifted our joined hands and pressed her lips against the soft skin of my inner wrist. An imperceptible shiver ran through me. I prayed she didn't notice.

"Nah," she corrected when we met eyes again. "I'm actually terrible at pretending."

My breath caught in my throat when I realized what she was saying. Or rather...what it *sounded* like she was saying. *When was the last time I'd cleaned my ears?* I needed to dust off my beeswax candles as soon as I got home. I was going off on a tangent. Shaking my head to clear away my errant thoughts, I craned my neck to face her.

"Kris—"

"I was the first person in the history of my school to fail drama," she stated, interrupting me without shame. "Ask Rhea. The first and only kid to be kicked out of theater class."

Laughter bubbled up out of me. "You're silly, you know that?"

Grinning, she leaned over and dropped a quick kiss on my neck. "You love me though," she murmured in a voice so low that I might not have heard it if it hadn't been directly in my ear. Her voice hitched just a tad on the *l*-word, the slight warble making it sound like a question. Despite implying that it was an indisputable fact, she truly wasn't sure, and *God Almighty* the hope in her words was so endearing that my heart ached.

"Yeah," I sighed, pure contentment making my words sound light and breathy even to my own ears, "I do."

Kris froze. Completely stopped breathing until the rhythmic thumping of her heart against my shoulder was the only indication that she was still alive. Painstakingly slowly, she lifted her head. My own heart was pounding out a West African drumbeat in my chest as I stared at the door across the room, too chickenshit to face her for fear of her expression being anything other than something that reflected the words I'd inadvertently admitted. I really, honestly, and truly hadn't meant to say that.

Slender fingers grasped my chin as Kris forced my attention on her.

"Say that shit with your chest, baby."

I licked my lips. "I— Isn't it— It's not too soon?"

"We're getting married in less than two weeks."

Well, when she put it like that…

"Okay, well…I know it's only been a few weeks and this is supposed to be fa—"

Immediately, her brow furrowed. "Uhn-uh," she interrupted fiercely, "I don't want a preface. No disclaimers. Tell me straight-up what the deal is, and stand in that shit if you mean it."

Sucking in a breath, I twisted in my seat until we were face-to-face. "Kris Zavala, I love you. Painfully. And, also I am *in* love with you."

One of those panty-melting slow grins came across her face and her eyes crinkled into slits. She cupped my cheek and brushed a thumb over my bottom lip before sliding her hand to the back of my neck and pulling my face toward hers. She nibbled on the spot that she'd caressed, and then soothed the sting with a flick of her tongue. My lungs protested, but I was ready to risk it all because who needed oxygen when the woman that you accidentally admitted you loved—probably more than you should considering the short amount of time you've known each other, even though you said you wouldn't acknowledge the *l*-word—was in your arms making love to your mouth?

"Yo también te amo."

The words ghosted over my lips, and I wanted to stick out my tongue to catch them as if they were tiny flakes of snow falling from the sky. Assuming they meant what I thought they meant. Pulling back a few centimeters, I gulped in a lungful of air as I rested my forehead against hers.

"Amo is from amar right? The verb, I mean." I knew what amar was and what it conjugated to, but it was better to know for sure than to assume. And I also wanted to hear her say it again in another language.

Chuckling, Kris nodded, making my head move as well. "Yes, baby."

A smile started at the corners of my mouth and bloomed until my cheeks had puffed and rose upward.

"Okay," I whispered. "But just to clarify, you should probably say it again in English…" I trailed off, waiting for her to just pick it up and tell me what I needed to hear.

"What happened to all of that Spanish that you knew?" she teased.

I shook my head. "I know un poco. What you said was advanced. The conjugations are at least three tiers above my skill level, so you should probably translate. For science."

"Oh, for science huh?" Leaning away from me, she smirked, one of those dark-brown eyebrows lifted in challenge.

I was terrible at playing coy and as impatient as a toddler sitting in front of a bowl of fruit snacks. "Or you could say again for me. So that I can hear it again and can know that I didn't imagine it."

Her smirk fell and brows knitted. She went from cupping the back of my neck to cradling my face between both of her hands, stepping closer until our knees knocked and feet tangled on the floor.

"Can you hear me?" she asked, her voice low but firmer than a whisper.

Her eyes were on mine and I was *gonegonegone* in those deep pools of dark liquid. There was a seriousness there. It was insistent and determined and I think she meant for me to understand her clearly but I was so, *so* gone, having fallen into her eyes and floating on a cloud of my own unquantifiable emotions. The whispering from my own mind followed me there, telling me that it was too soon, that it was too thin, that it was not enough. I could have sunk under the whispering for an eternity and a day, trying to find the right words to make it go away.

But she was waiting for me to respond, so I nodded.

"I. Love. You."

I'd watched her lips form each word, so I knew that was what she said, but I still felt a moment of confusion when nothing else came after that. That was it? Three words and the proper amount of punctuation? The whispering rolled around in my mind.

Too soon.

Too thin.

Not enough.

I'd asked her to repeat herself, so why did I suddenly feel so disappointed? Had I been expecting some grand declaration complete with a laundry list of reasons why? *Yes!* Foolishly, I had. We hadn't known each other long enough for the hair on my legs to grow back after shaving them for the cast party, yet I found a way to be disappointed that all Kris had said was that she loved me. If it was too soon to think of reasons why, wouldn't it also be too soon to feel that way at all? Was she only saying this because she was determined to "find love"? Or was it because we were being filmed? Because it gave great TV? Was this calculated? Had I fallen right into her plan? Was any of it real?

I'd gone from feeling euphoric to questioning my own feelings and ruining my mood. Sighing, I let my eyes flutter closed, hoping that Kris would believe that I was simply content instead of on the verge of fighting back tears. I felt like I was once again in that space of wanting someone to choose me and being left in the cold. The sound of wheels rolling on the unfinished floor alerted me that someone had entered the room. Instead of releasing me, Kris touched her lips to mine in the gentlest of kisses that was so tender that I did cry.

It felt so real, so sweet, and so…loving that I was unable to hold back my liquid emotions. A tear slipped from the corner of each eye and rolled slowly down my cheeks. I expected her make a noise in the back of her throat and wipe them away with her thumb or press a tissue to my face, but she once again bowled me over with a double combo of unexpected tenderness and caring that seemed like it couldn't be fake.

"Baby," she murmured low in her throat, before literally kissing away my tears, her lips catching the droplets before they dove off of the rounded cliff of my chin. Then she kissed up the trails they'd left behind until she reached my eyes where she left the most delicate, featherlight kiss on each of my eyelids.

I stood as still as I could manage, white-knuckling the table behind me, my bottom lip trembling as I choked back a sob. *You didn't kiss away the tears of someone you didn't love, right?*

"You two are so stinkin' adorable," Jae gushed. "I love working with clients who are so obviously in love with one another."

"Thank you." Kris bowed her head graciously.

That assessment made me crack my eyelids and my gaze flew from Kris to Jae. *What exactly did she see?* Kris had scooted back into her chair, but her eyes were on me. She wasn't smiling, but not frowning either. She was just...staring at me. I met her gaze wondering what *she* saw when she looked at me, but I could only maintain direct eye contact with her for a few moments before a dull throbbing began to make itself known between my thighs. That's what her attention did to me. Made me wet at the drop of a hat. I shifted in my seat and gave Jae my attention.

Well, part of my attention.

In my peripheral, I saw Kris's nostrils flare, her eyes narrow, and then she scooted her chair right up next to mine. She dropped her left hand onto my right thigh, just below the hem of my dress, sliding it into the crevice between both. With her thumb, she began to draw circles over the fabric of my tights. I gave her a sharp glance, but she faced Jae, nodding at the right moments as if she was truly listening intently about bulbs and blooms. As if her hand on me wasn't purposely stoking a fire inches away from where her fingers rested.

I worked at controlling my breathing and kept my eyes on Jae. She was telling us about arches when I realized something.

"Do you happen to know where our parents went?" I asked, interrupting her midsentence. They'd been gone for over twenty minutes and I was suddenly ready to leave as soon as possible.

Jae looked up from the green foam blocks in her hands and blinked in surprise.

"Oh!" she exclaimed, blinking in surprise. "I showed them some portfolios of past work and I guess they got caught up. I'll go get them."

She placed the items on the table and left out of the room, once again leaving me and Kris alone. Standing, I picked up one of the boutonnieres from the center of the table to distract myself from the rumblings in my mind and between my legs.

"Why painfully?"

The question had come out of nowhere, aggressively breaking into my thoughts. I looked up from the flowers in my hand to find Kris's eyes on me.

"What do you mean?" I knew exactly what she meant. Simply put, I was not built for confrontation.

"You said that you loved me. Painfully. Why painfully?"

Dang. I hadn't thought I'd have to explain that part.

"Um…" I placed the tiny arrangement on the tabletop and picked up an arrangement of lilies, stalling for who knows what.

Kris saw right through me, walking the few steps toward me and pulling the arrangement out of my hand. She turned, leaning against the table as she maneuvered me to stand between her legs. With her hands on my waist, she grabbed my gaze and held it with her own.

"Damn," she chuckled. "Is it that bad?"

Cringing, I shook my head even though the answer was a resounding yes.

"What? No! Of course not!"

Her eyes widened and the teasing smile disappeared. "Aw shit."

"Oh gosh," I muttered. I was fucking it up by being ridiculous. Blowing out a fortifying breath through my nose, I squared my shoulders. "Loving you is a little painful, Kris. Mostly because I don't know what to do with these emotions, but also because it feels too big for its britches."

The side of her mouth tilted up. I quickly averted my eyes. Her entire everything was distracting in the most pleasurable way. No wonder all of those people online stalked her pages for the next post.

"There's an egg timer on us and it's not stopping for nothing and nobody. Trying not to think about what I'm supposed to do with all of these…feelings when the show is over hurts. And trying to figure out what's next hurts even worse. Falling for you seemed like the easiest thing I've ever done, but sustaining it is a beast I can't defeat." The words all fell out of my mouth in a tumble, with me not daring to even glance at her in my peripheral until I'd said them all. It was my truth, and though I hoped nothing I'd said hurt her, it was all I had to give right then.

"Wow," she breathed, the awe in her tone shocking me enough to swing my head back toward her. Her eyes were wide and amazed. Or were they amazing?

They were both.

I was so freaking gone.

"Wow what?" I questioned.

"I don't know. I guess I didn't expect all of…that."

Instantly, I started to step back, wanting to put some distance between us before she shredded me with her dismissal of my feelings.

"Yo, chill out," she admonished, gripping the skirt of my dress and using it to pull me back into the bubble she'd created for us. "Don't jump mad before I have a chance to finish what I'm saying."

To that, all I had was silence. I did what I was good at and worried on my bottom lip to keep from saying anything else. Her thumb was at my mouth within seconds, massaging the flesh until I released it.

"Now," she began, seemingly satisfied that I wasn't going to bite my lip again, "that was deeper than I anticipated, and I guess I have myself to blame for that. I could tell you were a thinker when I met you, so it tracks that you would go full deep-end the moment that things got serious between us. Look—" she released my waist and grabbed my hands, linking our fingers as she held them between us "—you don't have to go into this being pessimistic. Yeah, we both knew how long the show was going to be, but never did we say this was a show-only situation. I know that isn't what I want. What about you?" Her brows rose as she waited for a response. I shook my head.

"Good. So how about we just dead that in the water right now? Let's go ahead and make it plain that the end of *Instant I Do* doesn't have any bearing on what D'Vaughn and Kris have going on. We're doing this with or without the show. Is that cool with you?"

I nodded again because it was almost exactly what I wanted to hear. Almost. So, *so* close.

She smiled. It was big and indulgent and put all her teeth on display. That hurt too.

"Good," she said again, this time punctuating the word with a slow, meaningful kiss to my lips. She doled those things out like candy on Halloween and I *lived* for it. I couldn't get enough and my hunger for them stung a little. She pulled back from the kiss and landed several pecks along my neck. "I'm going to run to the restroom. When I get back, I'll call Mami to see where she and your mother disappeared to, and then we can wrap this up." Reaching up, she brushed a thumb under my eye. "You coming home with me tonight?"

I nodded, unable to find a few words that wouldn't tug the stopper on more of my "deep-end" observations.

"Okay. Be right back." With a pat to my hip, she straightened and waited for me to step back so that she could exit the room.

As soon as she was gone, I released the shuddering breath I'd been holding. I wanted to cuss. That conversation hadn't eased my fears at all. All it did was make me take notice of the way there was never anything concrete in the words Kris spoke. She had a way of managing to skirt the issue while making it seem resolved that terrified me.

What was the *"this"* that she'd referenced and how would we continue doing it when *Instant I Do* wrapped in less than two weeks? Were we supposed to carry on the farce of our engagement until eternity? Did we announce that we'd called off the engagement but decided to stay together? They seemed like straightforward and easy enough questions, but to ask them was to risk everything. If I put voice to the worries in my head—and heart—and Kris became offended or angry, it could affect how everyone saw our relationship, bringing this house of cards tumbling to the ground just before we made it to the judges' table. On top of everything, it would ruin the little time I had left with her.

No matter how much I wanted a clear answer from her about what we planned to do when the *for-public-consumption* side of this ended, I had to hold my tongue until Kevin either placed a check in my hands or tapped me on the shoulder and asked me to clock out. Even if the money was never the goal, I'd come too far to let a few hurt feelings keep me from the prize.

Chapter Thirteen

Kris

Word From the Wise

I stepped out into the hall, heading left as Jae had instructed when I'd first arrived. When I turned the corner that would lead me to the bathrooms, I spotted Kevin and Joe having a conversation at the end of the hall. It had been a few days since I'd seen Joe, and I started to call out to them, but then Kevin put his hand on Joe's waist and I realized that they were standing far closer than was probably necessary for discussing work.

It hit me that their positioning was rather intimate. Kevin stood in front of Joe, who was leaning back against the wall. Although Joe's arms were crossed in front of him, he didn't seem closed off. He seemed to be listening, his head slightly bowed as he nodded every few seconds. After a moment, Kevin stepped in closer, used a finger to nudge Joe's chin up, and leaned down to kiss the older man. My eyes widened at the scene, but when Joe uncrossed his arms and reached around to palm Kevin's ass, I quickly looked away, not wanting to be caught creeping on a clearly private moment.

The sound of a throat clearing made me look up. Joe was coming down the hall, a satisfied smile on his face. He shot me a wink and dropped a hand on my shoulder as he passed me.

"Hey, Joe. Missed you these last couple of days."

His smile grew, making his deep-set, dark brown eyes crinkle. "I had to check on the other couples and their teams. Can't be out here showing favoritism like Kev."

I grinned, looking down the hall at Kevin, who was now leaning his shoulder against the wall, his legs crossed at the ankle as he watched us. "Oh? Are we getting special treatment or something?"

Joe glanced back at Kevin, and the tender look that came across his face as he took in the other man hit me right in the feels. When he turned back to me, his smile had softened a little. He nodded.

"Or something." He cleared his throat. "I'll be seeing you later, Kris."

"Yessir."

The moment that he disappeared around the corner, I rushed over to Kevin.

"Let me find out you mackin' on old man Joe."

Kevin glared, but it was devoid of heat, and dripping with amusement. "Hey, watch your mouth! Joe is *not* old. He's only fifty. That's barely seasoned."

Trying—and failing—to hold back my giggles, I nodded. "Oh, my bad. So, you're saying he's just a teaspoon of adobo instead of a quarter cup?"

He squinted at me. "No matter how much adobo you use, you're winning."

Lifting my shoulders, I tilted my head to the side and nodded. "I won't argue with you there. But, uh… Can I ask you a question?"

He quirked a brow. "Another question, you mean?"

I grinned. "Yeah, man. I'm curious."

"Ah, hell," he murmured, straightening against the wall. "Let's hear it."

"Bet. You look like you're only a couple of years older than us, and Joe looks closer to my parents' age. So…is he your sugar daddy or nah?"

His mouth spread into a toothy grin as he barked out a laugh. "Ooh! Thank you, dearheart! That's cute," he admitted with a chuckle, "but Joe isn't my sugar daddy; he's my husband. We've been together for almost twenty years and married for ten."

I gasped as my eyes tried to pop out of their sockets. "Did you say twenty years? As in veinte años? You're a motherfucking goddamn lie!" I swung my head from left to right, desperately needing to search for my flabber because, without a doubt, it was trembling in a corner somewhere, gasted out of its mind. There was no damn way that they'd been together for more than two thirds of my life.

Eyes sparkling, Kevin chuckled. He was having a ball shocking the shit out of me.

"I'm forty-six."

"Forty-six?!"

"Joe and I met at Splash in the nineties."

"Splash?!" I exclaimed dramatically. *"The nineties?!* Was I even *alive?"*

He narrowed his eyes. "You know what? I really don't like you right now."

Wiping under my eye, I tried to catch my breath. "It doesn't matter. Joe already admitted that I'm your favorite."

"D'Vaughn is my favorite," he corrected swiftly before pointing at me. "You're just the stud she ended up with."

My mouth fell open and I started wheezing, tears coming to my eyes as I laughed harder than ever. "Damn, Kevin! That almost hurt my feelings."

"Now, honey," he murmured in a voice that was condescension dipped in Texas wildflower honey, both of his hands on his hips as he pursed his lips. "Social media influencers don't have *feelings*. You have *content* and *algorithms*. Followers and brand endorsements."

Fuck! He was roasting the shit out of me and I was laughing so hard that I couldn't even take in a breath long enough to defend myself.

"You're judging me so hard right now. I'm starting to get offended."

"Au contraire, dearheart. I'm not judging you any more than you were judging me for being born in the seventies."

"I was definitely judging," I mumbled under my breath. Louder, I added, "Don't act like you aren't on social media also. Everyone is."

He nodded. "Of course. This is the technology age, after all. The difference is that I care more about the life I've created off camera, than the number of followers I have. They're just bystanders that I share bits and pieces of my life with. They don't know me—hell, most of them wouldn't even be able to pick my face out of a lineup—they just see the blue check and assume I must be someone important. You, on the other hand, are curating a life for the purpose of entertaining people on the other side of the screen. This isn't a judgment of your career, because I understand that people are going to do whatever they can to make money."

Nodding, I remained silent as I worked to not feel attacked by his accurate assessment of what I did on social media. My seemingly instant rise to social media fame might not have started off that way, but it was now exactly as he had observed. Every single post that I made was planned, drafted, and shot with the intention of getting a response from my some-odd two hundred and fifty thousand followers. Even the more casual—and especially the "impromptu"—posts.

"Even with the awards and accolades I received for producing shows like these," Kevin continued, waving a hand in the air, "I can't deny that sometimes, the shows with my name on them do more harm than good. In a room back there, you have a beautiful soul who is quickly realizing that she's in love with you. I hope you are more concerned with making sure that she doesn't regret those feelings when she sees the person you are on social media, because we both know that the Kris Zavala online isn't the same woman that's standing in front of me right now."

My head bobbed again, making me feel like one of those dolls with springs for a neck mounted on a dashboard, but there was nothing for me to say, and thankfully, Kevin knew that. Wisely realizing that I was likely to spend the next few moments absorbing his words, he squeezed my shoulder.

"Take a minute if you need to," he said, reading my mind completely. "I'll let Jae know I held you up and that you'll be back soon." Then he exited the hall, leaving me with so much more to think about than I'd expected when I'd left D'Vaughn.

Suddenly, I understood what Joe had meant by Kevin showing favoritism. The talk we'd just had, everything beyond the banter and teasing, felt out of place on a show like this. With *Instant I Do* essentially being a race to the finish, this wasn't a place for mentors or life advice. Anyone could rationalize that a show built around planning a wedding definitely, probably, maybe had romance at its core, and I had been one of those people when I initially auditioned. Now that I was in the trenches, I realized that was an illusion. The show was cut and edited to seem that way, but the weekly tasks put the focus on our loved ones and left us with scant moments to be alone and really get to know each other.

Kevin had given me a new perspective and a renewed sense of my original mission. It was no longer a broad sense of finding love, but making sure that D'Vaughn knew that the love I found with her wasn't something I was willing to go without. I had to make the next couple of weeks count.

Jitter Cam 10-Kris

What is there to say?

The flowers were beautiful. Mami did a great job with choosing. She knows all about this floral stuff. D'Vaughn and I had no problem letting her take the lead today and thankfully she heard our suggestions and we all were able to agree.

I was a little concerned in the beginning about having to have my family's input at every step, but this has been such a rewarding experience. They all have had my best interest at heart and that means so much to me. I love those people, man.

What do you mean, 'and'? *And* I love that they love D'Vaughn.

Come on, man. Don't look at me like that.

*And...*and...I love D'Vaughn too.

I just... I told her that I loved her, and she looked like she'd been hit by a truck. There haven't been many opportunities in my life to confess my feelings like that, but I know that the expression she wore isn't the response you hope to get. It was like she couldn't believe what she was hearing, and not in the *'OMG, that's so amazing!'* kind of way. Like damn, was it really so shocking?

Of course I really love her. Why would you ask me that? What do you mean *'You have to wonder'*? Wonder about what? I came into this ready for love, so why would that even be a question?

I'm just saying, if I'm open to it, it'll happen. Obviously, D'Vaughn was open to it as well...but for some reason she isn't happy that it actually happened. That's what has me confused.

Wait. Do you think she's questioning my feelings too? But why would she? I don't know. I have to talk to her. I don't like that look in her eye after I said I loved her too. I'll do whatever I have to do to get things straight between us.

I have work to do if I want this to last beyond the finale.

Week Five

D'Vaughn & Kris,

We're nearing the finish line. This week is all about the calm before the storm. You get to relax with a party for you and your loved ones. Make it a good one!

—Kevin

1. Conduct joint bachelor/bachelorette party

Chapter Fourteen

Kris

All the Single Ladies

We were expected to plan a bachelorette party in three days. Of all the things that we'd been tasked to do over the past six weeks, I shouldn't have been as surprised as I was when I read that on the postcard. I thought that getting a custom wedding gown made three weeks before the wedding was insane, and although this wasn't on that same level, it still felt impossible. How in the world were we expected to not only plan the party, but ensure that people would be able to make it? Most people needed several weeks to prepare for such an event. Folks had jobs. Full-time, overnight, weeks-at-a-time jobs, and yet somehow we were supposed to gather all of our family and friends to a venue with three days' notice. Oh, and the icing on the cake was that the party had to take place on a Wednesday. Whoever heard of a bachelor or bachelorette party taking place in the middle of the week?! It was complete madness, but it definitely tracked with everything else we'd had assigned to us over the past few weeks.

"This might be the easiest thing that we've had all month," D'Vaughn said, a little excitement and surprise in her voice as she read the printed card. I gave her a disbelieving look.

"Easy?! How in the world is *this* easy?" I waved my card in the air.

"Uh, because all we have to do is find a club or a lounge and rent it out for a few hours. Shoot, we could even go to a strip club and put together a few sections. It's extremely easy."

I lifted my eyebrows in surprise. "Wait. Did you just say a strip club?"

D'Vaughn surprised me every single day. Of all the things I might've expected her to say, suggesting a strip club was not one of them. But now that she'd said it, it made a lot of sense. We didn't have to do anything special for our joint bachelorette party; all we needed was a venue. And since it was *supposed* to be a party, a club would be a perfect place. Strip clubs were normal for the bachelor side of things, so I got why she would suggest that, but is that what she really wanted?

"Do you seriously want to bring your mother to a strip club?"

From the look she gave me, you would've thought that I had snakes growing out of my head. "My mama is *not* invited to my bachelorette party! Are you inviting your parents? Seriously?!"

I lifted my eyes to the ceiling as I thought hard on what we were talking about. When it hit me, I busted out laughing. "I'm tripping. You're absolutely right. My parents are *not* going to be there, so it can be at wherever or whatever location we choose. If you want the strip club, we can do the strip club."

Tossing the card onto the table in front of us, D'Vaughn climbed into my lap, straddling my thighs as she settled on top of me and wrapped her arms around my neck.

"I don't really care where we have this thing," she murmured as she leaned down and began pressing soft kisses along my jawline and down my neck. "My only concern is getting to the good part."

Gripping her back, I slid my hands down her body until I reached her ass. "And what's the good part?"

"The slightly tipsy sex that we have once we get back home. After we've been flirting, and touching, and getting turned on by women shaking their ass all in our faces and grinding in our laps."

It was in the way she casually said "home" that brought a thump to my chest. For the past week, D'Vaughn had been spending nights at my house, sleeping in bed beside me, showering with me in the morning, and eating breakfast along with me and Rhea. It was becoming all too familiar seeing her in my space. And I was steadily wanting it to be *our* space. I didn't want to point out what she'd said because I didn't want her to correct it, so I simply patted her cheeks and nodded.

"Yeah, that does sound like the good part."

Finally her lips made their way towards mine. She ground down against me at the same time that she sucked my tongue into her mouth in that way she always did, just before her hands found their way inside of my pants.

"Do we have time for a little of the good part before you have to be to work?" I whispered, leaning back just a little so that I could gauge where this was going. Her sexy grin was all the answer that I needed. I slid my hands underneath the T-shirt that she'd slept in and prayed that I didn't end up late for work.

Three nights later, we got all dressed up and piled into a limousine to take us to the VR Club and Lounge downtown. We'd opted for a lounge instead of a strip club because it was such short notice, and on humpday of all days. We didn't want to cart a couple dozen people to watch talented women dance if they weren't financially able to make it worthwhile, and since no one got paid in the middle of the week, we scratched that idea.

I'd never heard of a bachelor or bachelorette party taking place on Wednesday, but we'd signed a contract and therefore had to do whatever we'd been tasked, whether it made sense or not. There were a few grumbles when we started telling people about the party, but almost everyone we invited somehow made a way to be there.

The club's event planner had done an amazing job. When we walked into the building there was a large sign with mine and D'Vaughn's names on it, letting patrons know where they could find us if they were there for our event. As D'Vaughn had predicted, we were able to rent out the top three private sections of the club for our entire party. There was more than enough space for all of our guests to chill and have a good time, and the DJ was playing the right kind of music for people to slide down to the dance floor and enjoy themselves.

D'Vaughn and I were grooving in the middle of the dance floor when I felt a tap on my shoulder.

"Hey, Kris!"

The voice gave me pause and I turned slowly, hoping I wasn't about to see who I thought I was about to see. When my eyes connected with the woman I'd last been involved with before I auditioned for the show, my heart plummeted although I smiled easily.

"Mara, hey. What are you doing here, girl?"

I might have gotten too comfortable over the last couple of weeks, because setting eyes on my ex had truly surprised me. After she initially reached out to me on social media, we burned hot and heavy for a few months before sizzling out. Mara had always been no-nonsense from the very beginning; when she wanted me, she didn't hesitate to let me know, and when she was done with me, she made that clear as well. Her presence was undoubtedly the work of the show, and while I couldn't imagine that she'd be here under normal circumstances, there was no question in my mind that this appearance was solely for the sake of shining a spotlight on her brand. I'd taught her well.

Mara surged forward, rubbing her hands up and down my back as she hugged me tightly. When she released me, I stepped back and slid an arm around D'Vaughn's waist. Mara's bright eyes tracked the movement and she quirked an eyebrow at me.

"Well, I had to hear through the grapevine that you were getting married. I'm sure you can imagine my surprise since we were just together six months ago."

"We weren't together anymore. As a matter of fact, you broke things off with me once you started your own page and gained about ten thousand of my followers, so nah, I can't imagine why you'd be surprised."

Mara's smile tightened. "You didn't tell me you wanted something serious when I first slid into your messages! I said I wanted to fuck and you said you were with it. Nothing more. So what is all of this animosity about?"

D'Vaughn's brows shot up. "Oh, so it really does go down in the DMs." I shot her a startled glance but her amused expression was aimed at Mara.

Mara giggled. "Oh, girl you have no idea. Apparently there are quite a few of us who've been able to hit that after just a few messages exchanged. Don't think you're getting something exclusive. Kris is for the streets."

Clucking my tongue, I shook my head. "You sound real bitter right now, Mara. It's not a good look."

She sneered at me, before turning a sympathetic smile toward D'Vaughn.

"Good luck, girl."

With that she slunk away, disappearing in the crowd and leaving me to clean up the mess she'd made. I licked my lips as I turned to D'Vaughn and slipped my arms around her waist.

"About that—"

D'Vaughn shook her head. "No need to explain. I think I got the gist of it."

I eyed her, wondering if her amicable tone was authentic or a front.

"Are you sure? Because I can tell you exactly—"

She interrupted me with a kiss. "I'm sure. And I'm not mad, if that's what you're worried about."

I was less worried about her anger, and more concerned about what she thought of me after hearing that information. She'd already known that I'd dated women I'd met through my page in the past, but Mara tried to make it sound like I was fucking anyone who slid through, which wasn't too far from D'Vaughn's earlier thoughts in regard to why I'd come on the show. That was far from the truth, and while I believed D'Vaughn and I had moved past that—that she understood that she alone was who I wanted—I couldn't deny that this felt like a setback. The urge to defend myself was strong, but if D'Vaughn said she wasn't bothered by it then I needed to trust her and let it go.

"Okay," I acquiesced, tightening my arms around her and taking another kiss.

We got back to dancing and I let the moment fall to the back of my mind. The only thing I was concerned about was enjoying the party and making it to the "home" portion of the night. Jada Michael's "Freak" came on, and I was in the process of grinding on D'Vaughn when I felt another tap on my shoulder. I stiffened, praying it wasn't another of my exes as I turned around. The moment that I noticed Kevin standing behind me, I started to frown. I already knew what time it was, but I hated to leave when I'd just managed to get us back to having a good time. Kevin had the absolute worst timing.

"Kris, can I get you for a moment?"

Groaning, I ran a hand down my face. "You asked that like I even have a choice, man."

Both he and D'Vaughn laughed, but I wasn't feeling particularly amused. I didn't want leave D'Vaughn yet. She was smiling like everything was fine, but I sensed a change in her demeanor.

"You'll be right back, I promise."

"Yeah, yeah," I mumbled. I planted a quick kiss on D'Vaughn's lips before following him across the dance floor and through a door that I hadn't noticed before. It was painted the same color as the walls and blended almost seamlessly.

"Right through here, Kris."

I followed Kevin into the empty room and took a seat in the sole chair that was in the center of the room. After a few weeks of this, I just about knew the drill by now, but in addition to the usual setup of camera facing the interview chair, there was a twenty-inch television sitting on a stand next to the camera.

"What's this?" I questioned, shooting Kevin a look as he dropped down into the chair behind the camera.

"You're going to watch a quick video before our final Jitter Cam."

"Aight, cool."

Kevin fiddled with a few buttons on the camera before the screen of the television lit up and an image of D'Vaughn appeared. That caused me to straighten in my seat and pay more attention. The video started and the voice I now looked forward to hearing every day poured from the television's speakers.

"I'm D'Vaughn Miller. I'm thirty years old, five feet five inches, and two hundred and fifty-five pounds. I live in Houston but I was born and raised in Mo City where the girls are all pretty. I'm single—have been single for a while, actually—and I'm a lesbian."

I realized then what I was looking at. It was D'Vaughn's audition tape! Sitting forward, I balanced one elbow on my knees and propped my chin on my fist.

"I think I'd be a great contestant for Instant I Do *because y'all need to diversify your contestants. The show is amazing, but every year y'all have these slim, racially ambiguous, aggressively heterosexual girls and I promise it's okay to switch things up. Guess what? The gays can marry legally, now. Put us in, Coach!"*

I laughed at how she clapped with each word of her last sentence. She was so animated in her audition video and I loved it. In the beginning, D'Vaughn came off more quiet and reserved, and I remember thinking that she was too shy for us to pull this thing off, but the more I got to know her, I realized that wasn't it. Shy didn't even belong in D'Vaughn's vocabulary. I learned that she waited until she felt someone out before deciding they were worthy of her full personality.

"I'm ranting, sorry not sorry, but obviously I feel strongly about this. Mostly because going on the show would push me to come out to my family. Yep, that was me heaving a large, ancestral sigh. As close as my family is and as much as I love them, they have no idea I'm a lesbian."

Her smile fell and she looked off camera, twisting her lips to the side. I felt a pang in my chest at her expression. Yeah, I'd witnessed how difficult that moment was for her, but seeing it on her face however long before she was able to change that narrative was hard. I wanted to reach through the screen and pull her into a hug. I wanted to kiss her temple and tell her how I'd support her through that moment.

"Anyways, I'm very, very single, and while it's incredibly likely that's because I would never introduce my girlfriends to my mama, I also have this fear that I'm...I don't know. Like, maybe there's something about me that's not worth sticking it out for? I don't know why I phrased that as a question. My best friend just stepped out of the

room because whenever I say this she always starts cussin'. Look, I've never asked anyone to jump in the closet with me. All I've ever asked of anyone is that they respect my decision. It's always fine at first but then they start getting restless a few months in, and I just wonder if it's deeper than just wanting my family to know we're sleeping together.

"So anyway, this is only supposed to be half an hour long and I'm already over time, so I'm gonna wrap it up. Put me on your show so that I can serve some beautiful, Black, lesbian hotness, and also so that you can help me come out to my family!"

She blew a kiss at the camera and then the video ended. Immediately, I shifted my gaze to Kevin, who was watching me with an unreadable expression on his face.

"What was watching that supposed to do?"

Blinking slowly, he just stared at me.

I huffed a laugh and shook my head. "You gotta be the worst e.p. on the planet, bruh."

"Worked with many of us, have you, dearheart?"

"That's not the point."

He shrugged. "For someone who has said—multiple times, mind you—that they've seen the show before, you sure do ask a lot of questions that could be answered by just…watching the show."

Groaning, I dragged my hands down my face, stretching my legs out in front of me as I slunk down in the chair. "You're worse than my brother."

Canting his head, he eyed me. "Which one?"

Lifting my head, I glared at him. "Raymond."

Throwing his head back, he let off a bark of laughter. "That's a damn lie and you know it!"

His laughter was contagious and I started cracking up. "Your ass hasn't been around long enough to know that. You trippin'!" He was right, but I didn't like how confidently he'd said it.

"And yet, somehow, I know it. Funny how that works."

"Yo, kill all that and answer my question."

He rolled his eyes toward the ceiling and shook his head disappointedly before facing me once more. "It's just to remind you of her motivation."

Frowning, I chewed my bottom lip for a second as I contemplated that. "Okay, but how does that—"

"That's enough questions for the night. You can go now."

"Wow, Kev? That's how you do your boy? Just put me out midsentence? That's rude as fuck."

"Trust me; it's a lot nicer than what I do to my actual brother. Now kindly get the fuck out so I can continue to do my job. Don't you have a fiancée out there waiting for you?" He gave me a pointed look and all I could do was laugh. He was such a fucking smartass.

"You're right. My baby prolly watchin' the door right now."

Surprisingly, he didn't respond as he stood to his feet and led me outside of the room, back into the main area of the club where the dance floor was steadily filling with patrons. I had no idea that the club went up on a Wednesday like this. I was impressed. I glanced around the room but honestly, I doubted that D'Vaughn was looking for me. She hadn't said anything, but I just knew that she was pissed about the encounter with Mara. There was no way she couldn't be. I never would have invited a woman I used to fuck with to my bachelor party, and had no idea how they'd even heard about it, which meant that the network likely had something to do with it. Every time I thought things were going well, they threw a wrench in the machine to try and fuck things up. Clearly, they didn't want to come off of that $200,000 D'Vaughn and I were pretty much guaranteed to win at this point, at least not without a fight.

Stepping onto the dance floor, Kevin and I parted ways as he likely headed to wherever Joe was holed up so that he could continue watching the party through the cameras that dotted the room. As soon as I reached the spot where I'd left D'Vaughn, I heard familiar drumbeats followed by shouts of excitement around the room. I didn't even have to look around to know that there was a surge of people rushing onto the dance floor to do the Wobble. With a smile on my face, I swept my gaze over the room, searching for the one woman who I hadn't been able to stop thinking about since I first laid eyes on her almost six weeks ago. My heart crashed against my chest when I found her.

She stood at the bar with her back to the room, her asymmetrical dress showing off a lovely expanse of the smooth, brown skin of her legs. Her head was tossed back as she laughed, and she held a drink in her hand, all of which would have been fine if Tanisha hadn't been standing too close to her, speaking directly into her ear. My jaw was already clenched before I started to make my way over there. As far as I knew, D'Vaughn had seen neither head nor tail of the other woman since that day at the bridal shop, but seeing her now brought all those possessive feelings, that may or not have been dipped in green, rushing to the surface. I was halfway to them when Rhea grabbed my arm and pulled me off of the dance floor and to the side of the room.

"Cálmate, bro."

Blinking, I frowned at her. "What are you talking about?"

"I'm talking about you breathing fire with rage in your eyes. You look like you're about to go tear some shit up, and since it's nothing but ladies up in here, that ain't a good look."

Heeding her wisdom, I took a minute to relax my jaw and roll my shoulders back to release the tension in them. Glancing back at the bar, I felt my blood pressure spike again as Tanisha touched D'Vaughn's hair.

"This chick is taunting me. Look at her!"

Rhea followed my glare, but she didn't react the way I expected. She cringed and shrugged, tilting her head to the side as she observed the scene. When she turned back to face me, her expression wasn't the least bit comforting.

"I see two women having a conversation. ¿Cuál es el problema?"

"The problem is that one of those women wants to fuck the one that belongs to me!"

"*Right.*" She smirked. "And does the one who you claim—" she made air quotes "—*belongs to you* know this?"

Licking my lips, I had to look away and get myself together. If I blew up, Rhea would go off, and the last thing I wanted was to be standing at my bachelor party, getting fussed at.

"You gon' answer me, or stand there huffin' and puffin' ready to blow down an innocent man's house?"

Rolling my eyes, I turned to her. "Man, D'Vaughn knows what it is. We're together."

Rhea nodded. "Right. Everyone in here knows that you're engaged, which is why the exchange over at the bar isn't that big of a deal. It's pretty tame. The chick isn't even touching D'Vaughn."

"But she wants to!" I insisted.

"Why does that matter?"

"Because she wants what's mine!"

Rhea canted her head and observed me. "Entonces. ¿Ella puede tomarlo? Tell me. Because, if she can, then maybe D'Vaughn isn't yours. And if she can't, then you need to calm the fuck down and figure out why you're so hype to begin with."

Rhea had unknowingly spoken my secret fear, and my chest heaved as I tried to get myself under control. Despite our declarations of love, and all of the time we were spending together, and the way my day brightened as soon as D'Vaughn's face popped into my mind, it still felt like a possibility that Tanisha could move in and take her from me. Not because I didn't think that D'Vaughn really loved me, but because it didn't seem like she fully believed that *I* truly loved *her.* And I didn't know how to change that.

After taking several deep breaths, I felt my heart rate slow down and I looked at my sister. She assessed me for a moment and then grinned, squeezing my shoulder.

"Good job. Now, politely go and get your woman. Don't start no shit."

Chuckling, I shook my head and did as she'd instructed. I offered an amenable "Hello," To Tanisha, who smirked at me, and grabbed D'Vaughn's hand to lead her back onto the dance floor. Burying my face in her neck, I wrapped my arms around her and squeezed her close, wishing I could impart all of my feelings inside of her so that she wouldn't have to question them ever again.

"I don't like her hanging around you," I mumbled against her skin. "She doesn't even try to hide her attraction to you and has no regard for our relationship at all."

D'Vaughn's laugh made me look up. I found her peering up at me, her eyes low as she grinned. "You don't even need to worry about Tanisha. I don't want her and she knows that."

Blinking a few times, I jerked my head back. "She does?"

"Yeah. I told her after the dress fitting. She was disappointed but said she'd get over it." She shrugged. "She doesn't really have a choice."

"Damn. So if you already shut her down, why has she still been getting too close for comfort?"

D'Vaughn giggled. "Because you don't have a dang poker face. You showed her how pissed you get when she stands a little too close to me, so she does it on purpose cause she's petty."

"That's fucked up."

Lifting a shoulder, D'Vaughn just smiled and slid her arms up and around my neck. "I thought it was funny."

"Mmhm. Is that why you let her get away with that?"

Raising her heavily lidded eyes to meet mine in the darkened room, D'Vaughn drew her bottom lip between her teeth. She knew exactly what it did to me when she pulled that move. Moving closer, I kissed the corner of her mouth, and then her cheek, before trailing my lips across her skin and leaving a lingering kiss below her ear.

"Why are you tryna start something when we're in public and I can't do anything about it?"

I squeezed her closer to me when she trembled in my arms.

"You started it," she accused, "when you got all green-eyed. You know how I feel about your possessive side."

Chuckling, I nodded. "So *that's* why you let her get too close for my comfort? You wanted to see me get agg? And for what? Now you wet for nothing."

Her lips parted and she blew out a soft breath, smiling as shook her head. "Not for nothing. Follow me."

Stepping back, she grabbed my hand and pulled me toward a dimly lit hallway in the corner of the room. I slipped into a sort of tunnel vision as I followed her wordlessly. There was something about the way that she instructed me to follow her that had my heart pounding. It was in her low tone; the twinkle of mischief in her eyes. The lights were low just like in the lounge, and the music was muted. Midway down the empty hall were four unisex restrooms with frosted-glass doors, two on each side, and at the end of the hallway was a low settee, bookended by large potted plants. D'Vaughn pushed me down and immediately lifted the front of her dress to her thighs as she climbed onto my lap. With her knees planted on either side of my hips, she bent down to take my mouth in a passionate kiss.

Reflexively, my hands found purchase on her body, landing first at her waist, before sliding down over her hips to settle at the back of her thighs. I was slowly inching my way up to her ass when she grabbed one of my hands and brought it between us, deftly maneuvering it underneath her dress. The moment that my fingers brushed the edge of her panties, my eyes popped open and I broke the kiss, leaning my head back to look at her.

"Babe, what are you doing?"

Her white teeth gleamed as she grinned down at me in that dim hallway that was lit only by electric sconces on the wall, which gave the dark walls an orange glow, and was empty except for the two of us tucked off at the end. From the look in her liquid brown eyes, I knew that I was about to give in to whatever she was requesting of me, exhibitionism be damned.

"Making good use of the wetness down there. What are *you* doing?"

With the hand that wasn't underneath her dress, I cupped the back of her neck and brought our faces together, stopping when our lips were just a hair's breadth away.

"Whatever you want me to," I murmured before sealing it with a kiss as I slid my fingers beneath the elastic at the juncture of her thighs and sought out the slickened lips that I had now become intimately familiar with. She gasped and clenched around me when my fingers breached her, but that only lasted for a second before she sank down, taking in my digits as she sucked my tongue into her mouth.

As I dug my thumb into her clit, D'Vaughn quickly undid my belt and unzipped my pants. We were completely exposed, and maybe I should have been trying to stop her, but our wedding was in a week, and I was still feeling a little possessive after seeing Tanisha, and the last thing I wanted to do was stop her when she was in the zone. I scooted down on the cushion a little more to make it easier for her hand to make its way into my pants just as that thought became realized and made me pause.

Less than seventy-two hours were left before the final week of *Instant I Do* began. The six weeks were just about over. I had no idea what was on the agenda for the upcoming week, but something told me it would be jam-packed with opportunities for us to fuck this thing up, which meant less time for us to be alone together like this. Once that perspective hit me in the gut, time seemed to speed up, with the seconds whizzing by at lightning speed and the minutes reduced to milliseconds.

The deliberate smacking of her fingers against my clit made my eyes snap open. Her brows were knitted as she frowned at me.

"Uh-uhn," she murmured. "I need you right here with me."

Grinning, I licked my lips. "I'm here, babe."

She shook her head. "No, you weren't. You disappeared somewhere in your head, and I need you to stay focused. We don't have a lot of time before someone eventually comes looking for us and I need you to make me cu—*ah, shoot!*"

Surging forward, I captured her bottom lip between my teeth as I started fucking her. She was right; we were on borrowed time and, by my calculations, barely had enough time for her to nut.

"Yeah," I whispered, releasing her lip and kissing along her jawline. "Ride my fingers."

She obeyed immediately, dropping her head onto my shoulder as she started rotating her hips back and forth.

"How does it feel?"

She mumbled something into my shirtsleeve, but between her muffled words and the increasingly rapid circles she was winding on my clit, I didn't hear her.

"Tell me," I commanded—no, pleaded—as I sank my fingers into her nape and pulled her head back so that I could see her eyes. Those dark brown pupils were slightly blown out and glossy. She was close.

"I said," she breathed, "'Good, baby, but I'd rather be riding your face.'"

The erotic image filtered through my lust-addled brain and pulled a groan from my lips. I was suddenly hit by the first stirrings of my orgasm and I bucked my hips.

"Soon, preciosa."

Her lids were low, and she began jerking above me. "You promise?" she asked on a whine.

"*Shit.* First night…of the honeymoon. I promise."

My legs stiffened in front of me and I clenched my teeth to keep from crying out as I climaxed. D'Vaughn leaned in and inhaled any sound I might have let escape with a kiss that did double duty to muffle her own cries as she came all over my hand. It was good, it was *so damn good*, but it wasn't enough. I wanted her naked and writhing beneath me. I wanted her ass on my face as I ate her for dinner. I wanted—

"Oh. My. God. Y'all are so nasty!"

Kiana's laughing voice immediately brought my gaze over D'Vaughn's shoulder. My baby sister stood between the restrooms with her arms crossed atop her massive belly.

"I know you ain't talking," I husked, deftly extracting my hand from between D'Vaughn's legs, grateful for the dress she wore and its ability to mask our actions. "You're the one who let a man turn you into a dessert."

For a second, she frowned, and it was like I could see her brain whirring to figure out what I was really saying, but then D'Vaughn dropped her head to my shoulder as she busted out laughing, and that's when I could see it click for Kiana. Her eyes widened to saucers and her mouth fell open.

"Ugh! You're disgusting and I hate that you're right!"

Laughing, she shook her head and entered one of the restrooms.

When the door shut, D'Vaughn quickly pulled my shirt down over my pants and pulled me to my feet.

"C'mon. Let's clean you up."

Jitter Cam 11-Kris

Y'all are really good at hitting me with something unexpected right when I'm the least prepared to handle it.

Watching that video felt like fate. Like…everything happens for a reason. Because I was supposed to be here and she was supposed to be paired with me. We were supposed to meet, and fall in love, and get married for real, and stunt on you boys for the next five years *at least*. Rhea clowned me, judged me, and then clowned me again for saying that I was going to find the love of my life on this show, but I knew I wasn't trippin'. It wasn't for nothing that I felt that way, even if I couldn't explain it. When I met D'Vaughn, a little of the puzzle became clear and it was obvious that she had a lot to do with that strong feeling that I had. Now that I've seen her audition video, can't nobody tell me that we aren't meant to be.

We have a week left and I know it's about to be some shit, but I feel like we got this in the bag. Get ready to crown us.

Week Six

D'Vaughn & Kris,

You've made it to the final week in the show. Congratulations! Although we're nearly at the end, things aren't easier from here. Now, more than ever, you have to ensure that your family and friends will support your journey to the altar. This week, all plans fall to them.

Good luck!
—Kevin

1. Complete rehearsal

2. Host rehearsal dinner

3. Meet at the altar

Chapter Fifteen

D'Vaughn

Remind Her

We were down to the wire.

I'd somehow managed to convince my family that I was marrying a stranger and they'd believed it so intensely that they'd assisted me in planning a wedding. The next seven days were crucial in maintaining the farce, and while I didn't see an issue coming from me and Kris, this week's tasks made my heart pound with worry. We were supposed to leave the arranging of the rehearsal and rehearsal dinner to our families and just show up at the appointed time. The logic was that they'd been present for every step and should have more than enough knowledge on how things should go. It was sound thinking, but still my stomach was tied in knots.

We'd been holding their hands at every step of this thing and now we were supposed to just let them run off without supervision? What if they'd only been pretending to get along this entire time? Or what if they didn't really believe this was real and were just holding their tongue to be polite? Or, what if someone revealed something about one of us that made the other family want to stop us from getting married? On top of that, Cinta was allowed to join in on the planning, but wasn't able to tell me anything at all. What was the point of having inside intel if they couldn't spill the beans? There were so many variables and I couldn't figure out what was worse.

No, that was a lie.

The worst of it is that Kris and I were under instructions not to see each other until the rehearsal. We weren't even supposed to call or text. So, not only was I suddenly outside of the loop, but I couldn't even be soothed by her kisses and reassurances. This of course meant that we were unable to discuss what happens after we make it to the altar. We'd come this far without either of us bringing it up, but it had been on my mind since the moment I realized things were becoming more intimate between us. This far in, with only days standing between us and The Big Day, would've been the perfect time to have that conversation—but apparently the *Instant I Do* producers had thought of everything, because now we wouldn't speak again until I met her at the altar. It was the pits.

I wasn't at all surprised to find Kevin at the door when Cinta and I were preparing to head to the rehearsal on Thursday. At that point, I'd been expecting him every day and was surprised when he didn't show up. He asked for a moment of my time and I agreed, following him to a Sprinter van that was parked in the lot of my apartment complex. Inside was a variation of the setup that I recognized, with a camera mounted onto an arm which was attached to a pole bolted to the floor of the van. There was a second arm that extended from the pole which held a monitor. After sitting in one of the two chairs that sat opposite the equipment, I looked to Kevin for further instructions. His face was kind as he regarded me.

"How are you feeling?"

"Right now? I'm nervous as all get-out."

He chuckled. "I can understand that, but if it makes you feel better, you have nothing to worry about."

My eyes widened as I stared at him. "Was that…are you saying—"

I stopped when he held a finger to his lips and winked. Sinking back against my seat, I sighed. Okay. If Kevin was saying that I had nothing to worry about when it came to the rehearsal, then I could work with that. He would know better than anyone.

"Okay," he began, "you're going to watch a quick video and then we'll do your final Jitter Cam."

Blowing out a breath, I laughed lightly. "Wow, is it really my last one?"

"Yep. Unless something happens and the whole thing falls through tomorrow."

My face fell and he quickly shook his head.

"It was a joke, dearheart. Breathe."

"That's not funny."

"It was, but you're feeling sensitive right now so I'll apologize."

Like clockwork, I began to worry my bottom lip. "So, about that video you want me to watch?"

"Ah, yes." He pressed a few buttons on the camera and the screen lit with a frozen image of Kris. I shot a quick look at Kevin but he nodded at the screen, urging me to pay attention. The video started and I quickly recognized the space around her as her living room.

"Whassup. I'm Kristin Zavala, but I go by Kris. I'm twenty-eight, five-ten, and—I'm not telling you my weight because I think it's fucked up that you ask for that. Why should how much I weigh have any bearing on whether or not I can convince mi gente, my people, that I'm getting married? It shouldn't, and if you don't pick me because of that then it is what it is."

As she shifted in her seat, leaning back and tossing an arm along the back of the couch, she licked her lips in that incredibly sexy way she always did. I felt a smile start to build and I sucked my bottom lip into my mouth to hold it back. Kevin's eyes—along with the camera—were on me and I didn't want to appear so dang lovesick if I could help it.

"I'm single and looking. My sister, Rhea, calls me a hopeful romantic because I'm always looking. I'm a lesbian; used to be a teddy bear stud but then I lost about fifty pounds and now I'm just a regular-ass butch. I documented my accidental weight loss on social media and gained a pretty big following from it. Now, I'm a content creator and influencer. I stick to weight-lifting and food, and it's working well for me. I also showcase my family a lot. There are a ton of us and we're pretty close, so it's impossible not to. I wouldn't call myself an IG hottie but others have, so do with that what you will.

"I want to be a contestant on Instant I Do *because I'm looking for a wife. Shit. That sounds wild when I say it out loud. Does anyone ever say that? Probably not, but it's the truth. This single shit is for the birds and I'm ready to start a family. I know what you're probably thinking, but I can assure you that the women in my DMs are not wifey material. I love it when women shoot their shot, and I respond to all of the messages in my inbox but that hasn't served me well so far. Man, I give these women a chance and every single one of them has left a sour taste in my mouth. Most of them hit me up and pretend that they want something real, but when it all boils down, they just want to be able to say they got with me. It doesn't even make any sense because I have way less than a million followers and I'm not even verified."*

She sighed, dragged both hands down her face, and licked her lips. I could hear the frustration in her voice and my heart went out to her. Everything she'd told me over the past few weeks stemmed from the emotions flitting across her face on the screen in front of me. It wasn't game curated especially so that I'd help her make it to the altar. She wasn't using me as a launching point for her business. She hadn't been lying that first night with everyone. *It was real.* What was building—had built—between us was real. My bottom lip trembled, and I quickly brushed away a few tears that were hell-bent on streaming down my face before I could stop them.

Kevin held a box of tissue out to me.

"Thank you," I murmured, a fresh wave of heat blowing over me at the reminder that I was crying on camera.

"Are you okay?" he asked, his voice comforting, caring.

Stuttered laughter fell from my lips. "I'm in love with someone I just met six weeks ago. I am definitely *not* okay."

He waved a hand in the air. "That's normal stuff. That's not what I'm talking about."

I gaped at him. "What's normal about falling in love with someone you just met? Please explain it to me. I would love to know."

"Love is unpredictable," he started. "It's messy; it does what it wants regardless of what you think people are supposed to do or how things are supposed to go. You can't control it. And because of all of those things, what you're experiencing right now is normal."

"Well since you know so much, why don't you tell me what to do?"

He chuckled, sitting back in his chair as he crossed one leg over the other. "Now, that I can't do."

Poking my bottom lip out, I pouted.

"Why not?"

I was whining and there wasn't a shred of shame in me. I'd been careening down this hill for a nice little minute with no brakes in sight, and if he was going to point out my impending crash, the least he could do was give me some airbags.

"Well, dearheart, if I tell you what to do, how will you know that it was the right move for *your* heart? What might seem like the obvious next step to me might not be the path that takes you to your rainbow."

"Rainbows are overrated," I murmured, causing him to release a bray of laughter.

"You hush your mouth!"

I giggled. "I didn't mean that."

"Oh, I know. Not with Ms. Kris Zavala waiting for you to arrive at your wedding rehearsal."

Just the mention of Kris's name brought a smile to my face. Ducking my head, I dropped my gaze to my lap.

"Has anyone ever said I do?" I held my breath as I waited for him to give me the answer I already knew. I hadn't watched the show, but I'd pored over the wiki pages. I knew how this thing had played out time and again.

"Not yet."

There was something in his tone that made me raise my gaze to meet his. "Not yet, huh?"

He winked. "There's no time like the present."

Sighing, I lifted my shoulders. "How foolish would I be to turn down one hundred thousand dollars for a woman who might tell me no?"

His smile was tender, almost paternal. "Not any more foolish than the one who takes the money because they're afraid to try for a yes."

A fresh round of tears fell from my eyes at the thought. Over the past few weeks, Kris and I had discussed a million and one things, but managed to avoid the one topic that would put my mind at ease about our future. We'd fallen into a sort of routine, becoming more comfortable settling into each other's lives, learning each other's schedules, but hadn't put one word toward what would happen once we made it to that altar.

I knew what I wanted.

I wanted Kris. I wanted her to choose me and love me

and make this tiny romance budding between us grow into a bountiful garden. The problem was communicating that to her without making her feel pressured to choose something she doesn't want. All of the "I love yous" in the world can't make someone want to be in a place not of their choosing.

"What are you so afraid of?" asked Kevin. Kris's audition video was paused, and his eyes were trained on me.

I shook my head. There was no way to verbalize my thoughts. It would sound bonkers on camera and they'd for sure edit it into the episode, and then I'd spend the rest of my life having to deal with people pitying me for being afraid that the girl I love doesn't love me enough to turn away six figures. Actually, it sounded bonkers even in my head.

"I'd rather not say."

"Okay, dearheart. I won't push."

Pursing my lips, I stared at him. One of the many things I'd discovered about myself over the past few weeks was that I really, really hated when people didn't push for information. First Cinta, and now Kevin! They forced me to share of my own volition and that robbed me of blaming them when I would then have to confront my problems after spilling the beans. I hated it.

"I'm scared that Kris will only say yes because she's tired of being alone. She's wanted someone long before she met me and now that I'm here, what if she thinks this is her only opportunity and she just…settles?"

I felt Kevin's penetrating stare for several long moments before he finally spoke.

"Has Kris ever made you feel like she was settling for you?"

"Well—"

He shook his head. "Nope. Don't answer that. I want you to think about it. Go back over everything that you two have experienced together over the past few weeks. Think about how she treats you when no one is around and the cameras are off. When you do that, I think you'll know if your fear is rooted in fact or fiction."

"This whole show is fiction!"

Smiling, he nodded. "You're absolutely correct, dearheart. The show *is* fiction. But you and Kris and your feelings for one another; what about those?"

Jitter Cam 12-D'Vaughn

When I came onto the show, my sole purpose was to come out to my family and boost my self-esteem a little. What I got was so much more than that. I'm not in a place to do a lot of talking and you've already gotten plenty of tears from me, so I'll keep this short.

I'm going to marry the woman that I love on Saturday.

Chapter Sixteen

Kris

The Big Day

My heart was pounding. I paced back and forth in front of the door, wishing desperately that I could go to D'Vaughn and talk to her before I walked into the room where the ceremony would be held. She'd been pretty closed-lipped during the rehearsal and I'd been stewing on that for the past two days. Ms. Miller was a traditionalist and insisted that we not see each other after the dinner on Thursday, so I was going into this blind. Despite the declarations of love we'd shared at the end of dinner, worry was still sitting heavily on my chest, and I didn't want D'Vaughn to make her way to the altar without knowing how much she meant to me, and how much I wanted this with her. I just needed a few more minutes.

"Oye, can you please stop pacing? You're starting to make me seasick."

I ignored Rhea, my mind too full of thoughts for me to even think of a comeback. We'd gotten dressed, taken pictures, and had moved to the sitting area of the dressing suite I'd been assigned.

"Hey now! Looking sharp there!"

Glancing toward the familiar voice, I noticed Kevin and

Joe coming toward us. Kevin looked dapper in a tailored suit, his hair braided back into a small bun with the sides of his head shaved. Joe wore slacks and a button-down, but the same work boots I remember him wearing at that first brunch six weeks ago were on his feet. After shaking both of their hands, I backed away and tried to keep from pacing again.

"How you feeling?"

I gave Kevin a wild look. "Nervous as fuck."

Joe let off a bark of laughter that was echoed by everyone else in the room. Along with Rhea—who was my best man—Raul, Ray, and Darren were all standing with me. Glaring at all of them, I turned back to Kevin.

"Do you have any news for me?"

He quirked an eyebrow. "What kind of news?"

"Uh, I don't know. Maybe a heads-up on whether or not D'Vaughn is gonna meet me at the altar in her white dress."

Raul laughed loudly. "You tweakin'. Why would she wait 'til the last minute to run off on you?"

"And not for nothing," Darren added, "if she were gonna run, I wouldn't be here right now. That has to count for something."

I pursed my lips and said nothing. I know they were trying to help, but they didn't know the stakes. Kevin dropped a hand onto my shoulder.

"I just came to get you because it's time. Let's go."

We followed him out of the suite and down the hall toward the area where the ceremony would be held. Soft music was playing and I could see through the open door that the room was more than half-full, with both sides of the aisle packed with people. My gut twisted. The plan was for us to proceed inside as rehearsed, but before the officiant began, Kevin would come in and make the announcement. It sounded easy enough, but was a disaster waiting to happen.

Taking a deep breath, I met Rhea at the door and we walked inside, moving at a moderate pace down the aisle as we made our way to the platform at the end of the room. I pasted a smile on my face, waving at the family and friends who'd come to witness what they thought was a conventional wedding. Shortly after we were settled in place, the attendants began to enter. Instead of pairing everyone off, our families had decided it would be better to have everyone walk inside in a single line, in alternating order, and then fan out toward their assigned sides as they reached the end of the chairs. Ray was first, followed by Cinta, then Raul, D'Niesha, and Darren. As soon as Darren took his place, "For You" by Kenny Lattimore began to play and my eyes zeroed in on the entrance.

D'Vaughn appeared in the doorway and my bottom lip began to tremble. She was a vision that I would never forget as long as I lived. The white princess gown was all tulle and lace perfection, wrapping around her elegantly and sweeping the floor as she made her way toward the altar—toward me. We locked eyes, and I knew then that there was no way I was letting her leave this building not knowing that she was mine from here on out. She ascended the steps of the platform and came to stand in front of me and I just…stared at her. Her thick hair framed her face, hanging around her shoulders in a blown-out twistout. She wore a crown made of flowers and half a dozen tiny blooms were pinned in her hair. The thin straps of her dress were covered in lace flowers which ran all over the bodice of her dress and faded out as the skirt fanned around her legs.

My heart was so full and pumping so quickly, and my throat was tight, and I wanted this to be real so, so badly that I didn't know what to do or say or if I was even at liberty to say anything just yet.

I just knew that I loved her and that this couldn't be the end for us. It wouldn't.

"We made it," D'Vaughn breathed, her eyes trailing my body from head to toe.

"We made it," I parroted. Unable to help myself, I reached out and touched one of the flowers in her hair. "You look... breathtaking."

She grinned, those dimples making an appearance as she ducked her head.

"Thank you." Lifting her gaze, she eyed me once more and I felt a thrill zip through me at the shine in her eyes. "I'm sure you already know this, but you look good enough to eat. With my hands. No utensils necessary."

I chuckled, swallowing back the lump in my throat. "Look at you, being nasty in public. Let me find out you wanna put ya lips on me."

She started to bite her bottom lip but caught herself before she could ruin her lipstick.

"My lips...amongst other things."

A murmur went up across the room and we looked over to see Kevin strutting up the aisle. I glanced over my shoulder at my family and found a sea of confused faces.

"Here we go," I murmured as Kevin jogged onto the platform.

He pulled a microphone from the inside of his suit jacket and shot us both a wink before addressing the crowd.

"Good afternoon, beautiful people. I apologize for crashing the party, but we've got some matters to address and announcements to make."

"Ooh, girl. *What the hell is this?*" Ray's whispered question was funny, but I was too nervous to laugh.

Kevin turned to us.

"D'Vaughn. Kris. For two people who only met six weeks

ago, you've managed to convince your families that you were not only madly in love, but eager to enter matrimony with one another. You not only convinced your families and those most important to you that you were indeed getting married, but you managed to convince me too, and for that you have won *Instant I Do* season three. I have here for each of you, a check for one hundred thousand dollars."

The noise level grew as our families and friends registered what Kevin had said. My stomach tightened further as I glanced from Kevin to D'Vaughn, who stared back at me with a soft smile gracing her beautiful face. We stood in front of a few dozen people, but was it too late to tell her that I'd give up the money if I could have her instead? Licking my lips, I leaned toward her.

"Baby, I—"

"But, wait, there's more!" Kevin's excited voice interrupted mine.

Annoyed at the interruption, but too nervous to shirk a moment to think, I glanced from D'Vaughn to Kevin, and back again. Her brows were knitted contemplatively, and I wondered what she was thinking. *Was it anything along the lines of what I'd been wracking my brain over?*

Turning toward our guests, Kevin smiled wide.

"For the first two seasons of the show, we've presented the winners with checks and that was it. This season, we've changed things up a bit."

Surprised, I shared a questioning glance with D'Vaughn before we both turned to see what the hell Kevin had up his sleeve.

"With season three," he continued, "we've decided to see just how close the contestants have gotten." He turned back to us, smiling widely as if he was delivering the news that we'd won the Powerball and didn't have to pay taxes on the money. "I can give each of you these checks *or* you can get married and the show will cover all expenses for this wedding *and* your honeymoon. The choice is yours."

The volume in the room became deafening as those murmurs turned into full-out conversations.

"Oh my gosh," D'Vaughn whispered, bringing a trembling hand up to her mouth.

My jaw fell open, eyes bucked. "Are you fucking serious?"

Nodding, Kevin lowered the checks. "Rebecca is going to get in my ass for saying this on camera, but I've never seen a couple who seemed more in love than the two of you. I know people say that things don't always work out in situations like these, but if my opinion means anything, I think that you're the real deal. The bond you've managed to form in these past six weeks is as solid as they come."

"You'd better take the damn deal!" I heard D'Niesha yell. "Weddings aren't cheap!"

Laughter rang out, and I looked out over the crowd to see my parents nodding their agreement. I met eyes with Mami and felt my throat tighten. She stood on her feet, her hands clasped over her heart, and I could see that her eyes were glossy.

"Marry her," she mouthed to me, bringing a smile to my face.

Before I could turn around to do just that, people started shouting and then cheering. Mami began jumping up and down as Papi began clapping. When I saw tears trail down his cheeks, I turned back to D'Vaughn and felt the world stop. I dropped my gaze to find her dress hiked up as she balanced on one knee in front of me. The prickling at the corners of my eyes gave way as tears instantly formed and marched their salty way down my face.

D'Vaughn gazed up at me, a bright, hopeful smile on her face and tears in her eyes that had yet to fall.

"I knew you were trouble from the first moment I laid eyes

on you," she began, making me laugh. "You were the most exquisite being I'd ever seen, and I gasped, which made me choke on my drink. You showed me kindness by giving me water and waiting until I told you that I was okay before leaving me to join everyone else. You stood by my side and held my hand, offering me more strength than I knew I needed as I came out to my family, and told them in no uncertain terms that regardless if they accepted me or not, I would never be alone because the Zavalas had made me their own. You have affirmed me, supported me, and loved me, and more than anything, completely ruined me for any other woman. Would you please, if you are so inclined, finish what you started and marry me for real, so that I can aspire to make you even a smidgen as happy as you have made me?"

Dropping to my knees, I wrapped her in my arms and took her mouth in the sweetest kiss I'd ever been privy to sharing. I was *fallingfallingfalling*, losing myself in her mouth, in her lips, in the taste of her love on her tongue until Mateo's telltale wolf whistle brought me back to the present.

D'Vaughn pulled back, shaking her head dazedly. "That was nice and all, but um…are you gonna answer me or nah?"

Eyes low, I gave her a silly grin. "Oh, that wasn't answer enough?"

Her hair swished around her shoulders as she gave a vigorous shake of her head. "No, ma'am. You gotta tell me what you want."

Cupping her face, I leaned in to press another kiss to her lips. "I want to be your wife, and I want you to be mine in return."

Sighing, she let her eyes drift closed and nodded. "Done."

I tilted my head to the side, twisting my lips as a thought occurred to me. "You sure you wanna give up a hundred k for me? That's a lotta bread."

Immediately, the satisfied smile on her face morphed into

a glare. "Do you not see me down on my knee on this filthy floor in the gorgeous, custom-made dress that my best friend sewed in three weeks?! None of this other stuff matters if I can't have you, Kris. I love you."

"I love *you*," I emphasized, because I did.

I had no idea that she'd started choking that first night after seeing me, but I did notice her from that moment on. I'd been strategic with my conversations at that event, but I'd had her in my peripheral all night. Standing, I grabbed her hand, giving Kevin a nod of thanks when he moved to her other side, supporting her elbow as she rose. When he stood back, we turned to him, linking our hands together as we faced our guests. D'Vaughn glanced at me and I gave her a nod. Smiling, she made the announcement.

"We're going to get married."

Kiana whooped loudly from her front-row seat, and the sound was immediately followed by the cheers of everyone else. It was clear they supported our decision. I hadn't realized how much that meant to me until right that moment. D'Vaughn and I had spent the past few weeks working to convince them that we were something authentic, and had managed to fall in love for real, but now that they knew we'd lied to them all, the fact that not one face around us held anger made my heart swell.

"Alright," I laughed, nearly yelling to be heard over the noise, "let's get back to this wedding!"

We started to turn around when Kevin cleared his throat.

"One more thing."

Halting midstep, it was almost comical the way me and my soon-to-be wife slowly spun back around. I could feel the tension radiating out of her and squeezed her hand in response. No matter what Kevin said, we'd already agreed to get married; nothing could top that.

"Aww man," D'Vaughn pouted, "don't tell me there's an-other plot twist!"

Laughing, Kevin held up his hands in surrender. "This is another good one, I promise."

"Just hit us with it, man," I said with a wave.

Bowing his thanks, he turned toward the front of the room, where someone was coming up the aisle holding another large check. Audible gasps went up around the room, and my eyes were wide with anticipation. *What the hell was going on?*

The guy reached Kevin and handed him the check before doing an about-face and scurrying back down the aisle.

"What is that?"

"This," Kevin began, acknowledging D'Vaughn's question as he lifted the check over his chest and spun back toward us, "is a little gift from the network for being the first couple from *Instant I Do* to turn down the money for the marriage."

D'Vaughn was squeezing my hand so tightly I thought she might break a couple of bones, but I understood completely. As my eyes roved the larger-than-life check in front of me, my heart rate shot through the roof.

It was written out to D'Vaughn and Kris Zavala-Miller and was for *two hundred fifty thousand dollars*.

"Oh. My. Gosh!" D'Vaughn shrieked. "Are you serious right now?!"

"Yo," I whispered, unable to form another word. I was completely shocked.

Kevin nodded. "When I said that you two were different, I meant that. We've had at least one couple make it to the altar every season, but everyone always takes the money. There's nothing wrong with that, of course, but it's a breath of fresh air to come across two people who've mutually decided to choose each other over everything else. This is what the show was about when we first pitched the concept and I'll never forget how you've shown us that real love doesn't always need years of cultivating in order to grow."

He held the check out toward us. D'Vaughn didn't make a move, so I grabbed it and handed it to Rhea before turning back to Kevin.

"Thank you."

He dipped his chin. "No. Thank *you*." Clapping his hands, he took a step backward. "Okay! Now that that's established, I'm going to disappear and let you two get married. For real this time."

He jogged down from the platform and I helped straighten the train of D'Vaughn's gown as we once again faced the officiant. She smiled at us.

"Ready?"

I nodded. "Absolutely."

D'Vaughn gently squeezed my hand. "Of course."

"Well," the officiant began, "I do believe that D'Vaughn's proposal was better than any hand-written vow I've ever heard, so why don't we skip all of the traditional stuff and jump right to the good part? Kris? Would you like to say your vows?"

Facing each other, I took D'Vaughn's hands in mine as I stared into her eyes. Her smile was so joyful, full of content, and I couldn't believe I was moments away from getting to wake up next to it every day for the rest of my life. Taking a deep breath, I spilled my heart out before her.

"D'Vaughn, I knew from that first night that you were something special. It was why I made it a point to stay away from you. I didn't want the producers to see that I was interested and match me with someone else on purpose." She gasped, making me smile. "You were kind to everyone that night, even the most obnoxious and annoying of the group, and even though you avoided me, I never got the feeling that you didn't like me. That next morning, after I saw that it was you, I made up in my mind that I had six weeks to make you fall in love with me, and the both of us standing here right now proves that I was successful. You have such a pure and loving soul. When I brought you to meet my family, you didn't hesitate to meet them where they were, speaking Spanish to let them know that you respected them and their language, especially in their home. That was huge and meant so much to me, and to my family. When you left, Papi took me aside and said, 'Estoy orgulloso de ti.'" I broke off, shaking my head and grabbing the tissues that Rhea handed me, wiping the tears from my eyes before folding the paper and wiping those that fell from D'Vaughn's as well.

"He said that he was proud of me. That you were a good woman and that I needed to take care of you, and he was absolutely right. I know that six weeks isn't enough time to learn everything there is about a person, but I think that's good, in a way. For us, it's perfect. This means that every day I get to learn something new about you to add on to my love. I want to continue to grow what we've built, to create a life that brings us both more joy than we could have ever imagined, and most of all, to have you by my side as we experience everything life has to offer. Thank you for allowing me to love you; for loving me back, and for making me the happiest woman on the planet by becoming my wife."

"Beautifully said," murmured the officiant. "Do you, D'Vaughn, take Kris to be your lawfully wedded wife? To have and to hold, through sickness and in health, as long as you both shall live?"

"I do," she breathed. "A thousand times, I do."

My breath hitched at the love I saw shining brightly in her eyes.

"And Kris, do you take D'Vaughn to be your lawfully wedded wife? To have and to hold, through sickness and in health, as long as you both shall live?"

"I do forever."

"By the power vested in me from the state of Texas, I now pronounce you wife and wife." She shot me a wink. "Ladies, you may kiss your soul mate."

Cheers exploded around us, followed quickly by catcalls as I swept D'Vaughn into my arms, bent her backward dramatically, and planted a gentle kiss upon her lips. She wrapped her arms around my neck and licked along the seam of my mouth until I opened for her, promptly tangling her tongue with mine, seeking out my flavor as I simultaneously siphoned hers greedily.

"I know that's right!" shouted D'Niesha. "You betta tongue your wife down!"

Her impassioned shout cut through the noise to grab my attention. Dialing back the kiss, I grinned, my lips only a breath away from D'Vaughn's mouth.

"Happy six-week anniversary, wife."

Her responding smile was so wide, so seraphic, that it brought instant joy to my already full heart.

"Happy anniversary, my love," she whispered, "and I look forward to many more."

Epilogue-D'Vaughn

Season Finale

We were all required to be present at the live airing of the season finale. The stipulation had been a part of our initial contract before we'd even recorded one minute of the show.

The network had managed to squeeze six weeks and hundreds of hours' worth of video into twelve forty-eight-minute episodes that were stretched to an hour with the help of commercials. The highly anticipated finale took up a two-hour slot. All ten of the original contestants had to sit onstage for two hours and answer questions and explain what was going through our head at any given moment in the show. I was exhausted before we'd even arrived to the studio, but knowing the trip that would follow pumped me up.

It was exactly one year since Kris and I had said *I do* for real, and after the finale, we were going on a five-day vacation for our anniversary. My excitement was just slightly overshadowed by my nerves. Kris told me that I had nothing to be nervous about since we'd already won and were happily married, but that had nothing to do with millions of eyes on you. Season three of *Instant I Do* had broken records with ratings and viewership, and had already been nominated for several diversity and inclusion awards. All that told me was that more than a handful of people would be watching the live show.

Our lives had already changed so much in just the past three months. Kris finally received that coveted blue check, with her followers growing from a quarter of a million to more than two million after the first episode aired. Now she was sitting at eight million followers, with several six-figure brand endorsements paying her yearly salary ten times over for a handful of sponsored posts. Her and Rhea had even done a commercial.

Although I'd been nervous about the fallout at my school, the reception after the show aired was phenomenal. I had so many students stopping into my office throughout the day to tell me how seeing me come out on prime-time television had given them the strength and courage to come out to their loved ones that I'd lost count after the fifteenth. The outpouring of love from parents and others in the community had been overwhelming, to where I'd had to filter emails containing certain words to a different server. I still counseled students on their course selection, but now my principal had asked me to dust off my psych degree and consider taking a new counseling position. I'd been talking it over with Kris and Cinta, and while I'd yet to make a decision, I had a pretty good idea which direction I was leaning.

Smoothing my hands down over my dress, I folded my hands across my knees and kept my attention on the host. Ansel, the polished socialite who moderated every season finale, had been bringing us out one by one in the order that we'd been eliminated from the show as the final episode progressed. We were to wait in the green room until we were called, and then walk out onstage when it was our turn. We'd been an hour into the live show when I finally made my way in front of the studio audience along with Kris, Hosea, and Bryce. The four of us were the last ones to make it to the final week.

Tanisha stood to her feet as Kris walked near her and the crowd started booing.

"Aye, y'all chill out!" Kris called out, shaking her head disappointedly as I hung my head in shame. I felt like it was partly my fault that Tanisha had been painted as a sort of home-wrecker, and nothing Kris said had been able to get that thought out of my head. Using the side of her finger, Kris tipped my chin up and I lifted my head just as Tanisha opened her arms wide.

My mouth fell open as Kris stepped right into the circle and they embraced, rocking left and then right before Tanisha kissed Kris's cheek and pulled away, winking at me before taking a seat on the couch opposite the one Kris and I were headed for.

"Well," exclaimed Ansel, "that was quite a reunion!" He'd taken the words right out of my mouth.

Tanisha shrugged. Kris laughed. I eyed them both.

"Hold up, hold up, hold up! We *all* saw that clip from week three, and the blood was very bad, honey, so what is this? Are y'all friends now?" Diamond would always have my heart for asking the question that sat heavy on my tongue.

Lifting a shoulder, Tanisha shook her head. "We just came to an understanding, is all."

Diamond sat forward. "Which is?"

Kris smirked. "That what's mine is mine, and mine alone."

Like a band of instigators, the audience oohed right along with half of the contestants. I might've swooned a li'l bit. Just a tad. No falling over or anything like that though.

"Tanisha is a home-wrecker!" someone shouted from the audience.

"Oh my!" exclaimed Ansel at the outburst, his hand to his chest in faux scandalization.

"I'm not paying them no mind. Go ahead, Ansel." Crossing her legs, Tanisha smiled widely.

Ansel chuckled and tapped the sheaf of cards in his hand on his thigh. "After every episode we polled our viewers via the *Instant I Do* website and texting. We like to know what they thought about what they saw, and it's always fun to go back and take a look at early predictions, don't you think?"

The audience collectively shouted, "Yes!" Ansel's unnaturally straight and sparkling white grin widened.

"I thought so too. Let's take a look at some of those, shall we?" Twisting in his seat, he swept an arm toward the large projector screen on the wall behind us. Everyone fell silent as we turned our attention to the screen.

The opening montage from season three played before several clips from episode one. The audience showed their own biases for the contestants with their responses to the clip of each of our entrances to the party the night before we were matched. I cringed at the terrified look on my face as I moved at a turtle's pace down that hallway, and the collective "aww" from the audience didn't make me feel better. If they all pitied me, did that mean I was the season's weak link? There was one every year. The person was a fumbling mess, who couldn't get anything right. *Had that been me?*

Whistles and the audience murmuring "ooh" made me blink out of my reverie. Kris had walked in on the screen and a large chunk of the audience—of *all* genders—had a visceral reaction to her presence. Thankfully, the camera cut before I'd started choking. I shot up a prayer for small favors. After every contestant was shown, clips of us finding out who we were paired with began to show. Some of the reactions were… rough to watch. Others were hilarious, and a couple were tooth-achingly sweet. My heart pounded as I waited for Kris's to show, but when it did I felt my eyes sting a little. That sexy, slow grin of hers bloomed across her face and she nodded. Even without saying a word, it was clear that she was pleased.

"I told you that I wanted you from the beginning."

Dropping my gaze from the screen, I turned to my wife. Her eyes were on me, as if she'd been watching me watch her on the screen. Warmth crept up my neck and settled onto my cheeks. There was a knowing look in her eyes, but she didn't seem annoyed. After being together all of this time, she had a pretty good idea of how my brain worked and likely figured what I'd been thinking.

I nodded. "You did."

"I always knew we'd make it here."

She'd told me that too.

"I know."

"Good."

She wanted to kiss me; it was all over her face. And I wanted to be kissed by her right then. But we'd been instructed by the e.p. backstage to keep the PDAs down. The way the show was edited, it wasn't clear who ended up married, and they didn't want us to give anything away ahead of time. So, instead of taking my mouth, she winked at me and returned her attention to the screen. After a moment of taking her in, I did the same.

When the recap of episode one came to an end, screenshots of the different poll questions popped up. Ansel read along as they appeared.

"We asked our viewers which pairings they thought would make it to the finale. The top answer was Kirk and Jerri, with Kris and D'Vaughn coming in at a close second!"

That surprised me. After showing a clip of my Jitter Cam where I focused on Tanisha, I'd expected that we'd be in the bottom. I should've known that Kris's sex appeal could take us anywhere.

"We also asked which contestant was their favorite so far. They said: Kris, Diamond, and Bryce."

"The girls have taste, honey," Diamond declared, bowing her head graciously.

Chuckling, Ansel read on. "Those three stayed in the top until week four when Diamond and Nicolas were eliminated."

With her nose in the air, Diamond sniffed and looked away. Nicolas grabbed her hand and tried to kiss it, but Diamond snatched her hand back and twisted so that her back was to him. My brows shot up when I saw the crestfallen expression on his face. They'd been knocked out when an ex of Nicolas's had hacked into his email, found his communication with the show, and told everyone that it was a farce. That had been a hard episode to watch because he and Diamond had seemed to have real chemistry.

"Kris and Bryce remained top two after that." Ansel continued on. "Let's take a look at the final episode and guess who came out on top. No pun intended."

The audience laughed as we all turned to the screen. My face heated as I appeared. We all watched as I cried while viewing Kris's audition tape, but then my shortest Jitter Cam of the six weeks played and shouts went up around the room. I felt several pairs of eyes on me, but the only pair that mattered were the ones that belonged to my wife. After all of this time, she knew exactly how I felt about her, but getting to see how it played out was a whole different animal. I understood, because the moment that I saw her expression when she learned I was her match did something to me as well.

I met Kris's gaze and held it until Ansel called my name. I had no idea how many minutes had passed, only that I couldn't wait until I was free to put my hands on Kris again. When I turned to Ansel, he wore a knowing smirk.

"What was going through your mind when you said that?"

I laughed. "Exactly what I'd said. That I was going to marry Kris."

"So, you knew?"

"At that time? I was positively certain."

An impressed look crossed his features before he pointed back at the screen. "Let's see how that played out, shall we?"

I held my breath as the last ten minutes of the episode played. When the camera showed me going down on one knee with the help of Cinta, people shot to their feet, screaming cheers. My cheeks hurt from how hard I was grinning as I watched us say *I do* on that big screen. When I felt Kris's fingers touch my chin, I turned to her, noting the gloss in her eyes.

"That moment will forever be etched on my heart."

"Yo también," I whispered, although it didn't matter because every grunt and breath we released was picked up by the microphones we wore.

"Oh my!" Ansel said. "Well, I guess I don't have to ask how you two feel after seeing that."

I shook my head as I shared a smile with my wife. She brushed her thumb over my cheek and licked her lips. The minutes were too many before I'd get to taste them again.

"I feel like the luckiest woman in the universe."

★ ★ ★ ★ ★

Acknowledgments

While the world raged around me, this beautiful story poured from me like water from a trope-tastic faucet. I often joked that guiding D'Vaughn and Kris toward their HEA was the only thing keeping me sane, but it was really the support from a number of people that helped me make it to the other side. My family; my backbone; my heart. Your love and grace as I disappeared into this story was priceless. My own personal Captain America and IronThor, Angelique and Ashley. Y'all already know, it's up and it's stuck! Jeanette, you were there with a rhema word whenever I didn't know I needed it, and I can't explain how much it meant to me each and every time. On the publishing side, my editor John, who blew me away with their care for these characters, and Kerri and the entire team at Carina who saw the value in this story. Thank you all.

Discover another great contemporary romance from Carina Adores

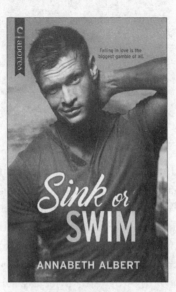

Navy chief Calder Euler loves to win big. His latest score? A remote mountain cabin. Checking it out is supposed to be a quick trip, but Calder's luck abruptly turns when a freak injury and a freakier snowstorm leave him stranded.

Oh, and the cabin isn't empty. A silver fox caring for two young girls claims that the property is his, but Calder's paperwork says otherwise.

Felix Sigurd is on a losing streak, and his ex-husband risking the cabin in a reckless bet is only the latest in a series of misfortunes. He'll tolerate the handsome stranger for a couple nights—even care for his injuries—but that's it.

Calder doesn't know a damn thing about kids, but making pancakes for Felix's girls is a surprising delight. Trapped in the cabin, the four of them slip easily into the rhythms of a family. But when the ice melts, they'll have to decide if a future together is in the cards.

Don't miss
Sink or Swim by Annabeth Albert,
available wherever Carina Press books are sold.

CarinaAdores.com